George Frederick Pardon

Tales from the operas

George Frederick Pardon

Tales from the operas

ISBN/EAN: 9783337174002

Printed in Europe, USA, Canada, Australia, Japan

Cover: Foto ©Andreas Hilbeck / pixelio.de

More available books at **www.hansebooks.com**

TALES FROM THE OPERAS.

EDITED BY

GEORGE FREDERICK PARDON.

AUTHOR OF "THE FACES IN THE FIRE, ETC., ETC., ETC.

NEW YORK.

CARLETON, PUBLISHER, 413 BROADWAY.

LONDON: JAMES BLACKWOOD.

MDCCCLXIV.

TO
MAX MARETZEK,

PREFACE.

THE want of a book, which, while preserving all the force and spirit of the original Operas, attempts the relation of the several narratives in a graphic and pleasing style, has often, probably, been felt by the patrons of the lyric drama. To supply such a want, and to provide all classes of readers with an accurate and succinct knowledge of the incidents on which are founded our most celebrated Operas, is the object of the following pages. Whether the experiment has been successfully carried out, the public, and the critics, must decide. Few who have listened to the tragic story of Lucrezia ; few who have wept with Norma or laughed with Figaro, but will, it is believed, welcome their old favorites of the theatre in their new literary costume. As it was manifestly impossible to unravel the plots of *all* the famous Operas in one little book, only such of them have been detailed as are intimately known to American audiences.

It is but right to add that these tales have had their origin, mainly in the published Books of the Operas, aided always by a familiar acquaintance with the Operas themselves, as they have been placed on the boards of European and American theatres.

CONTENTS.

TALES FROM THE OPERAS.

LUCREZIA BORGIA. (Donizetti.)

CHAPTER I.

When Satan fell, some of the essence of the god-head pityingly clung about him — hence those of men whose faces turn towards the darkness have ever something of the god within them, which raises them above the poor animals who eat and die.—*Montaigne.*

The Venice of nearly four hundred years ago was a great, splendid, gay, and powerful city. Gold was every day showered into the coffers of its merchants from all parts of the earth, and every night there was feasting, laughing, and dancing in Venice, the richest and the gayest city in the world.

On the night when our story opens was being held at the Palazzo Barberigo a masqued ball. All Venice, masqued, was there. The lamps hanging in the trees, laughed at the water as it threw back the gay colored rays of light which kissed it, in tremulous softness and beauty.

And there below on the still canal, the Giudecca, glided the silent black gondolas, bearing gaily dressed cavaliers and dames to and from the fête.

So silently the gondolas passed, that not a soul upon the shore knew a boat had gone by, a boat, perhaps, from which peered out a jealous eye.

The gardens of the palace were large, and ever when the music ceased, there were seen in all parts of it gay masquers, courting, talking, singing, flirting, or watching.

Among the guests was Gennaro, young and beautiful as the nights of Italy. With him was one of the great Orsini, even younger than himself, and far gayer. Nay, he was but a boy. These two were ever together, in peace or on the battle-field, at fêtes, or quietly at home.

So now amidst the group wherever walked Orsini, Gennaro had a place. These two as they sauntered along with their friends, all either carrying their masks in their hands, or else tied to their belts, these two were deploring, and being pitied, for they were to leave Venice on the morrow.

"Alas!" said one, "You will never like Ferrara, as you like the poorest street in Venice."

"But, still," cried another, "'tis something to form part of an ambassador's suite."

"Faith," cried a third, "I would sooner be as I am and in Venice."

"Let me tell you Signors," said a fourth, who was called Gubetta, a Spaniard, and not in good repute, "let me tell you the court of Alfonzo is superb, and as for Lucrezia Borgia " —

"What!" cried one, "name *her*, here, at a fête?"

"Pray ye be silent," cried another.

"The Borgia," said a third, "I abhor her very name."

"In faith," added another, "'twould not be saying much for thee to say that thou lovdst her."

"As for us," said the Orsini, whom they called Maffio, "we should dread her more than any of you, if the sorcerer spoke truly."

"Again a tale, Maffio," said Gennaro. "Leave the Borgia alone, who cares to hear of her."

"No, no, Gennaro, let us hear the tale. Go on Maffio."

"Then I'll fain go to sleep," said Gennaro. "Faith I could fall asleep standing, when Orsini begins his long tales."

"Signors, 'tis a good tale, though my friend has heard it before. See, now, he has flung himself down on that seat. Well,— well, 'tis but two ears the less. In the fatal battle of Rimini I was wounded; and while lying on the ground, and dying as I thought, Gennaro found me, helped me to horse, and bore me in safety from the

field. In the shelter of a wood he was dressing my
wounds, and we had both sworn to live and die together,
when an aged man, clad in a dress falling to his feet,
stood before us. 'Youths,' said he, 'shun the Borgia,
go not near Lucrezia, she is death.' Then he was gone,
gone. And the wind thrice whispered the hated name.
There — what think you of my tale? See you, Gennaro
would not listen to it, because he loveth not to be praised.

"A good tale' but it does not prove thou shouldst
shun the Borgia."

"Whereof in proof, we go to Ferrara to-morrow. Bah!
what Venetian need fear the Borgia, while the dreaded
lion of Venice can roar? Yet still, sometimes, Signors,
I fancy there may be some truth in the prophecy."

"Let us wake Gennaro, let us ask him if he believes
in the solemn warning."

"Oh, let him sleep. If he would rather dream than
hear my tales, let him dream."

Here the swelling dance music reaching their ears,
they gaily sauntered to the palace, and soon the only
person in the garden was Gennaro, peacefully sleeping
on a marble bench, his head resting on his arm, and his
face as tranquil as a little child's.

There is a ripple o'er the dark canal — the reflexions of
the colored lamps are all broken up and scattered. 'Tis
a gondola, silent and sombre, which, in a little seething
of water, stops just below the terrace stairs.

Then from it steps a woman all clothed in heavy black;
a black mask on her face, a black fan in her hand. Nay,
the very cross upon her neck is jet.

The gondola from which she has stepped glides silently
away, and leaves her standing hesitatingly in the garden.
Then she starts as she sees the sleeping face turned
towards the moonlight.

She moves towards the sleeper, darkly, noiselessly,
her shoulders drawn together; she is so desirous she may
not be heard, that she might be about to murder him as
he sleeps. At last, close to him, she bends over his
sleeping face. Her hand is on his forehead. Lower and
lower bends her head. Awake, awake! But there is no
fear. She has but kissed him. A soft, noiseless kiss.

As she moves a few steps from him, her eyes still on his face, her arm is touched.

"Signora!"

"Thou, Gubetta!"

"I fear for thee. Venice may guard thy life, but she cannot save thee from insult."

What does this mysterious woman think as her head droops? Truly she should be insulted, all breathing men and women, and small children even, abhor her name. Yet she was not born to such a fate. But the past, the past, who shall recall the past. And then the vision of an aged man, clad in a robe falling to the ground in heavy folds, comes before her, and she trembles. As she looks on the sleeper, she asks herself how long was it since she had slept so peacefully?

"Thou gazest upon the youth, Signora. Vainly have I sought to learn the reason of thy secret journey from Ferrara here to Venice — perhaps this youth."

"Thou seek to read my acts — thou! Leave me."

The man — a fair-looking man enough — bowed, and with quiet, measured steps withdrew.

Then she came back to the sleeping man.

"How beautiful he is," she thought. Never in her dreams had she imagined him so beautiful. She almost cried with rapture as she looked on him. Was this love? Yes. Guilty love? Nay; wait and read. Should she wake him? No.

She removed her mask to wipe away her tears (fallen to good purpose — as nearly all tears fall), and in those few moments her face was seen — not by the youth upon the marble seat, but by the scowling eyes of a tall, haughty-looking man, glaring from a treacherous gondola, which had quietly stolen up, under cover of the night, and there lay still below the terrace. Beside him stood a mean-looking creature whom he called Rustighello. "It is she!"

"Truly, Signor."

"And the youth, who is he?"

"A poor adventurer, without parents or country; people say he is brave."

"What will not people say, good Rustighello? Try every art to lure him to Ferrara, and to me —"

"There is no need for art. By chance, he will set out with Gruirani for Ferrara."

Slowly the gondola stole away with its watching secret.

"Sleep, sleep, poor youth, and good dreams wait on you. For me are naught but sleepless nights and bitter watching." She stooped again to kiss him. He woke.

"Heavens! whom do I see?"

"I Pray thee let me go!"

"Nay, nay, fair lady. On my faith—"

"Again I do implore thee, let me pass."

"Nay, but a moment to admire thee, for I feel thou'rt beuatiful. Oh! be not afraid, I will not harm thee."

"Surely not, Gennaro."

"What! thou knowest me?"

"And thou couldst love me!

"Who could not love the owner of so sweet a voice?"

"And thou couldst love me, Gennaro?"

"Surely, but not so dearly as I love one other I could name."

"And she—and she?"

"Is my mother."

"Thy mother! Oh my Gennaro, thou dost love her?" And she trembles greatly, this unknown woman.

"I love her as I love my life."

"And thinkst thou she loves thee?"

Alas! I never saw her."

And yet thou lovest her?"

"It is a wretched tale which I do hide from all; but ah! to thee it seems that I must tell it; for in thy face I read thou hast a noble soul."

"A noble soul!"

"I thought myself the son of a poor fisherman, with whom I spent my early years. But one day came a noble stranger; he gave me money, a splendid steed, bright arms, and, best of all, a paper. It was my mother—it was my mother who had written it. The victim of a mighty man, she feared for both our lives, and so would hide herself from me. She bade me never seek her name; and to this hour never have I sought to learn it."

"And this paper!"

"See here!" and he took it from the bosom of his dress; "it never leaveth me."

"Perchance, Gennaro, she wept when she wrote it!"

"And have not *I* wept, too, my mother—O my mother! But methinks I see tears on thy face, lady."

"Ah! yes, I weep for thee—for her."

"For me! for her! Indeed, I think already that I love thee dearly."

"Oh! ever love thy mother, youth; cling to her with all thy soul. Never think ill of her when thou dost doubt most strongly; think ever how she loves thee, and pity her, and hope that she may one day press thee to her heart."

"Ah! lady, no need hast thou to teach me this! I see her near me always—gentle, loving, pure; she is my guardian angel. When I would do ill, she comes upon me in my dreams, and smiles a welcome to me."

"I hear footsteps, I must leave thee."

"Why shouldst thou tremble?"

'Twas Orsini and the friends coming to seek for Gennaro. The youth Maffio, seeing a lady near his friend, ran gaily forward to them; but within a few paces, and just as the lady was rising her mask to her face, he saw her—saw her, to start and turn pale, brave as he was; saw her, to call on Heaven, and ask himself her name.

He ran back to his companions, uttered but two words, and each man was amazed. One laid his hand upon the spot where his dagger would have been, but that at fêtes all arms were rendered at the door. Another placed his hand upon his mouth and gazed in horror.

"Gennaro," whispered the unknown lady, "I must leave thee."

"Yet deign to tell who thou art?"

"One whose life is loving thee."

"Thy name!"

"I will reveal it," cried Orsini, coming forward, and speaking savagely, unmercifully.

As the woman heard these words, and recognized the voice, she flinched, and strove to run from the place.

But they stopped her; each way she made a step, on each side stood a stern, unyielding man. They stood about her, yet not near her.

"Gennaro, Gennaro; help!"

"Signors!" cried the youth, "what wouldst thou? This lady I protect; he that insults her is my friend no longer."

"We would wish to tell the lady who we are, and tell thee who she is," cried they earnestly, and yet with something of mockery in their tones, "then she may go; we shall have no wish to keep her with us."

"I, for one, am that Maffio Orsini, whose brother you murdered as he slept."

"And I, I am that man whose aged uncle you destroyed on his threshold."

"While I, fair lady, am the nephew of one who died quaffing your wine."

"I, Petruci, O lady, am cousin to him whose dominions you stole."

"And I was the friend of the man, who sleeps, by your will, beneath the Tiber."

Hopeless all her appeals, hopeless that she falls on her knees before them. Each strikes the air with his arm as he addresses her; not one feels pity.

"Who, then, is this woman?" said Gennaro; "dare I hear?"

"Gennaro, do not believe them; they mistake me."

"Oh! no mistake, lady," cried out Orsini; "remove thy mask. She is the woman who hath shamed all women; she is the woman whom all ages shall abhor; whose breath is poison, whose look is death, whom Heaven pities too much to destroy."

"Spare me! spare me!"

"As thou hast spared."

"Be merciful; there is yet time. Gennaro, see, I cling to thee; forbid them. Be merciful, signors! spare me!"

"As thou hast spared."

Then the Orsini tore the mask from her face.

"BEHOLD HER — LUCREZIA BORGIA."

What! is this the gentle face that wept over the sleeping youth? Look on it! like a demon's as she springs from her knees — defiant, fearless, no longer suppliant; degraded, but not ashamed. "Beware!" she cries, as tho gentlemen shun her, turning away from her — as Gennaro turns from her. " Beware, you who have shown no mercy ! beware ! "

CHAPTER II.

IN FERRARA. No longer in the city of waters, and palaces, and gay feastings. In Ferrara, where the Borgias reign. Where the cruel Duke Alfonzo reigns, where also his cruel wife is Duchess, the terrible Lucrezia Borgia.

See, in this grand square, there is the palace of the duke. Mark his arms carved over the gateway, the awful name Borgia swelling from the stone beneath.

The new Venetian ambassador with his suite had arrived.

It is night-time, and plot and murder are awake.

Look! is not this the figure of the tall, proud-looking man who watched the Borgia from a gondola in Venice. And the man with him, 'tis he who told of Gennaro.

They are walking slowly across the square.

" So, then, he has arrived in the ambassador's suite."

" Surely ; I have been his shadow. That house is his abode."

" Ah, she would fain have him near the palace."

" And in it, Signor, if Gubetta speaks the truth."

" It shall be his tomb."

" The Signor hears that music, 'tis from *his* house, The youth makes merry with his friends. 'Tis just the same each night, they only sleep at dawn."

" Let him take a long farewell of them, 'tis the last time they shall carouse with him."

With angry strides he went up to the ducal house. No need to knock. Too secret-loving was this man for that. Slowly a small door opened, and he and his companion entered.

Far different from these two gloomy men were the half dozen laughing youths who now came trooping away from Gennaro's wine cups. He came from the house with them, willing as host to show he did not love to part with them.

"Good bye, good bye, dear friends."

"Good bye Gennaro," cried the others; and Orsini added, "Thou hast the gravest face amongst us, thou art ever sad."

"No, no." But, truth to tell, his thoughts were ever with his unknown mother.

"Now I tell thee that this night thou shalt be gay. The Princess Negroni gives a ball to-night, where a thousand beauties shall be found, and thou must come, Gennaro. And if any one of you be not invited, let him speak. He will speak well, for on my word, I keep the ball-room door."

Said they, one after the other.—"I am bidden, and I, and I."

"And I also, Signors," said a fresh voice.

"What, Signor Bevarana!"

"Or Gubetta," said Orsini.

"That man seems every where; indeed, I do begin to doubt him," said Gennaro, softly to Orsini.

"Oh, fear not," said the other, carelessly. He is a man of pleasure, like ourselves, and fain not be alone if he can find him company. Thou art still sad, Gennaro."

"Oh cried one laughingly. "Perchance the Borgia has enchanted him."

"That woman's name again. I swear, Signors, I hate the sound of it."

"Ha! ha!" laughed another. "How darst thou speak thus so near her palace?"

"Her palace. I would I could brand her forehead, as I can and will the wall that bears her name."

As they wondered what he meant, he unbuckled his sword, took hold of it as it was sheathed by the point, and running to the palace door, clambered from boss to boss of the carved stone work till he got near the name "Borgia," jutting from the face of the doorway. Then he raised the sword, beat its hilt down upon the "B" commencing the name, and in a few moments the letter, splintered to fragments, lay upon the ground.

So those who stood below read on the proud door,

and beneath the proud arms of the Borgias, the meaning word "Orgia."

"Great heaven, Gennaro!" Even the brave Orsini was frightened, and the others looked at each other in terrible inquiry, as they read the terrible truth — "Orgia."

Said Gubetta, whom they had insolently called Beverana, "In faith, that jest may cost thee dear."

"In faith, I can pay my debts, Signor."

"See, Gennaro, there are eyes watching us," said Orsini; not meaning Gubetta, but two men, dressed in the flowing black cloaks of the time, like shrouds for sin, who met some little distance off in the square, and seemed to defy each other.

The youth Gennaro made no reply to the warning, but gaily saying "good bye, good bye;" turned to his house, and entered it, while the roysterers dispersed in different directions.

The men of the cloaks still seemed to defy each other furtively; still remained; not standing quiet, and yet not walking with a purpose. The sounds of the tripping footsteps dying away, these two men approached each other, each with his arms wrapped in his cloak, and, perhaps, each with his right hand on his sword.

"Why does the Signor wait here?"

"The Signor is waiting for thy going. And Signor himself?" —

"Is waiting to see thee leave this square."

"Prythee, why art thou here?"

"Perhaps the young Venetian who lives here, and for whom *thou* art waiting!"

"I?"

"Yes, where goest thou with him?"

"Stand back, in the name of the *duchess*."

"Stand back thyself, in the name of the DUKE."

"The duchess is powerful!"

"The duke is death."

"Now who shall conquer?"

"We will see."

A sharp, yet low whistle, from the lips of this last speaker, who stood beside the duke, when he watched his duchess away there in Venice, and watched her from a gondola.

Barely had the whistle whispered through the air, than a score of soft-footed men, each like each, enveloped in a shroud-like cloak, surrounded him who had spoken by the duchess.

"Beware — the duchess."

"Be silent, and depart. This youth hath offended the duke. Be silent, and fear not."

They carried him away with them, and in the wide square only stood the duke's servant, watching Gennaro's house.

CHAPTER III.

Go we now to the grand palace, where the husband and wife watched each other ceaselessly, each ever fearing death at the hands of the other. A happy palace, truly.

See, standing there, in that splendid royal room, are the duke and Rustighello, who had stood watching Gennaro's house.

" Well? "

"All is done, sire. The prisoner is now within the palace."

Keeping his eyes fixed upon the other's face, the duke drew from his waist a small golden key. 'Tis to unlock the hidden door of a hidden staircase, to be crept up, till a little chamber is reached. Then there are two vases, one of gold, and one of silver, each filled with wine, to be brought down, carried to the next room, and there be ready. Let not the golden vase tempt him, for it holds the wine of the Borgias. Then, if he be called, let him bring the vases; but if there be no call, then, good Rustighello, thy sword.

Then this mighty duke starts as a servant at the door announces "the Duchess."

Forward she comes, sparkling with rage and diamonds; no longer dressed in heavy black, but in rich rustling brocade, a sweeping coronet of jewels round her head.

" The duchess seems unquiet."

" Enraged. I come here to call for justice. A shameful crime hath been committed, the name of thy duchess has been degraded."

" Softly, duchess, I know it."

" And thou dost not punish the offender; doth he still live ? "

" Live ? Yes. That thou mayest destroy him, duchess. Nay, he will be before thee in another minute."

" Let him be whom he may, I demand his life, and in my presence, duke. Thou wilt give me thy word for this, my lord ? "

" I do, most heartily, dear duchess. I give thee my sacred word."

Then, to a page, who has entered after the duchess:

" Let the prisoner be brought forward."

" Duchess, thou tremblest, thou dost know this man."

This man is Gennaro, brought in before the angry duke and duchess, and standing fearlessly.

" I — I do not know him."

" Pray, may I ask the duke why I am here — why I have been torn from my house? May I dare to ask the meaning of such rigor ? "

" Good captain — draw near. Some coward wretch has dared to touch the noble name of Borgia written on this palace door, nay, to destroy the name. The duchess, even as I speak, trembles with anger at the act. We seek the guilty one; perhaps thou knowest him ? "

" It was not he — my lord — it was not he," cried Lucrezia.

" Ah ! duchess — duchess — how shouldst *thou* know? "

" He ! he was elsewhere when it was done. 'Twas some of his companions dared ——— "

" No — no — that is not true."

" Thou hearest, duchess. Now tell me, captain, and sincerely — art thou not he who dared to do this act."

" I'm not much used to hesitate, therefore I say *I* am the man."

Slowly he turned to the miserable duchess. " Thou dost mark his words " (how lowly the duke spoke !) " Thou dost mark his words, and I gave thee my sacred promise."

"Alfonzo, Alfonzo, I would speak with thee alone."

"Oh! surely. A moment, captain, but a moment. Well! duchess mine, we are alone. What wouldst thou ask?"

"The life of this poor youth."

"Do I hear rightly? And but now such anger as thou didst show!"

"I pity him. 'Twas but a passing anger. I acted but in jest; he is too young to think of consequences. Again, to what good his death? Pardon him. Have pity on him. Let him live."

"No, no, dear lady mine, my word is pledged. I never break my word."

"Nay, dear duke, but *I* insist. And why, thou seemest to ask? 'Twere ungenerous to refuse thy consort a poor favor such as this. What is the youth to me? Pardon him. Have pity on him. Let him live."

"No, no. What! pardon him who hath insulted *thee!* No, thou didst ask his death. And if *I* could pardon him, — nor could I — for thy dear sake I would not."

"Let us both pardon, and be clement, duke, for clemency is glorious in us all, and most of all in kings."

"No king am I, but a poor duke. I cannot spare him, duchess."

"Why shouldst thou be so angry with this same Gennaro?"

"Dost thou not know?"

"I?"

"Dost thou not LOVE him? Ah! thou dost start, Lucrezia. Even now I read in that face of thine thy crime."

"Don Alfonzo!"

"Nay, do not speak — "

"If I swear?"

"It were useless. What! shall I *never* be revenged on thee? If I may not strike thee openly, shall I let pass this hope of wounding thee?"

"Pardon, Don Alfonzo."

"Pardon!"

"For pity's sake."

"What, canst *thou* speak of pity — thou, Lucrezia?"

"Don Alfonzo, dear husband." On her knees to him, clinging to him, her eyes dilated, her lips dry and white.

But he stands immovable. Looks down on her un-yieldingly. Why, her very humiliation enrages him. For does not this poor unknown wretch, this Venetian, beat down her pride as he, duke and powerful, hath never, never beaten it down yet!

"Thou dost not answer. BEWARE!"

Once more she is the terrible duchess, and if the duke wear opal, let it warn him.

"I know thee, duchess. I have known thee long, Lucrezia. But forget not I am duke, and in Ferrara. Thou art in my power. Ah! well, I'm not unrea-sonable. I grant thee somewhat. Thou shalt choose the manner of his death. Or poison, or sword. Pray now choose!"

"I — I cannot."

"Let him then be — stabbed."

"No, no."

"Stabbed — stabbed."

"No, not blood, not blood."

"The poison. *Thou* dost choose his death. Pray be seated.— Enter captain, enter. The duchess is all-powerful with me. Why, I cannot tell, but she pardons thy crime, and bids thee go in peace. Italy would grieve to lose so handsome a son."

"The duke pardons me. Ah! well, now that I can speak without the look of cowardice and hope of mercy, I may tell the duke that his clemency has fallen on a man who doth deserve it. For thy father, surrounded by the enemy, would have died but for the arm of a poor adventurer."

"The adventurer, good captain, was —"

"My very self."

"Duke, duke," lowly, and pulling his dress, "he saved thy father's life — spare him."

"The duchess speaks to me, but so lowly that I scarce can hear her. So thou didst save my father's life — wilt follow his son's standard?"

"Pardon me, I'm bound by oath to Venice, and oaths are binding."

"Surely. Oaths are binding — is it not so, duchess? Well, well, good captain, take a golden present."

"No, I am not rich, yet rich enough."

"Thou art hard to please, fair captain. At least a draught of wine thou'lt drink with me. At last thou dost agree. The duchess, here, for once, will e'en turn cup-bearer. Nay, nay, nay, duchess, do not leave us; generous-minded thou hast been to him, and now be more so. Rustighello, bring us wine." He almost towered higher than his actual stature, as he looked upon the suffering woman. "Place the cups there — for me the silver one — the golden to the captain. Now, duchess, pour, pour. Nay, nay, duchess, the golden vase and golden cup do go together, and silver to the silver. Now, mark, good captain, the duchess will bear the cup to thee herself."

Slowly she takes the cup, slowly she carries it to the captain. And thus he holds it, wondering at the kindness of these people, whom he has always thought so harsh and full of hate.

"Lady, I did not dream of pardon, and, methinks, my mother, whom I know doth pray for me, hath by her dearest prayers inclined thee and the duke to gracious mercy. I drink to the duke and duchess."

Courteously the duke relieves the captain of the emptied goblet, lightly places it upon the table, then slowly creeping, like a reptile, he goes up to the duchess and says, softly, "Thou hast perchance somewhat to say to him. Permit me to retire."

Why does a hopeful flush rush over her face? Why does she touch her bosom with a trembling hand? Why again does her countenance express so much emotion?

The young captain sees her accompany the duke to the doors. The duke bows to him profoundly, and then his back is turned. What next? She stands listening for a moment or so, then rushes madly towards the youth, who looks alarmedly about the room in which are present only their two selves.

As she runs to him she takes her hand from her breast. "Gennaro, thou art poisoned; do not move; quickly take this phial, and begone. A single drop will save thee."

She stands a little away from him, and draws her dress on one side as she gives him the phial, so that it may hide her hand. When he has it, she presses his hand round it, so that it cannot be seen, and then she stands away from him.

What does he think as he stands there, now full of terror? Death faced on the battle field or on the scaffold may be met calmly; but to die poisoned, treacherously destroyed by a lie, it would make a god tremble. Fool, that for a moment he had trusted the court of Ferrara; and this antidote, perchance 'twas death; perchance the wine had *not* been poisoned! He had insulted *her* more deeply than he had the duke. Distrustful and terror-stricken, he stands hesitatingly.

"Drink, drink, he deemed thee his rival."

As he looks on her face his heart turns towards her — he knows not why, but he believes her — he seems to think she wills that he shall believe her, he sees in the proud face nothing but love for him, not a guilty love. No, she looks, this terrible woman, as his mother might look upon him.

"Drink, save thyself — for — *for thy mother's sake.*"

Ah! it has decided him, he raises the little bottle to his lips, and he is saved.

She knows now he will obey her.

She runs quickly to a secret door — for such a palace must have secret doors — and slides it open ; by a gesture she bids him enter, presses his long hanging sleeve to her breast as he passes her — and he is gone. Then, as she closes the door, she is a lioness guarding her young. She folds her arms and stands there waiting. The gentleness of face which bade the soldier drink the antidote is gone. She stands there — awful, terrible, alone. No one now — no one now beyond the known and hated LUCREZIA BORGIA.

CHAPTER IV.

THE night was come, and the Princess Negroni's palace was a blaze of light. The grand ball spoken of by Orsini, was taking place, and all Ferrara was there. At one table, drinking and singing, were Orsini, Gennaro, and most of the young lords who were present at the unmasking of the Borgia at Venice. They were chiefly in the suite of the Venetian ambassador, and now, as on the night at Venice, they were all together, as friends should be.

"Would you believe it, Signors," said the Orsini, gaily, "you see Captain Gennaro here by the merest chance. He was furiously preparing to fly us, when I came upon him. To Venice; would you believe it, he was departing for Venice. 'What,' said I, 'did we not swear to live and die together? and now dost thou leave me?' 'True,' said he, 'yet —' But, Signoras, I would not let him go. 'No, no,' said I, 'come thou to the fête with us, and I promise I will start with thee at dawn.' So, behold, we are both here."

Applause, followed by discussion of wines. One was for Madeira, another for Rhenish; but all were of one opinion, that every kind of wine was good.

The hours crept on, the guests departed, yet was the table of the Venetians occupied by the Venetians themselves, and by many ladies, amongst them the Princess.

Gubetta was there, and kept his watchful eye upon them all.

"I am tired already, and will go."

"'Tis he again," cried Orsini; "'tis Gennaro who spoke. Gennaro, hear my new ballad."

"Ah, ah."

"Who dareth to laugh at me?"

"I, Gubetta, and the rest of us. Thou art an eminent poet, truly."

"An insult, Signors."

"If laughing is insulting thee, I do; ah, ah."

"Castilian renegade!"

2

" Roman bully ! "

In a moment the place was in confusion. The women fled, the seats were overturned, and the Orsini and his enemy had armed themselves with knives from the table, for it was the wise custom to deliver arms at the door where feasts and rejoicings were held.

" Respect the Princess," said one, holding back the Orsini.

" The guard will break open the doors," said a second, restraining the Spaniard.

" To-morrow, Signors, to-morrow."

" When you may fight with swords."

" And not with knives like highwaymen."

" Signors," said the spy, Gubetta, now that his ruse for removing the women had succeeded. ' Signors, I was wrong."

" Truly ; and to prove it, Orsini shall sing us his song."

" Orsini *will*."

" Wine, wine."

" Truly, Signors, wine." Thus Gubetta. "There, cup-bearer. My faith, Signors, this is Siracusa, the noblest drink. Let me pour for you." And he took the tankard, no one wondering where the bearer of it sprung from. Nay, they took each a cup, and crowded round the Spanish spy, each calling laughingly for a share of the Siracusa.

" Nay, nay, Signors — there is enough for all."

" Thou hast poured all out, Gubetta. Thou hast none — now drink with me, Orsini, from the same cup. 'Twill drown our quarrel."

" Nay, Signor Orsini, as a punishment on me, drink thou the whole draught thyself."

" Obedience is good-will. Behold — the cup is empty."

" Orsini ! Orsini ! the song."

" Here 'tis."

> ' Oh, I'll teach you the secret I've taught me,
>   I mean the sure way to be glad,
> 'Tis — or cloudy — or freezing — or sunshine,
>   Oh ! never, oh ! never be sad.

> " Oh ! — oh — sing, drink, and laugh at the madmer
> Who give to the future a thought;
> Let to-morrow look after to-morrow,
> For double is trouble when sought."

Hark — as the last note dies away, there is a slow chanting without.

" THE JOY OF THE PROFANE IS A PASSING SMOKE."

As the solemn sound reaches them, the very light seems to pass away. For it is late, and the lights are dying out.

" What voices are these ? "

" 'Tis a jest."

" Bah — another verse."

" Oh — 'tis ready."

> " Let us smile on the youth that smiles on us,
> For youth of all joys is the crown ;
> While if death for a moment draw nigh us,
> And he should ungraciously frown.

> " Oh ! — oh — sing, drink, and laugh at that madman
> Who gives to the future a thought ;
> Let to-morrow look after to-morrow,
> For double is trouble when sought."

" THE JOY OF THE PROFANE IS BUT A PASSING SMOKE."

" Again those sounds ! "

" See — see, how the lights are going out."

" Gennaro, I can barely see thee."

" Orsini, Orsini, here."

" Methinks this is no jest," cried another.

And the six came close together. Amongst them was no Gubetta.

A moment or two of bated breath, still the lights are fading. Another moment, and the room is almost dark as midnight.

" Let us fly."

They drew to the great door, sped rapidly up the steps, and then the whole six stood motionless, their hands pressing against the unyielding doors.

They came down from the steps, but the next moment the doors swung open, and as they turned towards them, thinking, perhaps, for a moment, that it *was* a jest — behold there stood Lucrezia Borgia, looking down on them, proud, triumphant — a demon. Behind her were men-at-arms, ready to do her utmost will.

"Lost! — lost! — lost!"

"Yes, Signors. Lost. You gave me a ball at Venice. In return I give you a supper here in Ferrara. For you, my guests, I have prepared five shrouds, which shall enwrap you when the poison now coursing through your blood, hath diligently done its duty."

"Five did'st thou say? But here are six of us!"

"Oh heavens, Gennaro!"

Then rapidly she turned to the guard behind her; almost by a gesture she bade them remove the destroyed gentlemen, and coming down the steps, called to Gennaro to remain.

Helpless — lost — they showed no spirit. Hope had utterly left them. They embraced their friend Gennaro one after the other, and went mournfully from the hall. Gennaro alone remaining, she ran swiftly to the doors, bidding one close them, and ordering that whatever happened, no one should enter the room.

"Thou wert here, Gennaro, thou wert here."

"Near my friends, lady."

"Again thou art poisoned."

"And my friends, lady?"

Suddenly her face lit up. "The antidote, the antidote I gave thee."

Love of life is strong — so he felt for the little bottle, and he held it before her.

"Drink it."

"No — with my friends I either live or die."

She took the little bottle, looked at it agonizingly, and then said, "There is barely enough for thee. Holy virgin, he has cast it to the ground."

"But if I must die, thou demon — if I, my friend, my dear Orsini, if we all die, shalt thou live — thou? Ah! thou also hast reached death; none will come to help thee; hast thou not closed the door thyself. Prepare thee, thou shalt die!"

See how the knife glitters in the pale moonlight as it sweeps high up into the air.

"Gennaro! Gennaro! wouldst thou kill me?"

"On thy knees. I grant thee that mercy, die on thy knees."

"I forbid thee!"

"Thou forbid me, thou who hast destroyed me. To thy knees! To thy knees!"

He forces her to her knees. Again the avenging steel is high in the air. Another moment and he shall thrust it downwards through the air — down, down, into her wicked heart. But she speaks five words — and see! The steel has fallen from his hand, and is lying harmless on the floor, his hands are clasped upon his head, and she may kill him without fear and so save herself. What is it then she has said? The words were : —

"Hold — thou art a Borgia."

Hark to what he whispers. "I — I a Borgia?"

"Thy ancestors were mine. Thou durst not shed the blood of thy people."

"I — I a Borgia?"

"What have I said? have I forbidden thee to kill me? Rather I should bid thee kill me, for each day I die a thousand deaths. And thou, oh live, live, Gennaro. If thou canst save thyself, and if thou wilt not, thou dost destroy thyself. See, see, the phial is not broken. Thou canst yet be saved. Ah! thou takest it from my hand. Drink! drink!"

"I — I a Borgia?"

"Drink. No, do not hear that sound, 'tis nothing — 'tis but the wind."

"Oh Maffio, 'tis thy voice, the poison kills thy youth the first. Good bye, good bye."

"They shall live, if thou wilt save thyself. For thy mother's sake."

"How darest thou name my mother?"

"And who may name her, if not I?"

"Perchance, thou didst destroy her also."

"Ah, no! she lives."

"She lives, she lives, and I shall never see her."

Here the quick poison struck him so that he reeled against a high Gothic pillar to save himself from falling, and as his hands lay on his breast, he leaned his head slowly backward, and still he cried "Mother, mother, that I could die in her arms. Back, back, woman, do not touch me. Oh, mother! mother!"

"A woman, guilty, yet penitent, quailing and kneeling at the feet of him whom she has slain, who lowers her head as I do mine, and fearingly doth shut out sight by covering her eyes with both her hands, as I do, Gennaro. This woman is thy mother."

As she spoke, he was sustaining himself against the Gothic pillar, like a brave man as he was, willing to meet death standing — rocking round the pillar from right to left, and clinging to it with weak hands.

But the last words stay him. Rigid he stands for a moment, then as she flinches away from him, yet stretching out her arms, he falls down, and to her breast.

"In my mother's arms. At last in my mother's arms, I die."— And as her arms crept round him he was dead.

As he lay there, she looking on him, the doors were opened, notwithstanding her orders, and there at the head of the steps stood the duke and many ladies. No fear now had she of him, her Gennaro was dead. He might come and scorn, upbraid, insult her now. No matter, she did not care.

Hark! she speaks.

"He was my son, my hope, my comfort. He would have saved me. Where now is hope? All lost. All lost. Heaven hath turned from me."

Her head fell and her cheek lay against her child's.

They went to lift her. And then they learnt that she was dead.

So, destroyed by the only godlike evidence she ever had, the love she bore her child, lay Lucrezia Borgia, cold upon the palace floor.

[Note.— The general notion of Lucrezia Borgia seems to partake of the nature of a popular error. Though the sister to the great Cesare was not, perhaps, the most discreet lady in the world, and though drama, opera, and tale have represented her as " the great poisoner of the fifteenth century," no authentic account of a crime of this nature has yet appeared. It is true that she married thrice, and that tradition gives her a hand in the deaths of two of her husbands, but no criminal charge has been really substantiated against her. It is well that the truth be told of so famous a historical personage, even though a whole library of fine fiction be thereby destroyed. She lived in a profligate court, and was doubtless witness to many flagitious scenes, but that is all that can be said against her. On the other side of the picture we have her charities, her beauty, her wisdom, and her devotion, in the latter years of her life, to virtue and religion.— ED.]

DON GIOVANNI. (Mozart.)

(DON JUAN.)

CHAPTER I.

A TALE whispered and told to children all Spain through. And why should not a statue have power to speak?

Don Juan lived in a city of Castille, lived a godless, reckless life; and as for that matter so did his factotum Leporello. If the don climbed a ladder, Leporello held it; if the don had to be thrashed, Leporello often caught the blows. He might have had a better service, and he frequently complained of the don's, but he did not leave it till the don had no further need of a factotum.

One night he was watching as usual, and grumbling as usual, "what a life was his, to be harrassed day and night, blown by the wind, cut at by the rain, robbed of sleep, and all for what? no wages paid, and half starvation." For the thousandth time he had resolved to get him a new master, when the noise of footsteps made him discreetly retire.

Next moment where he had been standing, was a woman striving to detain a cavalier, and calling all the time for help.

"Let me go, I say, for thine own sake, let me go."

"Help, help."

A quick, heavy step, and a third person was there, an old man, his white hair streaming in the moonlight.

The lady let go her hold, as the new comer ran forward, his sword bravely out before him.

Yet he did not at once fall on this thief coming in the night time. He called on him to defend himself.

Said the other, placing himself, so that the golden braid about him glistened in the moonlight, "Begone, my sword is not crossed with such as yours."

"Defend yourself, I say."

"Ah! dotard, if thou bravest me."

A little sawing of the swords, a click or two, and the white hair is touching the dust.

"Dead, by the rood!" exclaimed the cavalier, wiping his sword. "Here, Leporello, here!"

"Sinner that I am — behold me, master. Thou art not killed — then the old man is?"

"Surely, the old can better be spared than the young."

"Rare, rare, my master, to break into the chamber of the daughter, and to kill the father, both in one night. Rare, oh! rare."

"By my faith, he thrust himself upon my sword. Come, let us go. See, torches are flickering near."

And without fear or hurry, the young don moved away, not swaggeringly, yet audaciously, followed by the trembling Leporello.

Another moment, and the light of torches was gleaming on the face of the dead. The old man's daughter, Donna Anna, had hastened away for assistance, and returned with it but to find her father slain, the warm blood gurgling out from his heart on to the cold and thirsty ground.

With her was the Don Ottavio, her betrothed, but he was nothing to her in her grief, as she leant over her dead father.

Then came the solitary procession, bearing one dead into his house, who but a little while agone was hale and strong, even in his age.

Meanwhile, the don was forgetting the tragedy.

Even the next evening he was in the streets with Leporello, seeking some new adventures.

"Well, Leporello, and pray what is it thou hast to tell me?"

"It is important — it is grave."

"Better and better."

"Now good master, promise not to be wrath."

"So that it doth not relate to Don Pedro."

"Unless thou art Don Pedro, it doth not relate to him."

"Speak out!"

"Verily, thy life is infamous!"

2*

" Rapscallion."

" And thy promise, good master, thy promise."

" What ! thou darst to suppose *I* keep promises."

" To *me*, yes, of a verity, I'm dumb, I'm dumb."

" The way to friendship.   Now, why am I here ? "

" An affair.   The name of the damsel, for my list, good master, for the perfectioning of my list."

" Write her down Venus, for she hath her form.   I shall whisper her at the Casino; but tarry a little, here cometh one — whom — "

" In truth my master hath a good eye."

" At a glance, I see she is handsome."

" And also she hath a brave eye ! "

" Let us retire a little."

" He hath fired already.   O rare."

Into the shadow they crept (the don dealt largely in shadows.)

'Twas a Spanish beauty, and a pensive beauty, who came slowly along.

" Lepo, 'tis a damsel who hath need of condolement."

" He hath condoled with many of them, this master of mine."

" Senorita, Senorita.   Heaven ! "

" Ha ! 'tis Donna Elvira; O rare — rare."

" 'Tis you, Don Juan — monster, robber ! "

" 'Tis an old acquaintance, as one shall read by the tongue."

" Donna ! quiet, quiet (what misfortune); if thou wilt not believe me, thou'lt believe this worthy gentleman."

" In faith ! that's Leporello — "

" He 'll tell thee all; I pray thee turn to him."

And the lady doing so, the don took advantage of the shadow, and was off anywhere.

" Well, villain, speak ! "

" In faith, good lady, it may be declared, seeing the world we live in, that a square is ne'er a round, or equally a round a square; and yet — "

" Cease, scrub; and thou, Don Juan — gone !   The monster hath gone !   Which way ? "

" Ah ! marry, which way ! though wherefore shouldst thou care ; he is not worth the kindness of so considerable a lady."

" Ah, he leaves me ! "

"By your leave, lady, 'tis not the first lady he hath fled from. Have I not here a book, which hath weight in it, I warrant thee ; and if it be not filled with the names of the ladies he hath fled from, with the particulars of their birth, parentage, and residences, the evil one hath played false with my handwriting, or some good angel hath, in pity to my master, wiped out the faithful record. See now, in Italy he flies me six hundred and forty ; in Germany, he hath ruined two hundred and thirty-one ; one hundred in France ; thou shalt repeat me that number for Turkey ; but here in Spain he hath destroyed the peace of one thousand and three."

Here the serving man dutifully followed his master into shadow, and scudded away harder and harder when he heard the pattering of little feet behind him.

CHAPTER II.

LITTLE Zerlina was a little country maiden, as happy as the sun was bright, and as fond of Masetto as the bee of sweet flowers.

As for Masetto, he loved Zerlina as honest natives do love, with his whole heart, and he thought nobody equal to Zerlina.

And that day was come when Zerlina and Masetto were to be nobody's business, and more, and were to be all in all to each other for life ; they were going to be married.

The country folk were blythe and happy, and full of the wedding, chatting, laughing, and wishing the bride and bridegroom happy, when a grand Don, accompanied by his servant, for he walked behind, caused the prattle to die away into silence.

" I'faith, pretty creatures ! a marriage, good friends ? Nay, go on with your sports — go on."

" Yes, good my lord, and I am the bride."

" A lovely bride ! And who's the bridegroom ? "

" So please you, at your service, here, I call myself Masetto."

"Spoken bravely!"

"O rare! he hath the build of a husband, hath he not?"

Here the little bride, who was a little vain, and who rather plumed herself upon talking to a grandee, said, "Masetto hath an excellent heart."

"And also have I, so we should be friends; and, prythee, what do they call thee?"

"Zerlina, so please you."

"And so please you, *I* call myself Masetto."

For truth to tell, the little rustic was growing jealous.

"And you two are to be married. Well, well; I do offer you my protection, aye, and my house. Leporello, show these good people to my house, give them what they will; and for the bridegroom, he is the guest of honor, Leporello — pay, if thou valuest whole bones, excellent attention to the bridegroom."

"I seize thee, master, I seize thee." Thus the man, speaking softly to the master. Then the man said to the lucky bridegroom: "So please you, walk by me. And all you rustics, follow heartily."

"But, good sir, Zerlina must come with me."

"'Tis not etiquette that thou shouldst be bound to her side. Good friend, come walk by me. The Senor himself will care for her right heartily. So please thee, walk walk."

"Oh! be not afraid, Masetto, the senor will guard me."

"But! — but! —"

"Verily, friend Masetto, thou art little better than a curmudgeon. Walk, I say, walk."

"Dost thou not breathe more lightly, Zerlina?"

"Wherefore, Senor?"

"That the clown hath gone."

"Nay — he hath my love!"

"A king should have thy love; those pretty lips, those eyes, those little fingers, were not made for clowns."

"Nay — but I love him!"

"And I love *thee*. A poor home, and a poor husband — is this thy lot? See away there, 'tis my house, 'tis my palace. I love thee, I love thee. Wilt thou be my wife, Zerlina?"

"Wife, Senor, *thy* wife?"

"Choose between us, Masetto or Don Juan."

"I — I, then, a great lady. Yet, Masetto."

"Come my love, come, my love."

But the don started and turned pale, for as he made a step forward with the simple little Zerlina, there was standing Donna Elvira.

"Thou seest," he said rapidly, before she could speak, "I am but toying with her simplicity, I mean no harm,"

"No harm, Don Juan, thou art destruction."

"Nay, believe her not, charming Zerlina, 'tis a poor forlorn creature, who followeth me because I cannot love her. Well, if she will not quit me, I will her;" and lightly he ran away.

She pitied him, did the donna, nay she still loved him somewhat; but for all that, she warned Zerlina of him and went away with that simple little maiden, hand in hand.

Barely had they left the spot, than Don Juan was upon it again, for he had determined upon keeping the little village maiden in view. But barely had he returned to the spot than he was accosted by one whom he would fain have not seen, Don Ottavio, the cavalier of Donna Anna.

The don was not easily abashed, so he came lightly to Ottavio's side, but he thought to himself that this was one of his unlucky days.

"This meeting is fortunate, Don Juan, if thou hast a generous heart."

"I hope for thy sake and mine own, that I have."

"For we have need of thy friendship."

"I breathe again," thought the don, who, brave as he was, had trembled in meeting the injured lady, Donna Anna. "Command me," he said aloud, "my arms are thine, if 'tis a question of arms. But Donna Anna, why these tears?"

"Do not hear him," said a voice; and the three turning, saw Donna Elvira, who had determined to keep Juan in view; "do not hear him, he hath destroyed me."

"Pardon her Ottavio, and you, Donna Anna, she is a poor deranged lady; leave her to me."

"Do not believe him!"

"Poor lady! You see!"

"Do not believe him!"

Donna Anna and Ottavio seemed puzzled by this meeting. The lady seemed sane, and yet Don Juan was a man of probity, said all the world.

He bade her be still; but she called out more loudly than before, that he was her destroyer; and as she changed color, and struck her foot upon the ground, Ottavio and Anna shook their heads as though deploring her.

Whereon, the poor lady seeing their error, turned from them, and walked away quickly.

The don took advantage of this incident to rid himself of the terrible company of Ottavio and Anna, and so saying that for her dear sake he would follow her, he fled away, not marking the terrified start that Donna Anna gave as he turned from her.

"Dear Anna, how pale thou art! What has happened?"

"I dare not say, and yet I dare not be silent."

"Speak! speak!"

"As I live — as I live, Ottavio, Don Juan killed my father."

"What sayest thou?"

"I am sure; I am sure. The tones of the last words he spoke — the very words themselves. Ottavio, as I live he killed my father; 'twas he who entered my room; whom I held, whom I followed, who turned and killed my father! I ask of thee that vengeance that is just, Ottavio. Be but sure, and then act; thy arm shall be strengthened to thy work by my love — by the memory of my bleeding father! Come, come!"

Barely had the couple left the spot, than Leporello and his master were upon it.

"If I fly him not, the foul fiend will have me!"

"Well my little Leporello? All well?"

"No, little Don Juan; on the other side, all ill."

"Wherefore ill?"

"Wherefore? marry, because 'tis. Have I taken them all to thy house? Yes have I. Have I spoken lies and flattery in thy service, that I am lost for ever? Yes have I. Have I beguiled Masetto till he is a very fool? The tempter knoweth that I have. The men I have set drinking, the women idem (as the lawyers have it), when, who cometh, if not my little Zerlina? And who with our little Zerlina, if not Madame Elvira, who prythee? She should be laid, master; she should be laid like a vexed spirit. And she hath abused me; my faith! hath she abused me — hath she laid about her uncivilly touching me!"

"And what saidst thou?"

"Marry, the best thing I could say. . . nothing. But when she hath worn herself silent, and when she is, if I may thus say it, so to speak, melting in tears, I take me her hand, direct her to the street, and there do I most gingerly leave her."

"Then, she being gone, I may be there. Now, my Leporello, wine, wine; bring us plenty of wine, for 'tis the persuader which smoothens my road wonderfully."

And, taking the factotum by the arm, he pushed him along before him.

CHAPTER III.

"But Masetto, dear Masetto."

"Get thee gone. What! thou wouldst caress me, thou false Zerlina!"

"But I love thee."

"Then hast thou a marvellous queer way of showing it. Thou dost bemean me. Thou dost make fingers to point at me, and then, forsooth, thou dost say 'I love thee.' Pish! for pure modesty's sake I cry 'shame.'"

"But I love thee. He did deceive me. See, if thou lovest me not, thou dost kill me. Wherefore turnest thou from me? I love thee, I love thee."

"Thou art encompassed with immodesty."

"Beat me, beat me, thy Zerlina, here she stands, beat me; and I'll kiss thy hands quite meekly. Beat me, beat me, but forgive me, for I love thee, dear Masetto."

"Thou hast the power of the evil one to overthrow me. Truly, man is weak."

"Beat me, beat me. Masetto, here's the don."

" Let him approach.   I defy him."

" I fain would hide myself."

"And, marry, I fain thou shouldst not.   Ho, ho — she fears I shall learn secrets; ho, ho, ho, thou art falsity.   I will hide myself."

" Nay, if he find thee, he will beat thee, as thou wattest not of."

" Let him fear me, my arm is strong."

" 'Tis hopeless to speak to him."   This she said softly.

" Speak loudly, untruthful woman, speak honestly loud. (I have mine ideas, yes, Masetto, I have mine ideas.)"

And he hid behind a tree.

Said the little woman to herself, " he hath a wry mind, Masetto ; " and then she ran to hiding herself, as she saw the don approach, accompanied by several peasants.

He dismissed those people immediately, and then called out " Zerlina, come thou here."

" So please you, let me go."

" My angel, I love thee too well."

" So please you, if thou art merciful, let me go."

" Masetto, come thou here also."

" My faith, he hath marked me," said the rustic, and came forward sheepishly.

" Thy Zerlina is unhappy when thou art not near her, why dost leave her? come, be merry, I will go with you and be merry with you," and he walked away between them, and entered his house with them.

Nor did he see three masked persons following him. Donna Anna, Donna Elvira, and Don Ottavio.   They were following him, marking him, bringing home his guilt to him.

Suddenly Leporello passing a window of the house within, saw the masks and called out, " O rare, my master, here is fit company for thee, my master ; here are ladies, and of a quality!   What sayest thou, invite them in.   Aye, marry, will I.   Masks, list, fair masks ; my master greets ye, and prays ye enter ; ye shall find good entertainment."

Still watching him, still tracing the crime to him, they entered the house of the murderer.

CHAPTER IV.

In the house of the don itself, the rustic feast, which he had improvised, was going on —

"Pray ye, Senors, drink; I, Leporello, who talk to ye, will sip chocolate, but ye shall take what ye will — sherbet, sweetmeats, as you like it — as you like it."

"My lovely Zerlina, thou charmest me."

"Thou art very kind Senor!"

"My faith," said Masetto, "she is as a fine lady!"

"Oh! rare, I love ye all, ye charmers."

"If thou touchest her, Senor Leporello, I will touch thee," exclaimed Masetto, who saw the factotum eyeing the simple, charming Zerlina.

"Methinks he's fallen out with me again," said the simple Zerlina to herself.

"Of a verity, I shall go distraught," said Masetto.

Here the masks entered.

The don bowed to them, then called out to the musicians, and went gaily up to Zerlina.

"That — that is the poor country girl," said one of the masks, in a low tone: and the three drew together.

"Verily, I tell thee, nor will I dance myself, nor shall she dance: I love not these pousettings."

"Verily, and I tell thee, Masetto, thou art a rare fool, a fool such as the world hath never seen. Be merry, I say be merry; nay, thou shalt be merry."

And the man of stratagem playfully thrust about the uneasy rustic, while the master led away the young girl. Then the dancing began, and soon the don had thrust Zerlina into a closet, unperceived, he hoped, but fully marked by the eyes under the masks.

At once they ran towards the door, as the girl called out loudly, "Help! help!"

"Verily, 'tis her own voice — help me, masters, help!"

Here the don entered by another door, and, sword in hand, fell upon the luckless Leporello. "What, thou wicked servant, thou destroyer, wouldst thou, in thy master's house, send thyself to perdition? Ho, ho! thou shalt die."

The simple folk were inclined to believe the don, and would have fallen upon the servant, who cried under his breath, " 'Tis the fiend himself."

But the wearers of the masks showed their faces — Don Ottavio, Donna Anna, and Donna Elvira.

And they unmasked him, too, for they pointed to him as the ravisher.

Then they threatened him, stood about him with angry glances. Nearer and nearer they came, and as though approving them, the thunder muttered high in the air.

But he was fearless; on heaven, or earth, or both, he cared not. Like a baffled tiger, he flew at his enemies, cut his way through them, and was saved.

CHAPTER V.

" I tell thee, master, 'twere death to stay with thee."

" Then thou hadst best depart."

" Verily will I, and quickly."

" Yet why desert me, thy old master?"

" What ho! thou beatest me, thou dost threaten to kill me; am I kicked, am I cuffed? Wherefore is it that I am kicked and cuffed? Now, tell me that, master?"

" Le-po-rel-lo!"

" So, my master — "

" What! shall we not be friends again? I say, yes. Ope thy hand."

" How much?"

" Four pistoles, Le-po-rel-lo."

" Good! rare! but I tell thee, that if thou thinkest a man of my mettle is to be bought with dirty gold, as thou wouldst buy of the weaker sex, thou thinkest mainly wrong, my master."

" Nay, drop thy hand, there be no more pistoles."

" Avaunt! the gold; but if I stay by thee, thou wilt promise to abandon women?"

" Aye, aye!"

" Nay, dost thou not harm them ? "

" I, who love them all! Is not he cruel to all who loveth but one ? I do abhor cruelty, therefore do I love all
women. And yet are there women who stand by thy
metaphysics, and call this love of mine perfidy."

" If thy love is benevolence, which is charity, then art
thou saved, and art sure of a cool heaven."

" But thou didst never see so sweet a woman. And I
had thy dress ? "

" Marry, is she so sweet that she loveth a patched jer-
kin ? "

" Her mistress is not a patch upon her; and her mistress
is Donna Elvira."

" What! wouldst make the maid weep also ? "

" I would rather the maid wept than Leporello. See,
'tis the house, and behold Elvira at the window. I will
speak to her — Elvira! dear Elvira ! "

" Who speaketh ? Methinks 'tis the voice of the per-
jured Don Juan ! "

" 'Tis Juan, who prays thee to forgive him."

" My faith ! Of a verity I believe she will trust him.
O rare! O rare ! "

" Thou art a traitor, Juan."

" Nay, descend, love, that I may kiss thy tears away."

" Methinks, I shall very fairly crack with laughing.
This is good. This is good, rare."

" Dear Elvira, come to me, come to me."

" She yieldeth now. By my faith, I would I had such
a deft tongue i' my head. She hath left the window."

" Friend Leporello, dost thou not admire me ? "

" Master, if thou comest not from heaven, of a surety I
know *thy* cradle — 'tis below, master, 'tis below ! "

" Now remember thee of this. When she cometh out,
smother her in thy arms. Speak as I speak, yet not fine
like a woman. Then deftly discourse her away."

" *Good.* But if she find me out ? "

" Then hadst thou best scarify thyself."

" *Good.* My faith, a pretty posture mine. I will leave
this master. I will leave him."

Here the luckless lady came from the house.

" Nay Juan, did I ever think my sorrow would melt thy
heart. Thou dost, then, repent thee of thy desertion ? "

" Aye, do I."

" I have sighed as the south wind sigheth all the long night through."

" Eugh."

" But thou wilt never leave me again."

" Angel, never."

" Thou wilt forever be mine."

" Eugh."

" And thou wilt never deceive me again ? "

" Ne—e—ver."

" Thou wilt swear."

" I swear by this kiss upon thy hand."

" Ha! ha! ho! the guard, the guard." Thus cried Don Juan, while the unfortunate lady ran quickly away.

The don was about to enter at the open door, when he stopped suddenly, as he saw Masetto come stealthily along, accompanied by some friends. For the young Zerlina's sake he was interested.

" Now, who goeth there ? "

" A friend; my faith, 'tis Masetto. Ah, Masetto! What, knowest thou me not ? "

" Why, thou art the very foul one's servant ! "

" Don Juan's; ah, 'tis a base man, Masetto; a base man. I have left him for a godly service."

" Truly? But canst thou tell me where I shall find him, for we would fain cudgel him to death ? "

" Good. I will help you, my master, to punish this sinner unparalleled. He is near at hand, my masters, and making love, for he hath a rare habit of making love. Go you — all. I and Masetto will follow you."

So the peasants went off stealthily on their toes, each hoping to have a hand in towelling the don.

" So, Masetto, thou wilt cudgel him to the death."

" To the *very* death ; good."

" Wouldst not be satisfied with a few broken bones ? "

" Talk not to me of broken bones only, he shall soon know of no bones, marry."

" Thou'rt well armed, friend ? "

" A cudgel, sir, i'faith such as shall make a broad-chested man fly before thee ; feel not its weight. Oh, oh. My head, mercy o' my head. My back, wouldst twitter my back to a jelly? Marry, now, 'twas an awful thwack to the elbow; help, oh, oh. See what 'tis to trust people. Help!"

Here the don finding his vicious arm quite weak, stole away in the dark, each of Masetto's "helps" growing fainter and fainter.

Now little Zerlina had followed her rustic affar off, and when she heard his yells, she came with quite a run to his side. Arrived there, she saw no one near him; but he was still yelling, and rubbing all of his back he could get at.

"Masetto, Masetto, what hast thou?"

"By my faith, what have I not? I am beaten to a jelly!"

"Who hath beaten thee?"

"A man of a foul tongue and a strong arm."

"Where is he?"

"I know not, but that he is gone. Why art thou here? Oh, gadabout, why art thou here?"

"Thou art jealous again."

"Why art thou here? Now answer me that, straightly and purely."

"Thou shalt see, O dearest, what my answer is. For a reason that no money could purchase nor art wrest from me — that thou mightst lay thy hand — thy hand here on my heart."

Whereon the jealous young rustic marched home appeased.

CHAPTER VI.

THE worthy servant and the worthy master were once more together; they met in the cemetery.

The don was wondering how his servant had managed with the Donna Elvira, when that valuable factotum ran up against his master.

"This master will destroy me."

"What! dost ruffle with thy master?"

"Yes, I say again — would I had never known this master."

" What, rapscallion ! "

" I tell thee I have rarely escaped a murdering business and I love not blood, my master; no, I love not blood."

" 'Twould be an honor to lose blood for thy master's sake."

" Faith ! I would sooner keep it for mine own."

" Come, I have rare adventures to tell thee."

" Good master, tell them me at home ; but, master, what devilment brings thee here ? "

" I have had a wondrous adventure."

" The poor woman ! "

" I met her in the street. Thou may'st guess, I briskly went to her. Take her by the hand, do I ? Aye, yes. When, thou dog, whom, thinkest thou, she took me for? Thyself was it? Yes, then."

" For me ! then, master, that woman hath abused herself in this, for I will have nought to do with the sex."

" But, faith ! she soon finds I am not Leporello, and then doth she yell so as to wake the happiest sleepers. I' faith ! I leapt over the wall, and here am I. Ha, ha, ha ! "

" Good ! rare ! my master. Ha, ha, ha ! "

" BEFORE THE DAWN THIS MIRTH SHALL DIE ! "

" Who speaketh ? "

" Master as I tremble — and I would not say I do not tremble ; for as I have a soul, I tremble vastly — 'tis some spirit from the other world who knows thee better even than I do."

" Peace, fool ! Who speaketh ? "

" MAN WEIGHED DOWN WITH CRIME, DEPART FROM AMIDST THE HOLY DEAD."

" Did I not say 'twas a spirit, master ? A very gentle spirit, most assuredly."

" 'Tis some one without the wall, who would affright us. But, prythee, is not that the statue of Don Pedro ? By my faith, 'tis the statue of Don Pedro ! Read the inscription."

" I pray thee spare me. My eyes are not diligent in the moonlight."

" Read, Leporello, read."

" Yes, master, yes. As I do spell it, it says, ' PATIENTLY HERE I AWAIT VENGEANCE ON MY DESTROYER.' "

"Master, good master, if thou upholdest me not, I fall."

"Bid him to supper. Ha! ha! ha!"

"Preserve us, ye saints, how he frowneth. Master, he hath life. He will speak. I would I were conveniently away from here. Master, why dost thou not look at the statue?"

"'Tis not handsome. Now, thou cur, obey me!"

"Softly, good master. This is woeful, this is woeful. So please you, gentle statue; nay, I cannot proceed. I have my heart in my mouth. I would I were at home, this master will most completely destroy me."

"If thou dost hesitate, I will warm this dagger in thy coward's heart. Now, proceed."

And he again laughed, still not turning his face to the statue.

"So please you, gentle statue, for I advise me thou art gentle, if thou art stonely — he hath turned his eyes on us: mercy, he hath remarked us."

"What, thou wilt die, recreant?"

"Master, laugh not. So thou hast thy choice of death, Leporello — 'tis more than many a sinner; either by fear or by steel thou fallest. Well, well, if I love blood, I know not my likings. Good, master, good. Most gentle of statues, my master, and I — prythee, mark well, 'tis my *master*, and not I, good statue. Oh Lord! he hath up and downed his head."

"Thou art but a pudding, friend Leporello."

"Granted, I am what I am, yet look, master."

"And wherefore?"

"The statue, which with his stony head goeth thus, up and down, up and down!"

Then suddenly the don turned and looked for the first time at the statue.

"Tell me, statue, wilt thou sup with me?"

"Yes."

The don started, but his courage was equal to his crimes, so he laughingly bade his servant come and prepare the meal.

"Anywhere and anything, my good master, so that we go from this place. Methinks I am half dead."

And the servant kept pretty close to his master's heels

till they had quitted the cemetery and the awful speaking statue.

CHAPTER VII.

THE supper was laid, the don seated. He had forgotten his guest. He sat lightly at table, leaning back in a great crimson chair, and chattering gaily to his servant and friend.

"Leporello, I shall eat a supper as large as thy eyes when thou art frightened."

"Rare, master, rare."

"This is a good dish, Leporello."

"My faith, but I would e'en eat of it too. I would he would ask me."

"Another plate, good Leporello. Pour out some wine, Leporello."

"Verily, if I do not eat, I shall fail in my strength. Faith, I will steal, 'tis not much more on my conscience."

"Leporello, my friend, whistle."

"He fain would stay my eating."

"Marry, how doth a man whistle, master?"

"Not with his mouth full."

"Master, lay it down that 'tis no fault of mine. The cook is too good; he is a tempter."

Here there sounded a terrible tramp which shook the mansion.

"Preserve us, saints; what is that my master?"

Again the awful sound broke over the house.

"'Tis a wondrous uncouth noise, Leporello!"

Again the sound came, like the footsteps of an iron-shod giant.

"Go thou to the door."

Yet once more the footsteps sounded. Nearer now.

The servant ran from the room and then came staggering back, shutting the folding doors after him, as though for safety.

"Help, master! help! methinks I am dying!"

Yet once more the sound was heard. Then a summons at the door of the room called the don's attention.

"Leporello, some one knocketh — open."

Still this man's courage held good. Surely he was as courageous as wicked.

"Open the door, I say."

"Nay, master, I cannot move."

"Then must I."

And he went to the door, and opened it. There stood the white statue of the murdered Don Pedro. Implacable, destructive.

"DON JUAN, THOU DIDST INVITE ME TO THY SUPPER; BEHOLD THY GUEST!"

Still mighty in his courage at least.

"I did not expect thee. Leporello, fresh dishes."

"Master, master, we are lost!"

"MY PRESENCE HERE IS THAT I MAY SPEAK WITH THEE!"

"Thou art polite."

"THOU HAST INVITED ME TO THY TABLE — WILT THOU BE MY GUEST?"

Here the first evidence of fear showed itself, in nervously tearing a candle from its socket and quickly walking round the visitor. As he ended that tour, he trembled, and the wax-light fell from his hand.

But he suddenly seemed to find fresh courage, and he flung himself easily into a chair.

"WILT THOU BE MY GUEST?"

"By the rood, master, say thou we are engaged."

"I will come with thee; I will be thy guest. I never yet feared; I never will."

"THEN THOU ACCEPTEST?"

"Good master, if you love me, say no. This master of mine will surely destroy me."

"I say I will be thy guest."

"THY HAND UPON IT."

"Behold it!"

Then he trembled again, for as he touched the hand the chill of death crept through him.

"REPENT, AMEND THY LIFE, OR DIE!"

This was a threat, so it renewed all his fatal courage.

"I will not repent; I will not amend my life! Let me die, then!"

3

"Repent, I say, amend thy life, or thou shalt
surely die!"

"No, no, no!"

"Thy time has past—'tis too late to hope—die!"

"What is this sudden fear which weighs me down?
Lost, lost! I see the flames rising to me. Lost, lost!"

So, if we repent not we shall surely die.

LA TRAVIATA. (VERDI.)

(THE LOST ONE.)

("LA DAME AUX CAMELIAS.")

CHAPTER I.

[THE author makes no apology for laying before his readers the tale of this popular opera, for never yet was fester cured by covering it up. Whereby, he means to say that no social wrong will be remedied, if the mention of it be ignored. But "La Dame aux Camelias" does not only rest upon this justification, it has yet another, "morality" itself. Let any unprejudiced man take the younger Alexandre Dumas's play, (I do not say the novel of the same name, which is terribly inferior,) and read it through, and I think he will admit, if he has read thoughtfully, that it is perhaps one of the best homilies he has ever perused. Let us now consider the subject. The heroine was a notorious woman, rich, handsome, courted. Seen going in her carriage to the opera, seen at balls, at gardens, always courted, always fêted; did she not excite envy in the heart of many a pretty girl, leaning on the arm of a not rich father? Dead — her history before the world, on the stage — let this said pretty girl see the real life of this woman, and her envy will change to pity; surely, a better armor than envy to defend *her* virtue! Let her look into the depths of that life, with no hope, one brilliant blank, surrounded by selfishness, and almost without a friend, and it will be no worthless lesson. Observe that all through the play the heroine is sad, and even in her poor yearnings after virtue, she does injury. And setting aside this real character, however, the play is a magnificent exposition of the heartlessness of sinful life, which may be read with profit by us all.]

There were many present, great lords and gentlemen, and several women. They were waiting for Marguerite's return.

What Marguerite was, all knew. The reigning beauty and toast of Paris. The woman for whom men fought duels, and before whom jewellers bowed low. She had more diamonds than the richest lady at court. Her carriages were perfection, her house as sumptuously furnished as a nobleman's.

And yet how wretched was her life. Not a young mother toiling for her children's bread, but she envied; and though she had thousands of diamonds, she had not a single friend. To be sure her maid liked her, but she sighed for one nearer and dearer.

Rich men fêted her and named her with honor over their wine, but she knew how little their friendship was worth; and so, amidst all her admirers and female companions, she was as lonely as a land bird on a rock at sea, and she as often sighed as would the wind about that same barren rock.

Well, on this night her house was full of company, waiting her return from the opera.

She soon came amongst them, radiant, splendidly dressed, and apparently as joyous as any there. But now and then she coughed, for near her always sat an unseen skeleton, holding an hour glass.

This evening, a gentleman named Armand was introduced to her, who, it was declared, had loved her for a long time, but who was too timid to tell her so.

Some one proposing to dance, Marguerite started up and began waltzing, but soon her cough came upon her, and she was obliged to sit down half-fainting.

The youth Armand ran to her, almost stranger as he was. "You suffer," lady!"

"Oh! no, no! take no heed of me; leave me for a little, and I shall soon be myself again."

They left the room, laughing and chattering (so used were they to her attacks); but the youth called Armand came gently back, as this poor lady looked at herself in a glass, with affright.

"You are still pale —"

" Ah! 'tis you, Monsieur Armand! Thank you, I am better; besides, I have grown accustomed to these attacks."

" If I were your friend, your relation, I would say you are killing yourself, and would prevent you from continuing this wretched life."

" Bah! you could not prevent me; but tell me, why are you yourself so pale?"

" I am sorry, perhaps, as I look upon you."

" You are very gentle; you see the others take no notice of me — "

" Perhaps — perhaps they do not love you as I do, lady."

" Ah! I forgot, this grand secret love of yours."

"You are laughing at me, lady."

" No, no — no, no — not laughing; I have heard the same declaration so often that I do not laugh at it."

" Ah! well, make some return for it, so take care of your health."

" Take care of my health, my friend! If I did, I should die at once. Bah! I can but live in this feverish life. Truly, good women, with families and friends, may seek quiet and rest, not such as I. The moment we cease to attract, we are alone, and our days then are *so* long, *so* long. Did I not keep my bed two months? At the end of the third week my last visitor came to see me!"

He again urged her to watch over her herself. She laughingly told him his countenance was too long. When he asked if she had a heart, she said 'twas the only thing left to such as her to throw away.

He looked so sad at her jesting, that she grew grave herself, and she said, " So, this passion is real?"

He told her he had followed her from place to place, and when she lay ill, inquired each day after her health.

" Why did you not ask to see me?"

" What right had I to ask?"

" Right! Do men stand on ceremony with me? So, you say you love me? Now, let me be your friend, and give you this advice — shake me by the hand, and let us part good friends, and for ever."

" As you will — as you will, good friend, and for ever."

" Ah! you are so far gone as that, my friend! Many men have told me they would not return, but have come back on the morrow."

He was going towards the door, when she called him back. " See you, I shall not have long to live, and 'tis but right I should live as I choose through my short span. But I tell you, if I believed your protestations, they would live even for a shorter time than I myself shall. Well, well, perhaps you have a good heart — who knows? Not I. And you seem sincere; perhaps you are for the moment. For this you should have some reward; take this flower. You know they call me the Lady of the Camelias, because I always carry a bouquet of those beautiful flowers. Oh! I give it you that you may return it to me. When? When it is faded."

" And in how short a time will that be?

" The time in which all flowers fade, the duration of an evening, or a morning. Good bye, good bye."

She fell into a reverie as the youth left her, but she was soon startled from it by the cries from the other room.

The next moment they came running in, as he joined them, and was soon as merry as the merriest among them.

Yet not for one mere moment was she really happy.

CHAPTER II.

Away from the hot, crowded city—away from the brilliantly lighted ball room. Away to a peaceful cottage before which rippled a lake, while round the trees whispered sorrowing peace through the livelong day.

Living at peace, but not happy. No, not for one moment happy. Always before her flitting in the air, the menacing fatal future, always treading on a flowery path resting on a volcano.

Again, want stepped in. These ladies always live up to the extent of their means; so, if money suddenly fails them, they are quite poor. Not actual want of bread, but want of luxuries, which are necessities to them. Besides, she had debts: and when she deserted her gay life in Paris, her creditors, who knew of her miserable health, noisily demanded payment. She kept all this from the man whom she had grown to honestly love. So first her carriage, then her diamonds, then her cashmeres went to appease the raging creditors, and pay their daily bills. The youth was poor, there was no income now. So they lived, and she staved off debts by the sale of the presents of old admirers.

A wretched life truly, and useful only as a warning.

He learnt at last the sacrifices she was making, and grew ashamed of himself. He had a small fortune of his own, and at least he was honorable enough to make preparations to throw it into the common vortex. He wrote to his lawyer, desiring him to dispose of his entire property ; and a few days after, telling her he had important business in the city, and bidding her keep up her spirits, left the cottage, and came to Paris, meaning to carry his poor fortune back to her, and bid her place it in the common bank.

Gone. Marguerite sat dreaming of her past life and her present position : who, she asked herself, would have thought that she, the gayest of the gay, should ever love such a tranquillity as she now enjoyed — passing days as happy as hers could be wholly with one whom, but three months ago, she did not even know. She would sit for hours hearing him read, and wonder when those hours had fled. At times she doubted whether she was the same woman — pictured her other self, still living the old weary life. And — and then she perhaps hoped that, away there in the hot bustling city, they had forgotten her. She often pictured herself gorgerously attired, the brilliant center of a ball-room crowd, and then shuddering at the sight, she turned from it, and saw herself seated near this new lover in their boat upon the lake and quietly gliding on the peaceful moonlit waters. She asked herself, Who would take this to be Marguerite?

She sat thinking, thinking for a long time, and at last she had a glimpse of such a bright future that she feared she might never live to reach it. She would sell all she possessed, all that could remind her of the past, and then they would live quietly in a couple of little rooms, and live as honest as they might. This was the first break of light in her gloomy life. Nevertheless, a great storm was gathering about her. We set up our little plans, we poor mortals, and the wind passes by and blows them down as easily as a breath overthrows the houses of cards, that children build on winters' evenings.

The lawyer had, with great prudence, warned the young man's father of the proposed sale. Coming up to Paris, the old man learnt the whole dismal truth. Portions of it had filtered home, indeed, and had done harm there; terrible harm; but no idea had the father that his son actually proposed to ruin himself for this lost woman.

Duval, the father, immediately took steps to discover his son's residence; and upon the very day that Armand left his quiet country house for Paris, the father turned his face towards it.

Marguerite was still dreaming — now hopefully — when a servant came and said that a gentleman wished to speak with her.

Given permission to enter, an old gentleman came in with a quick, haughty step, and suddenly announced himself as the youth's father.

Trembling, she answered that his son was not in the house.

"I know that, but 'tis with *you* I would speak. I presume that you know my son is degraded, and is ruining himself by remaining with you."

"Pardon; I know that no one speaks of me, and that I have not ruined your son. I have received not one piece of money from him."

"By which you mean to say that my son is fallen so low as to dissipate with you what you have received from others."

Pardon me again; I am a woman, and in my own house; two reasons which demand your courtesy, and — and you will allow me to — to leave you."

"Truly, as I look upon and hear you, madame, I can hardly believe the scandals I have heard of you, you, who I have been told, are dangerous company."

"Dangerous to myself, perhaps."

"But this lawyer's letter, does it not prove my poor

son's ruin? does it not show he is realizing all he is worth?"

She took the letter in her hand, and glanced hastily over its contents.

"I declare to you I know nothing of this act. I declare to you that your son knows I would refuse to take money from him."

"You have not always spoken so."

"I have not always been the woman that I am."

The unfortunate creature then burst into an incoherent declaration of her passion for the youth, but the disbelieving gentleman merely shrugged his shoulders.

She added she knew the oaths of such as she were not believed, yet she could swear she knew nothing of Armand's collecting his fortune into his own hands; but M. Duval, still being in doubt, she nervously took from a drawer a folded paper, and gave it into his hands.

It was a paper on which she had noted down what each of her valuables would probably realize; and, as her visitor had come without warning, he saw that she could not have prepared it in anticipation of his present visit. Then, believing her words were true, he began to show a courtesy to her which an hour before he would not have dreamed of using. Indeed, he expressed himself sorry that he had entered so abruptly, and told her that he thought, perhaps, she had a good heart after all. "And," he added, "perhaps so good that it will prompt you to make a sacrifice greater than all you have yet made."

She trembled violently; but strong in his duty, the old man went mercilessly on.

Gradually as he proceeded, the place grew dark around her; gradually all happiness drifted away, and she was left tossing about on a sea of troubles quite alone, with no guide, no hope.

He began by saying he had more than one child — he had a daughter, whose happiness rested on her brother's will. She might be married, but on one condition — that her brother led an honest life. As Marguerite covered her mouth, that she might save herself from hearing her own cry of terror, he added, that away in the provinces, they looked more severely on sin than they did in large

3*

cities; and indeed he had that morning received a letter from the father of his daughter's proposed husband, which peremptorily said that if Armand did not at once break off his connexion with Marguerite, all intercourse between the families must immediately cease. "See," he continued, "refined as you may have become, even in my eyes, by your affection for my son, the world will only look on your past life, and will forever close its doors to you."

She said she comprehended, and would obey him. She must leave his son for a time — only for a time? And he might write to her?

He required more — she must leave his son altogether — for good.

She said, "Never, never!" And with pardonable selfishness she cried, "that dying, as she was, having but a few years of life left she had built upon these few years for peace and love near the man who had reclaimed her. To leave him, it would kill her."

"No, no my child, not kill you. Let us be calm and do not let us exaggerate. You take for a mortal disease that which is but the fatigue of a weary life; you will not die before that age when we are all prepared to die, I hope. I may seem severe, but consider that you have known my son but for three months, and I will believe that you love him; but shall your love supplant ours? Shall your love destroy a whole future, for in staying near my son, you do destroy *his* future. And again, are you sure this love will last? Are you sure of yourself? And if now, a little later, you should dethrone him. And, pardon me — your past justifies the supposition. Again, can *he* be sure of himself? Can you both, at your ages, be sure of yourselves — of your hearts. Consider this — he who loves you so now, but a little time gone by poured out his wealth of love on us at home. Hearts will change — does not a man love his wife more than he loves his parents? Then his children more than his wife? If nature gives prodigally, she extorts rigorously. I say, you may be deceiving yourselves, both of you. This is a probability. Now will you see realities — certainties, for you are listening to me, are you not?"

She answered him but with a look; a long, terrible, miserable look.

"You are willing to sacrifice all to my son, and what equal sacrifice can he offer to you? He shall bask in your best years, and later on, when he is sated — and satiety will come — what shall happen? If he be worldly, he will spread your past before you and leave you, saying, he does but as others have done. And if he be an honest man, he will marry you, or at least not desert you. And this marriage, or this life, not based on virtue, nor supported by religion, this life, pardonable, perhaps, in a young man, how shall it be named, when age is creeping on? For this man, for my son, what ambition dare he breathe, what path is open to him? What consolation shall this son then be to me — to me, who have watched and tended him for twenty years? Your love for each other — it is a passion, the most earthly and wholly human, it is born of the caprice of one, and the imagination of the other. Your love is a result, not a cause. What shall remain of it when you are both grown old and weary? Who assures you that the first wrinkle on your forehead shall not sweep the veil from his eyes? Who assures you his love shall not pass away with your youth."

"OH, THE TRUTH, THE TRUTH?"

"Then yours would be double age, doubly desolate, and doubly useless. What retrospect would you have, what happiness to look back upon? Ah, Marguerite, there are cruel necessities in this life, against which we must fight, if we would not be dashed to death against them. You and my son have different roads in life; chance has thrown you together for a little while, but reason must separate you. In the life you have entered, you saw not the end, and to your three months' happiness no more can be added. Keep the remembrance of this time, and let it strengthen you always. I speak harshly, but consider that I plead where I might command. It is a man of the world who speaks to you, a father who implores you. So, Marguerite, courage, and show you love my son truly, by leaving him to the care of those who have a family claim upon his obedience."

"So — she who falls shall never rise." (She was speaking lowly to herself.) "Heaven may pardon me, the world never. And truly, what right have I to a place in this

honest family? I love! What reason! And what proofs
can I give of this love? Who would believe them?
What, poor girl — thou to speak of heart, and future —
these are new words to thee. Look back on thy past,
what man would call thee wife? What child would call
thee mother?"

Then turning to her visitor, she said: "Nearly all
you have said I have half asked myself — oh, how often,
but never, never wholly. You are right, you speak kindly,
and you are very merciful. Ah well, I will obey you, and
one day you will say to the pure honest girl, your daughter — once there lived a poor erring woman who had but
one hope in the world, and at the invocation of *thy* name,
this erring woman renounced that hope, laid her hands
heavily upon her breast, and so died; for I shall die, I
shall die. You say, 'poor creature,' you pity me, sir, and
methinks you even weep. Ah well, I tell you I will obey
you; command me."

"Tell him that you love him no more."

"He would not believe me."

"Leave this place."

"He would follow me. You hesitate? Sir, lay your
hand upon my head as you would upon your daughter's
head. And now I promise you that in eight days he shall
be with you, unhappy perhaps, but wholly cured, and I
promise you that he shall know nothing of this visit; oh,
fear nothing, he shall HATE me."

Yet a little and the father was leaving the room.
"And," she murmured, "when all is ended, and I am dead,
I pray you tell him how I loved, and proved my love.
Good bye; we shall, perhaps, never see each other more.
I pray you may be happy."

Left to herself, she sat down, miserably, and wrote a
letter which was to destroy his love for her. But it was
still unfinished when he arrived. She hid the paper, and
trembled.

After a time she walked quickly from the room, saying
she should soon return.

And she was gone to return no more.

He waited as the night came on. Then, growing unaccountably frightened, called for lights. No one answered. Running from the room to the grounds, he shrieked out her name. No answer. He ran over the house; it was deserted. She and her servants had left the place, and it was silent and lifeless.

And still, hoping against hope, he wandered about the house in search of his lost love.

CHAPTER III.

BACK into the dreadful life she had left. Away from the placid lake and whispering trees. Again feasting, and heartlessness, and golden misery. Armand soon learnt that she had abandoned him for another. He cursed her very name; but she was wrong in thinking he would hate her; wrong in thinking he would hasten to the home where he was born. He came to Paris, and waited angrily for revenge.

Marguerite's new protector was a man immensely fond of pleasure, and in spite of her protestations, would drag her from theatre to ball room, and from house to house.

She suffered horribly. Her old complaint burst out anew, her cough came back again, and she was once more a poor ailing creature, whose great beauty grew each day less and less.

One night, a month after her flight, the poor woman, quite against her will, was present at a ball given by one of the reigning belles of wicked Paris.

Entering the room, she shrank back, for there sat Armand. He had not visited many of these gay places since she had left him, and his entrance here had created some surprise amongst the guests. Many looked to see how the old lovers would meet. As she entered he looked up from a card table. She smiled timidly; he bowed to her coldly. She told her companion that she would rather not remain; but he also, marking her old lover, said he would not be laughed at, and insisted upon her keeping in the room. She obeyed, and sat timidly down.

Armand played high, and some one remarking it, he said he was trying the force of the old proverb, " Unlucky in love, lucky at cards." " Oh, I mean to make a fortune to-night, then spend it in the country. And not alone; with some one who has lived in the country as well as I have — perhaps when I am rich."

Marguerite's companion hearing the player's menace, went up to the table, and commenced playing. He lost, and every time he lost, the other gained.

Soon afterwards, supper was called, and all the company made for the table where it was laid, all except Marguerite, who remained seated, depressed both in body and mind.

She had scarcely been alone a minute, before Armand came running to her. He loved her as fervently as ever. As she perceived his ardor, she felt almost tempted to tell him the whole truth of her flight, but the promise to his father stayed her. At last, he prayed her to fly with him again, saying he would forget the past. But no, she refused. Again and again he implored, yet she was obdurate.

Then he grew enraged — mad; he rushed to the supper room, screamed to them to see him do an act of justice; and, as they came streaming out and round about, he took from his pocket all his winnings, and cried, "You see that woman! well, do you know what she has done for me ? She sold her horses and her carriages, and her diamonds, that she might live with me — so much did she love me. Was not that noble ? And I — what did I do? I, a mean wretch, accepted the sacrifice, and gave no payment. But 'tis not too late, and I would repair my shame. See you all, I pay this Marguerite, and I owe her naught."

As he spoke, he flung a heap of bank notes and gold at the feet of this miserable woman, who fell heavily back upon a sofa, mercifully deprived of sense. Down they rained upon her, the notes and gold; down they fell crushing her as surely as though they had been jagged rocks.

CHAPTER IV.

CONQUERED, weak, and dying, she lay upon her bed in the joyous carnival time. While all Paris was gay and merry, she was drawing her last breath.

Misery, degradation, desertion, and consumption, had done their worst; they had destroyed her, but not wholly killed her beauty. Far, far from the brilliant creature who had ruled over so many but a short time before, she was yet beautiful as she lay upon her bed, awake, and heavily breathing through the dark hours of the night.

Now and then she would fall into a feverish sleep, but only to start back into wakefulness, as a bevy of masques returned home from their revels, singing as they went. What a contrast! the poor dying creature lying there, and below in the streets the heedless revellers, shouting their noisy songs, and dancing madly through the otherwise deserted streets.

She knew that she had not many days to live, and yet she had one glorious hope, possessing which she looked back upon her blank despair with horror.

It was three months since the catastrophe at the ball. Her protector and Armand had met and fought, and the former been slightly wounded. This was the joy: he knew the whole truth or would know it. His father had promised that when she died he should know all. But alas! after the duel he had left Paris, and no one knew where he had hidden himself. To think that he might know that her very love had bidden her leave him, and that he himself was now the only cause of his ignorance. Yet there was plenty of time, plenty of time; and before she died she should surely see him.

Many of her companions and friends had forgotten her by this time. But when her waiting woman came in that morning, she had half-a-dozen new year's presents for the patient; — so she was not forgotten altogether.

The faithful doctor soon came, he who had so patiently tended her, without fee or reward.

Asking her how she was, she replied that she was bet-

ter and worse, worse in body, better in mind. The night
before, she said, she felt so surely that she was dying that
she sent for a priest. She welcomed him heartily, she added smiling. How beautiful was religion, the minister
came to talk with her for an hour, and then leaving, he
carried away with him despair, terror, remorse. Then she
said she fell asleep quite peacefully. The doctor promised her health on the very first day in spring.

Smiling again, she said it was his duty to say so; an
untruth surely was not a sin in a doctor, for he must
speak one for every patient he saw.

For indeed she was much worse that day.

Moreover, want was tormenting her last hours. Her
creditors were again exacting, and almost every hour
brought one of them to the door. Indeed, the new year's
presents, jewels for the most part, were ordered to be sold
almost as soon as seen.

Left alone, she took from the bosom of her dress a
letter. It was one written by M. Duval, saying that his
son would soon be with her to entreat his pardon, and the
writer's own. It bade her be careful of her health, and
said that her courage promised a happy future. For six
weeks had she read this letter daily — for six weeks of
days she had watched for his return, and still she watched
— sickening with despair one moment only to glow with
hope the next. If she could only have a letter from him,
if she could only live till the spring — why then? She
got slowly up from the soft chair to which she had been
led, and eagerly searched her wan face in a looking-glass.
"How changed I am! yet the doctor has promised to cure
me. Oh! I must have patience. And yet, did he not
tell my waiting woman, Nannie, did I not hear him say I
was much worse? Yet, only *much worse;* there is, then,
still some hope, still a few short months to live, and if in
that time he comes to me, I shall be saved — I SHALL BE
SAVED. This is now new year's day, then surely I may
hope. And — and, besides, if I were really in danger,
they all of them, the doctor, Nannie, my old friends,
could not come laughing to my bedside as they do, nor
would the doctor leave me." Here she slowly wandered
to the window and looked from it. "Ah! what joy is

there not in a family, how beautiful now is that child playing with his toys — ah, I could die loving that little one."

Suddenly her maid ran quickly into the room, her face full of joy. "Madame! madame!"

"Well! well!"

"You are strong to-day — you feel quite strong."

"Yes, but why?"

"Pray be calm."

"Yes, yes, but why?"

"I would prepare you — a sudden joy is so heavy to bear."

"A joy? A joy for *me?* You have seen him — he — he is coming!"

With weak, rapid steps she staggered to the door, and called to him. Then he stood before her, pale and trembling. She fell upon his neck, and clung to him as though he were life. "No, no, it is not thee; not so much clemency can be shown to such as I am."

"'Tis I, Marguerite, and so repentant, and ashamed, so guilty, that I dared not to pass the threshold. I was afraid to enter; so I waited till Nannie came to the door, and then I spoke to her. My father has told me all. I fled, no one knew where, after that night; travelled night and day, without sleep, without hope, ever pursued by vague presentiments. If I had not found thee, I must have died, for should I not have been the cause of thy death? Tell me that you pardon me, that you forgive, too, my poor father."

"*I* pardon? *I*, the guilty one? And I did what I thought the best for thy happiness, even at the expense of my own. But now, thy father will not separate us again. Ah! look at me, I am not the creature that you left, yet — yet, I am still young, and I shall grow beautiful now that I am happy. We will forget the past and commence a new life from this good day."

"Never to leave thee again — never. We will quit the house. Quit Paris for ever. We will be happy, for our future is our own."

"Speak on, speak on, my soul burns at thy words, and each moment I gather new strength. I said this morning thou couldst save me, and I was right."

Then she said they must go together, and kneel in the nearest church, and pray, and be grateful; and as she spoke she staggered to her feet again, and called to her maid to bring her a shawl and bonnet.

As the girl came forward, the youth had a good word for her.

"Oh," continued the suffering woman, "Nannie and I talked of thee every day, and she always said thou wouldst come back, and she was right. So thou hast seen beautiful countries since that time. Ah! well, now we will see them together."

"Marguerite, thou hast turned quite pale, and thou art so cold!"

"Oh, nothing, 'tis nothing," she said, hurriedly, and nervously drawing a thick shawl about her. "The coming in of so much joy; why joy sometimes is as hard to bear as grief itself."

And then she dropped exhausted upon the nearest chair.

"Dear Marguerite! speak, speak to me."

"Be not afraid, you know I was always subject to these sudden fits of weakness, but they are gone almost directly. Watch me, thou seest I can smile already. And again I feel strong. 'Twas only the hope of life thrilling through me."

Taking her thin hand he said, "how thou tremblest."

"No, no. I *will* go out. Nannie, give me a bonnet."

He drew away from her for a moment in horror.

She again strove to stand, but could not. Then falling upon a seat, she tore off the shawl and cried "I am dying, I am dying."

As he flung himself down by her side, the serving girl ran from the room, and sped away, crying out that she would go for the doctor.

"Yes, yes, bring him to me, tell him Armand is here — that I want to live — that I WILL live. Why, if thy return doth not save me, nothing can!"

"Oh, thou wilt live, dearest."

Sit down beside me, close to me, my husband, and hear me." She spoke very quietly, very faintly. "But a moment since I raged against death. I am sorry for my fault. It is right that I should die, and I love death now that it has spared me to see thee once again. Ah, if my death had not been sure, thy father would never have bade thee come to me."

"Marguerite, speak not of death. I shall go mad. Say no more that you will die, say rather that you desire to live."

"Ah, what is my will? If I were a good girl, if I were honest, perhaps I should weep to leave the world, and leave *you* behind, for then the future would be full of hope; my past life would then let me hope. Dying, thou wilt hold me in gentle remembrance; living, there would ever be a gloom upon our love. Believe me, all is for the best; what is done, is well done."

In an agony of grief he clung about her.

"What then it is *I* who must give *thee* courage! Gently obey me. Open that little drawer, you will find there my portrait, when they told me I was pretty. Keep it, for it will help thee to remember me. But if some day, there cometh a kindly honest girl who will love and marry thee, as it should be, as I hope it may be, and if she should find this portrait, tell her it is the likeness of a friend who, if she may reach the obscurest corner of heaven, will pray for her happiness. If though she is jealous of the past (as we women are sometimes), if she demands from you this poor picture, place it in her hand without fear or remorse — it will be but justice. And now I pardon thee the act, for a loving woman suffers so much when her love is not returned. Thou hast heard me. Dying — dying — yet happy. Tell them to talk about me sometimes — and they will — will they not? and — and — give me your hand. Oh, it is not hard to die when one dies happily. But what is this?"

She stood up for a moment, smiling gloriously; then she continued, "Why I suffer no more. All pain has left me. Has a new life been breathed into me? I feel as I have never felt. Am I to live — am I to live?"

Then she gently sat down again, leant back in her chair, and, sighing softly, became silent.

"She is sleeping," said Armand to himself, his hand still pressed in hers. "Marguerite, Marguerite."

Still her hand was clasped in his.

" Marguerite — Marguerite ! "   Still she slept.

He uttered a loud cry, and started to his feet.   But his hand still remained clasped in hers.

" Marguerite," he again cried, and with a terrible energy, he tore his hand from her grasp.   Her own fell placidly to her side.

He flung himself down at her feet.

" Dead — dead — dead."

DON PASQUALE. (Donizetti.)

CHAPTER I.

Don Pasquale was an old bachelor, and as wealthy as he was old. He was saving, credulous, and obstinate. But for all that Don Pasquale was the best-hearted of dons.

Now he had a nephew, whose name was Ernesto. This youth had been continually either falling from the heights of his uncle's approbation, or to the depths of his displeasure, only to be raised again the next day. But at last Ernesto forfeited the don's approbation altogether, for he fell in love with Norina, of whom the don had no good opinion, though, in truth, he had never seen her. In the first place, according to the don, she was flighty; in the second place, she was impatient; in the third place, she was fiery; and the old bachelor had a horror of fiery women.

So when his nephew showed a disposition to speak in praise of his lady love, the don grew so obstinate and ill-tempered, that his friend, Doctor Malatesta, no longer recognized him as the old bachelor companion: Doctor Malatesta had known the bachelor don for more years than he would like to name, and known the nephew as long as the don himself, so he was like one of the family. It may also be stated that the doctor was a practical joker.

There is but a fourth party to this little tale — though she cannot be called one of the family — we mean Norina, a young widow, a delightful widow, perhaps impatient, as the don had declared, nay, perhaps even fiery, but for all that she was affectionate and sincere, and amazingly fond of Ernesto.

Well, it may be said at once, that the nephew persisted in adoring Norina; the old don then marked out a line of conduct, the effect of which was, that he sat in his breakfast parlor one fine morning, impatiently waiting for

his friend Malatesta, and snappishly looking at the clock.
Being old and a leetle deaf, he took the first sound he
heard to be the doctor's step — 'twas only the wind; then
he thought of the "pill" he had prepared for his obstinate nephew, moreover his insulting nephew, for that relation had gone so far as to indecently call him a donkey
— call *him*, Don Pasquale — a donkey.

In the midst of his silent anger, the doctor arrived, a
pleasant middle-aged gentleman, with a jolly, pleasant
face.

"Well, well," said the don.

"Well, indeed," said the doctor.

"What, you have found —"

"Yes, indeed."

The don embraced his friend in the Italian manner, and
thereupon did not see the laugh that spread over the doctor's merry countenance.

"Now for her portrait," said the don; "I am all attention."

"She is as beautiful as an angel who has missed her
way, and wandered to earth; she is as fresh as a newly-
blown lily, and her eyes are like darts that pierce the very
heart — and whether you shall most admire the blackness
of her hair, or the beauty of her smile, who shall say?"

"Blessed is the man who is blessed with such a wife."

"And her modesty, and her grace, and her charity!"

"Yes, yes, doctor; and her family!"

"Such a family!"

"And her name —"

"Her name is Malatesta."

"What! is she related to you?"

"A little; she's my sister."

"Oh, dear brother! when shall I see her?"

"To-morrow."

"'Tis an age! this very instant!"

"Ah!" said the doctor, "I can deny naught to a
friend."

Again the don embraced the doctor.

"This second embrace was not so long as the first. The
don ejected his friend from his arms, and said rapidly,
"Go, go, go."

Left to himself, it may be remarked the old don danced with glee. If you have not seen a gingerly old gentleman in such a situation, you have lost a sight. He was in the midst of this practice, when his nephew, Ernesto came running into the room.

"Good morning, nephew! You may sit down."

"Surely, surely, uncle!"

"Don't be afraid."

"Surely, surely, uncle!"

"I am not going to scold you. Tell me, did I not, precisely two months ago, offer you the hand of a lady, as rich as beautiful, and as noble as both?"

"Surely, surely, uncle!"

"And did I not promise to give you all I had?"

"At your death — surely, surely."

"And did I not say if you refused, I would marry her myself?"

"That is, marry somebody else — surely, surely."

"Well, you did refuse; now, I offer you this young lady again — will you marry her?"

"Surely, surely — NO."

"No!"

"No."

"You homeless fellow, you!"

"You turn me out, uncle?"

"Yes, I do, to make room for your aunt."

"You marry?"

"Surely, surely, nephew; I myself, the Don Pasquale, in very flesh and bone."

"You take my breath away!"

"Yes, I myself, the Don Pasquale, sane and sound, I marry."

"'Tis a comedy!"

"Is it? Till to-morrow; wait till to-morrow."

"Sir, I will."

"Yes, but not here, in Don Pasquale's house."

The youth here grew very disconsolate, for indeed he was thinking if his uncle cut him off with that proverbial shilling, he would have to resign the promised hand of somebody whom he had no objection to marry whatever.

Meanwhile the don was watching him attentively, and half hoping that the youth would consent.

Said Ernesto, after the dismal pause, " Uncle, just two words."

" Three — young man."

" Don't be rash — consult Doctor Malatesta."

" Sir — I have consulted him."

" And what is his advice ? "

" He is as willing for the match as I. Oh, you may look astonished — as *willing for the match as I.* In fact, nephew — between ourselves — SHE IS HIS SISTER ! "

" The doctor's ? "

" Well, he *said* so."

Poor Ernesto. The doctor had always been his best friend, and when the crashing announcement came, he thought Doctor Malatesta would be his man-at-arms, and now it seemed he had gone over to the enemy. And he looked even more dismal than before, for now, not only had his old love drifted away from him, but his old friend too.

The don saw these dismal marks of misery with dolorous satisfaction — the satisfaction arose out of his pride — and the dolor was buried in his heart. But for all that he showed his nephew to the door, though it should be said to his honor, that he did not dance when he was alone again.

———

CHAPTER II.

NORINA, the young widow who had caused all that commotion at the don's domicile, was *not* so rich as she was beautiful. If she had been, she would have been besieged with lovers ; but she was rich enough to have a home of her own, and she was sitting in it reading on that very morning when the don directed his young nephew's shoes to the street door.

The doctor had told her he should want her for a certain plot, though he had carefully only raised her curiosity without confiding particulars, and she had taken up the book to divert herself till the doctor, by appointment, should be there.

The book was a romantic old love tale, and she had got
as far as, " Her looks were so heavenly, so delightful, that
the Knight Richard, enraptured, fell at her feet, and vowed eternal fidelity," when she flung it down, exclaiming
to herself, that she did not want the heavenly lady's
instructions in the art of love-making. She well knew
the power of glance in time and place, the effect of a
smile, a tear, silence, a word; in fact, this vivacious little
widow believed herself a coquette, though in reality, there
was not a more earnest little woman in the whole world,
when it was a question of *her* love for Ernesto. She *did*
love him. She would plague him by flirting with third
parties; but she could always turn his anger into smiles.
Well, she was thinking of Ernesto, when a letter came to
her in the handwriting of that youth. Ah! how all the
bright looks went out of the face a moment after, and the
letter was opened. She read it through, and was reading
it again, when the doctor, without waiting for any ceremony, ran in and up to the little lady — for she was little.

" Good news," he cried, " strategem —"

" Not a word of it, doctor," and she thrust the letter
into his hands.

He read: " 'My dear Norina, I write to you with a
broken heart.' (The poor young man) 'Don Pasquale,
advised by that scoundrel ' (that's me, beyond a doubt,
poor young man), 'by that false, double-faced Doctor
Malatesta ' (as I thought) 'will marry a sister of his, and,
he turns *me* out of doors. And so love tells me I must
run away from you. Therefore, good bye, good bye.
May you be happy, 'tis the dearest wish of Ernesto.'
How glad you must be to receive this letter."

" Glad, doctor!" she exclaimed, in tears.

" Why, next time you see him, he'll be more loving
than ever."

" When will that be — perhaps, perhaps, he's *gone!*"

" And perhaps not. He shall know our plans at once."

" *Our* plans, what are they?"

" You know to punish his nephew, the don would
marry!"

" Is *that* our plan, doctor?"

" Well, well, seeing him determined, I seconded him!"

4

" Oh ! "

" To serve you, and Ernesto — I have spoken to the don of my sister. You shall pass for her. You appear before him, he falls in love with you ! "

" Well ! "

" Then he marries you ! "

" Oh ! "

" Don't scream. He marries you, and yet he does not. My nephew Charles shall personate a notary. Then, married, I leave the rest to you, 'tis your business to drive him mad, as of course you know. Then, then we will do with him as we please."

" Ah, ah, ah, ah ! " (no more tears now, unless from laughter,) " ah, ah, ah, ah, ah, oh ! Oh, how I'll teaze him — how I'll worry him — how he shall repent — ah, ah, ah."

" Oh but not at first ! "

" Oh, *dear* no ! shall I be merry, or downcast, or reserved ? "

" No, not at all."

" Shall I weep, or cry ? "

" No, you must appear a simple country lass."

" And I *will*. See how do I manage ? oh, thank you, thank you — no, that is — but I'd rather not — you're very, very humble servant, sir. Ah, ah, ah ! "

" Brava, that will do."

" And I must hold my head down, like a goose ! "

" And your lips pursed up."

" Like an old maid. Oh ! sir, I am ashamed. I'd *rather* not — your humble servant, sir ! Ah, ah, ah ! "

" Come, let us go."

" Yes, oh, I shall die of laughing before we get there. Sir, your most obedient — ah, ah, ah, ah, ah ! "

CHAPTER III.

Don Pasquale got himself up in such style for the reception of his bride that his own servants did not know him. In fact he hardly knew himself, and felt rather taller. But he was not comfortable, and indeed as he gave his servants orders to admit none but the doctor and the person who might be with him, he blushed rather red, which last word is superfluous, for no don in the world could blush blue! Well, the servants departed; he danced again, and then growing tired he was fatigued with waiting.

Soon they arrived. The doctor pushing his "sister" forward with angry jerks. As for her, with her veil down over her meek face, she was uttering cries of fright and mild opposition.

"Courage, courage, sister."

"Oh, dear me — that is — I can't — please, brother, do not leave me."

Here the don danced up to the young lady, adjusting his necktie gracefully round his neck.

"Something like a giggle was heard, but the next moment a voice from under the veil said,

"Oh, dear, dear, dear, I can't — that is, I'd rather go away. Please, brother, don't — *don't* leave me."

"Do not be afraid."

"Oh, I'd rather stand behind." And behind she went.

The doctor went up to the don apologetically, saying that the poor girl was but just fresh from the convent. In fact, he said, she was naturally of a wild disposition, and it was for the don to tame her.

"Oh, brother, brother, come here."

"Just one moment, sister —"

"Suppose some one should come in, I should faint." Here the young and bashful widow covered her mouth with her hand, and laughed.

Said the don to himself, keeping away from the lady, whose face had not yet turned towards him, "If her face is equal to her voice, Don Pasquale, you lucky man you, you have waited for something."

"Brother, brother, I don't like to be left alone."

"My dear, you are not alone, I am here, and here is Don Pasquale."

"Oh! oh! a man! — oh my goodness! a man, — oh take me away — a man! oh I never!" Here there was another laugh.

Here the don congratulated himself more than ever.

And here, also, the Doctor said to himself, "Poor old fellow."

"Then he added, "Don't be afraid, sister, this is the noble Don Pasquale."

"Oh indeed!"

Don Pasquale made as low a bow as a stout old gentleman could. The timid young lady made him a sweeping curtesy.

"Thank you, sir—your most obedient. Oh, oh."
Here the don was taking her hand.

"Oh loving hand," muttered the old don.

And while he pranced off after three chairs, there was another laugh, suppressed, from under the veil.

Each chair the doctor set down with a puff and a bang, and at last he sat himself down in the center one.

"What do you think of her?" (in a low voice to the don.)

"What indeed! But that veil?" (in a lower voice to the doctor.)

"Oh! she would not dare to speak to a man, unveiled. Talk to her a little; see if your dispositions agree. Then we will question the veil."

"Hum—hum—(courage, don, courage)—Am delighted—have the honor—your brother—Dr. Malatesta—pray did you speak?"

Here she got up and made him another curtesy.
"Oh—sir your most obedient—sir."

"I was going to say, no doubt you like company of an evening."

"Oh *dear* no. We never do at the convent. We always go to bed."

"Ah, but you *sometimes* went to the theatre?"

"Oh!—dear,—what—is—that? I'm sure—I never *wished* to go there."

"Delightful," thought the old don, and added, "And pray, now, how did you pass your time?"

"Oh, sir, in sewing, and knitting, and embroidering, and sometimes I played with the pretty little cats."

"Ah, ah." (doctor.)

"Dear me, doctor, pray be still; 'tis rude to laugh, even at one's sister. But doctor, that veil!"

"Dear sister, remove thy veil."

"Oh! no, I couldn't — before a man."

"But I bid you."

"Oh yes — oh yes, brother — I obey."

The don rose in honor of this act, but no sooner did he see the dove-like face, than he fell upon his seat again with a crash.

"Pray, Don Pasquale, what's the matter?"

"Can't tell, doctor. But it seemed to go right through me — speak for me, doctor. Tell her how I love her."

"Courage, old friend. She does not seem indisposed towards thee. Now tell me, sister — this gentleman — do you like him?"

After casting a glance at the don who was admiring his own legs, she said. " — I — I — I think I do."

"She consents, don; she is yours!"

"Oh bliss; oh joy; oh delight, oh!"

Here came another of those mysterious laughs.

Said then the don in a loud voice (when he had recovered it,) "A notary."

"Ah, don, a notary is not like a glass of wine, ever at hand; but anticipating this joyful moment, I have brought a notary with us."

"Quick, quick, quick," said the don.

"Yes, yes, yes," replied the doctor, and running; but he returned immediately, with the false notary, Nephew Charles.

Solemnly this functionary walked to a table, sat down a mass of black folds, and severely took up a pen.

Then said the doctor pompously, and dictating to the grave notary, "On the one part, et cetera, et cetera, Sophronia Malatesta, residing et cetera, et cetera, and the rest of it. And on the other part, Don Pasquale, et cetera, et cetera, residing at et cetera, et cetera, and also all the rest of it."

The notary, writing hurriedly, soon completed the work.

"Very good!" said the proud don, "and then continue — which above-named gentleman (I mean myself,) from this hour, makes over one half his goods and property, by a deed of gift made before his death, to his most beloved wife."

This was also written in a hurry.

"Bless you! bless you!" said the doctor

"Bl-l-less you, sir, your obedient," chimed in the lady.

The notary gravely held out the pen for signatures. Thereupon the don seized it, and speedily signed his name.

"Oh, dear sir, I'd rather not; no, don't brother."

For the doctor was again pushing her forward. The modest woman didn't like to sign, and again her face was buried in her handkerchief.

"Where are the witnesses?" said the grave notary.

And at this moment, the voice of a gentleman named Ernesto was heard at high words with the obdurate footman. The face of the lady thereupon grew very grave, and indeed she dropped her pen.

"Back, back!" shouted Ernesto, without the room.

And the lady was forced to confess to herself, that she now really began to tremble.

And so also did the doctor tremble, for Ernesto had not been informed of these plans, and he might in consequences spoil all.

At this moment there was a rush at the door, the next moment it was flung open, and in the doorway stood the young nephew.

"Sir," said this latter, "I came to take my leave of you, and I am debarred your presence as though I were a robber."

"We were busy, young man, *very* busy when you came to the door; however, now you are here, stop; sign — witness. Let the bride advance."

Tableau.

The "young man" was about explaining, when he felt his coat pulled. Then the doctor said quite solemnly, "This is Sophronia — my sister."

"So — who?"

"So that you be quiet — never mind who," said the doctor, lowly. "For your own sake, be still — be dumb: excuse him, don — the poor youth, I will explain all to him." And as the old don bowed in his own absurd fashion, the doctor led the youth on one side, and thus admonished him: "Now, if you wish to be your own enemy and Norina's, go on; but if you are not your own enemy and Norina's, don't."

"Just so — but —"

"Yes — exactly — don't, as I said before; come and sign the contract."

Which, with great doubt still, the jealous lover did.

Said the stern notary, rising from his chair, "You are man and wife."

The writer *would* respectfully have it understood that *he* is in no way responsible for this astounding free and easy marriage; far be it from him so to dispose of brides. But he opines that 'tis a way they have in Spain.

Upon that notarial announcement, the don was faint with joy, and the next moment he was nearly faint with surprise.

For hardly was the contract completed, hardly had the astounding notarial intimation been given, than the bride throws aside her veil, and with it her meek look. Let it not, however, be said she assumed a bold look — say rather, an easy, cool, pleasant countenance.

The don advanced towards the lady to give her a marital embrace, but she gently pushed him back. "Softly pray; calm your ardor; you should first entreat permission."

"And I do!" —

"And I do *not* permit."

The don fell plump upon his chair, and looked unmeaningly after the notary, who was quietly withdrawing.

"Ah, ah, oh," said the youth Ernesto, as he saw the blank expression on his uncle's face.

"Sir Nephew, how dare you laugh. Quit this house. Begone!"

"Begone, don, fie!" said the new wife contemptuously. "What rudeness! Pray remain, sir." Then turning rapidly to the don, she said, "I must teach you better manners."

"Doctor Malatesta!" said the astounded don.

"Don Pasquale!" said the doctor in the same tone.

"This is quite another woman, doctor."

"I am turned to stone, don."

"What does she mean?"

"By your leave, I'll ask her." And the doctor luckily turned away, for his red face was quivering.

As for the lady Norina, she marched with dignity up to and against the don, and thus terribly spoke. "You are too old, too stout, too slow, to take charge of a young wife through the streets; this young cavalier shall be my BEAU!"

"Oh, dear NO."

"And pray who will prevent it?"

"*I* will."

"You said —"

"*I* will."

"*Indeed.*" (Here she tenderly approached him, and stroked his friendly old grey head.) "Dear husband; now forget those horrid words 'I will,' or at least leave them with me, with me alone, for the wife *should* be obeyed."

"But — but!"

"But us no buts, dear man. Be still, I say. What, are you one of those men who will not be led by kindness? what, would you dare!"

Here there was a dull rap distinctly heard, it was a knock on the don's expostulating knuckles.

"Am I awake?" asked the don of himself. "What has happened? blows I think! Pray what shall come next?"

In fact, the don looked as though petrified — dreaming — struck by lightning, as though he were anybody but himself.

"Courage, don, courage," said the doctor.

"Courage, oh dear," said Don Pasquale, the married man sinking lower and lower in his chair.

Suddenly the new lady of the house flew at the bell, and rang it till the room seemed made of bells. As a servant entered, she cast the implement at him.

"Let all the servants come directly, rascal."

"Oh, heavens!" sighed Don Pasquale.

Two servants and the steward came running in a moment after at a tremendous pace.

"Three! *Three* beggarly servants. Three. As for you, steward. Bow lower, sir, bow lower" (stamp of the foot) ; " listen to these my orders. Turn those cubs away at once. Get new servants, good looking young men that will do us credit; two dozen will do."

" Oh, heaven ! " exclaimed Don Pasquale.

" Steward," (another stamp of the foot) how dare you turn away. Let there be two new carriages this very evening in MY stables; as for MY new horses, I leave the choice to you. And as for these apartments, they are frightful, they shall be rebuilt. And as for this horrid furniture, it shall be burnt."

" Oh, heaven! have you done ma'm?"

" No, man. Steward (greater stamp of the foot than ever,) how dare you not keep your eyes on me? Let everything, everywhere, always be in the first style, so that people may respect us. Begone, fool!"

" And pray now ma'm," suggested the don, "who pays?"

" And pray now sir, who should know better than you?"

" Oh, heaven! Pray am I master, or am I not?"

"You are not — master, where I am! Zounds!" She flings over a chair.

"Sister, sister," said the doctor, but the sister did not even look at him. She flew at the don as well as she could, seeing she was a wingless angel; and arrived within a quarter of an inch of his head, bade him, in the most impassioned language, depart.

"Tell me, some one, *have* I married her?"

"Ah, you poor man you," said the new wife; with a sneer.

Here the don went off into a roaring, yelping, yelling rage, tearing his own clothes, dilapidating his own walls with his own head, and damaging his personal appearance with nobody's hands but his own.

" Oh, brother, brother," shrieked the doctor, dashing after the don, who was taking a tour of destruction all round the drawing-room to the north, while his lady was doing precisely the same thing to the south.

" Oh, will anybody tell me," asked the don —"am I mad?"

Well, Norina in her rage worked round to where Ernesto was standing — and then she was wearing her own

4*

natural bright face, and reaching that youth she uttered this little speech. "Ah! well — Ernesto"— To which the youth answered — "Ah! dear Norina."

So it may be supposed that both were gratified.

The next moment she had recommenced her sail round the room : but by this time the doctor had run up to the don and deftly turned him away from this affectionate little duet of soft words.

"My goodness, don, what a pulse — eighty, ninety, one hundred and twenty, twenty-five — Don Pasquale you must straightway go to BED!"

CHAPTER IV.

THE don's pulse was moderate by a late hour the next day; and having obtained the permission of the doctor, who had sedately watched all night by the bed, to go down stairs, the poor gentleman crept down as though he had never danced in all his life.

And what a sight when he reached that drawing-room of his! To the right, dresses; to the left, dresses; in front, band-boxes; behind, the same; lace, bobbins, furs, scarfs, shoes, gloves and — bills! a large number, all in a nice little heap in the centre of the table. He sat down in the middle of all this invasion, and stared about him as though he was anybody else in a strange place, rather than Don Pasquale.

He was still sitting staring about when a hair-dresser passed quickly through the room. The next moment a lady's maid appeared at the door. "Good gracious," said she, "ain't my lady a scolding — do be quick with the diaments!"

"Please, miss," said a second servant to the lady's maid, "here's the milliner."

"Then let the milliner come quick."

The milliner rushed past the don, so to speak, smothered in boxes.

At the door she was met by another waiting-woman, dashing off to the carriage with a cloak, a bouquet, and a scent-bottle. All these paraphernalia were handed to a footman, and then back the woman came, and crashed up against the fourth body menial —" me lady's fan! me lady's gloves! me lady's veil!"

The second footman without the door fell upon, and bore away these things.

" Me lady's carriage!"

" Storms and ——" something else said Don Pasquale, and with an effort fell upon the pile of bills. " To dress-maker, 100 dollars— oh! dear me! To coach-maker, six hundred — worse and worse. Twice as much to the jew-eller. To horses — horses! I wish they'd carry all to ——," again the don used a highly improper atom of speech.

Then the don in an awful whisper said, " HERE SHE IS!"

In she came, like several ladies of state, and dressed as surely never pupil at a convent had ever been dressed before. She did not see him as she passed on, not she; but he stopped her — rather hoped he would excuse her, and faintly desired to know whither she was going.

She loudly desired to be informed what that was to him — she was going out!

Again he faintly and in a slightly sarcastical tone ob-served that a husband *might* take the liberty of objecting.

" A husband *might* take the liberty, and it certainly *was* a liberty; and indeed, a husband *might* even *object*, but that was no reason why the wife should *obey*. It was the duty of such a man to see, and hold his tongue; indeed, common sense would tell him to hold his tongue; for, she would ask him, was he listened to when he *did* speak?"

" Take care, take care."

" It were wise, don, to take care of yourself."

" Go to your room, ma'am."

" You were best in yours. Go to bed, and to sleep. We will talk about this to-morrow."

" You shall not pass."

" Ah! you fill up the door. Indeed — don."

" Yes."

" Pray, now move."

" I will not."

" Ah!"

What is it makes fire flash in the old eyes of the new husband? Was it a humiliating box on the ear — the right ear? Yes — yes.

She came out from the door-way.

Meanwhile the young Norina asked herself if she were not going too far.

"Then I may go now?"

"Yes, go where you like. Go anywhere, so that you don't come back."

"I shall then see you to-morrow — hem!"

"You will find my doors closed."

"Bah! be not a tyrant, poor grandfather. Sleep well, and when the morning comes, I will call you."

And she sailed out grandly.

"Divorce, divorce!" he shrieked out as the lady left him — "divorce! if this is wedlock — what's that?"

That was a paper which Norina had dropped on going out.

He picked it up, after some effort. "Another horrid bill, I find one in every corner — eh! what! ah!" —(here he read.) "'Between nine and ten I shall be at that part of the garden which looks to the north; for greater precaution try to let me in through the secret door. I shall warn you by singing. Adieu.' I shall go mad, I, Don Pasquale — I shall go mad. Malatesta, send for Malatesta. Here, some one — any one — ALL — go fetch Doctor Malatesta. All — I say — all." And out he tumbled from the room.

Then came the servant's parliament. "Up and down. Up and down. Did you ever? First a bell this way — then a bell that way. Who could bear it? Did you ever, now? Horrid. Not a moment's peace. A good house — yes, a good house. But still, why *she* made a piece of work when her breakfast went up, and when her dinner went up, too. Then there *was* a disturbance when she went out. *He* flies into a passion, *she* flies into a worse passion than ever, and then they fought! Lor! Oh yes! She hit him. You don't say so!"

When footsteps were heard approaching, the house adjourned.

It was the doctor and Ernesto, still plotting. Ernesto

was to appear at the secret door, and he was to take great care that the don should not recognize him. Here the heavy step of that luckless gentleman was heard coming towards the room, so that Ernesto fled like guilt.

The don came in paler, and colder, and more dejected than ever.

"Don Pasquale!"

"A living corpse, brother."

"The matter—what is the matter?"

"I wish," said the gentleman to himself, "I wish I had rather given a thousand Norinas to Ernesto."

"A good thing to know," thought the doctor, as the don thus spoke. Then aloud, "But pray explain yourself."

"Half my income spent in ribbons; but that is nothing."

"Dear me — go on."

"To the theatre she *will* go —but also that is nothing."

"Dear me — proceed."

"My ears she boxes with a will —*that* is nothing."

"Indeed — indeed."

"But just look here. I think that's something, surely."

Here he handed the horrid letter to the doctor, whose horror was unapproachable when he had read it minutely.

"Stone, don, I'm stone."

"So am I. Revenge! revenge!"

"Surely don. Revenge! revenge!"

"And I have the means. Sit down."

"The means."

"To the garden on tip toe — you and I — we softly go — on and on behind each tree — fearing one of them should see — then upon them straight we fall — and loudly for assistance call. Then to prison off they go — and thus am I avenged you know. And now doctor if you can — please devise a better plan."

"Very good; but," said the doctor, "he had a better plan, which he would divulge only on one condition, namely, that the don should agree to all he should propose."

The don was too fallen to oppose, so, with this arrangement, away they trundled towards the garden.

CHAPTER V.

In the garden, where the last scene of the don's married life was to take place, and in the moonlight, tripped Norina — a young widow again — to the secret garden gate. Click, click went the lock, and the next moment Ernesto was at her little feet, vowing in the warmest manner that he loved her.

Barely had he got through a dozen protestations when there was the flashing of a few rays from a dark lantern all up and down the garden walks, and there was the cranching of the don's heavy legs in the gravel, followed by the lighter walk of the intriguing doctor.

The doctor quite cleverly showed the little lantern rays as he slid behind from tree to tree, and as he did not see Ernesto glide away to the house.

All of a sudden, and with a terrific lunge, he dashed before Norina, and started open the dark little lantern full in her face.

" Thieves! thieves!"

" Hush, ma'am, where is he?"

" Who, the thief — thieves! thieves!"

" No, ma'am, he — who was whispering in your ear."

" Sir, how DARE you. There was no one here."

Whereon the don shot the dark lantern all round and about, like clock-work.

" Sir, I say again, how dare you, there was no one here."

" Pray what were you doing at this dark spot, at this hour of midnight?"

" Enjoying the cool air and the moonlight."

" Begone ma'am — out of my house, ma'am."

" Sir, what tone is this?"

" I say, begone ma'am."

" A pretty tale; this house is mine, and in it I'll remain."

" Ten thousand bombs, you won't."

" Ten thousand bombs I will."

" Don Pasquale, Don Pasquale," said the doctor, "pray leave it all to me. Sister, I would spare you."

"Would you, sir, indeed."

"To-morrow, a new bride will be brought to this house."

"How *dare* you, sir, indeed."

Don Pasquale paid great attention to the dialogue.

"And pray whose bride?"

"Ernesto's, Norina. That contemptible, coquettish, arrant widow!"

Don Pasquale felt some satisfaction, and cried out, "Bravo, doctor."

"That odious woman, here in spite of me. Norina and I under the same roof. Never, I'll leave the house first."

"DO."

"But stop, stop, brother. Perhaps this is a trick. I must be sure of it."

The doctor went up to the don and said, "Then Don Pasquale, you must let them marry, or she'll *never* go."

"*Never?* Will she when they *are* married?"

"Here—house! who is there? Why, as I'm a doctor, 'tis Ernesto."

"Well, well."

"I, Doctor Malatesta, speaking for Don Pasquale, grant you the hand of Norina, and an income of four thousand dollars a year."

"Dear uncle, is this true?"

"Dear nephew, yes it is."

"And *I* (stamp of the foot) oppose it."

"And *I* (don, shaking his head) do not. Go and fetch her, some one; go and fetch her straight."

Said the doctor. "No one need go far, for she, Norina's here."

"What—what—what—what—what!"

Here Norina made a full curtsey.

"THEN WHERE'S SOPHRONIA!"

"I'd not be sure, dear don, she should be in her convent."

"And the marriage, doctor."

"A glimpse, dear don, of what your future might have been."

"Dear—dear—dear—dear—dear! Thank heaven. Still—"

"Come don, be generous."

Need it be said where the two "young people" were at this particular moment — of course, at the don's stout feet.

The don blessed them in the usual manner, and the young people rose, happy.

THE MORAL OF THIS IS MOST EASILY GUESSED,
IN AGE TO SHUN WIVES, IS OF WISDOM THE BEST.

LA SOMNAMBULA. (Bellini.)

THE SLEEP WALKER.

CHAPTER I.

In a beautiful valley in Switzerland there lived a maiden whose name was Amina, a poor village foundling, who was as fondly loved by the woman who had adopted her as her own mother might have loved. There also lived in the valley a rich farmer whose name was Elvino. Not much wealth truly had he, but enough to make him the richest person in the parish, except the absent lord. Count Rudolpho.

At the village inn (as all villages are supposed to possess that appendage) lived Liza, its mistress, but alas! scandal said many cruel things of her; in fact, there were two or three *very* ugly tales about her, but they were all so dim that when any of her female acquaintances quarrelled with her, which thing frequently happened, the other one could only vaguely hint, but could never positively assert anything.

But whether or no, certain it is that young Elvino, who fell in love with Liza when he was young, but as he grew older, he shook that love off, and Liza herself declared with much warmth, that it was all owing to that chit of a child Amina; scandal *did* say that it was all owing to Liza herself.

Be that however, as it may, it is very certain that having abandoned Liza, Elvino soon grew madly in love with Amina, whom all the women declared to be very plain, an evident proof of the young creature's pretty face.

Amina worked hard and well for a living, and she laughed at Liza, as well she might, having certainly the best of the position.

The village was a very happy one throughout the day,

but when night came, it was quite the reverse. "The phantom" weighed the village down. It was clothed all in white, was very tall, and every villager trembled as he spoke or even thought of it.

It had been the ruin of Liza's best bed room, into which this phantom would glide in the dead of the night through the unfastened window, which opened down to the ground, and upon the flower garden; beyond which, and across a rickety, unused bridge, stood the little cot of Amina's adopted mother, Teresa.

Sooner than sleep in Liza's best bed room, any peasant would have slept out upon one of the mountain tops. Yes, the village was a happy village, if you took away the phantom.

Well, at last it was understood that Amina and Elvino were to be married, and the very night came when the contract of marriage was to be signed. 'Twas summer time, so the contract was signed in the broad street itself, just opposite Liza's house, behind which stood the old mill, the unused bridge, and Amina's cot, or, to be honest, Teresa's cot, though for that matter, everything that belonged to Teresa was Amina's.

Elvino endowed Amina with all his wealth. Amina said she could only endow Elvino with her love, and that youth was perfectly satisfied. Liza signed the contract, and very spitefully she signed it too.

The good-tempered fool of the village, Alesso, was rather fond of Liza, and he offered her the pen, but she took it with such a snatch, that he regretted his politeness.

"Never mind, never mind," said Amina, patting the disconsolate fool on the back; "'tis a way she hath of shewing her love for thee."

"Then I should like to know, Mam'selle Amina, how she would show her dislike for me."

All having signed the contract, the bridegroom presented his bride with the ring — a plain little fillet of gold, but how great a treasure when given between a couple, whose only difference of opinion is which loves the other the best.

" Take now this ring, I pray thee,
  In assurance that I wed
  She who once nobly wore it
  Was my mother, who is dead.

" O ! sacred be the gift, love,
  Let it aid thee in thy vow ;
  And ever, ever bid us
  Love, dear wife, as we love now.

It need not be said that the word "wife" applied by
Elvino was hardly right; for the church had to bless the
couple before he could fairly use the tender term, and the
church would not do that till the next day.

Well, the ring had hardly been given, when, with a
great smacking of a whip, a travelling carriage drove
into the village, up to the inn, and, as a consequence,
right into the heart of the contract-signing party.

From this carriage alighted a fine-looking gentleman.

"How weary the road is," said the stranger to his
postillion; "how many miles to the castle?"

"So please you three, monsieur, and' a *dreadful* road;
— have a delightful inn, monsieur — my inn — if monsieur
would do me the honor to walk in."

"True," said the handsome gentleman, smiling; "seeing your face, I recollect you and also the inn."

Alesso heard this admission, and immediately began
to puzzle his brains to find out who this new arrival was,
and for that purpose he went peering amongst the boxes
and portmanteaux.

"And pray, good people, do you ever think of this new
lord, whom you have not seen since he was a boy?"

The villagers immediately began talking about this
lord with great force; would he come? why had he not
come before? pray did the good monsieur know him?"
&c., &c.

The stranger laughingly said they would ask questions
till the evening was night; but this assertion Alesso
doubted; for he could assure monsieur that they would
not stop to question even the new lord himself when the
night came.

"Indeed, why not?"

What! what! had monsieur never heard of their
village spectre? Why, where had monsieur been? He,
Alesso, thought it was talked of all — over — the — world!

The stranger desired to have it described.

A villager then sang—

> " When day has gone — when night has come,
>   When howls the wind — when thunders roar,
>   Then on the hill-top, all dressed in white,
>   Thou'lt see this shade — thou'lt see with awe ! '

> " Without a step it glides along,
>   With hanging hair — with glaring eyes.
>   On — on it glides, and then 'tis gone,
>   And as 'tis lost, it utters cries ! "

The stranger laughed, and said he would soon find out
the mystery if he lived there.

It may be presumed that the stranger had been living
in Paris; but certainly he was very gallant.

He flattered Liza somewhat, but turning his eyes full
upon Amina, he forgot Liza altogether, and began paying
the young bride a great many compliments.

She smiled at the compliments paid her by the stranger,
and answered smartly; but at last grew timid as the count
grew bolder; and indeed she was not sorry when Elvino
came up, and accidentally stood between them. The
count requiring some explanation, Elvino gave it him by
plainly telling him she was his wife; whereupon the
count congratulated him on his good fortune.

Well, the contract business over, the notary departed
for home; the villagers also within doors; the count in
the village inn, and Liza retired, rather annoyed and angry; the two young people were in the moonlight,
bidding each other good night.

At last, after a long time, Amina's mother had the
opportunity of remonstrating upon late hours, and then
Amina went to bed for the last time in that little cot of
her adopted mother's.

CHAPTER II.

THE stranger looked curiously about the haunted room, when shown to it by Liza. There was the white-curtained bed standing near the window; the door-windows open to admit the cool night air; and beyond, the garden, and the unused rickety bridge.

He looked out through the open window, and then returning where Liza was standing, began talking gaily to her.

Liza not feeling gratified by his former conduct, answered rather pertly, and told him that the villagers had discovered who he was — Count Rodolpho; and further intimated that they were coming to pay their respects to their young lord. The "young lord" said he cared naught for the whole village, while so pretty a woman was by his side. Whereat Liza smiling, the count — for it was the count — grew bolder, and insisted upon having one kiss, when a noise frightened Liza, and she ran quickly behind the bed. But as she ran, some portion of the bedstead caught the light scarf about her shoulders, and tore it from them. She took no notice of this mishap, but ran and hid herself behind the curtains.

Certainly she had heard a noise. 'Twas a light footfall. Nearer — then nearer still.

The count went to the closed door, light in hand, and listened.

The step was not coming that way.

Still the slight noise continued; nearer and nearer still. Then a light flashed through the open window. He ran towards it, and then started back.

It was the phantom they had told him of — a white figure moving slowly along, with a lamp steadily held in one hand.

Nothing daunted, he moved towards the figure, as it silently entered the room, and put down the light. And then he saw that it was the village girl to whom he had spoken but an hour or so before.

He drew his breath silently, as he recognized her, for

he knew that she was a somnambulist, and that if woke too suddenly she might fall dead.

But he kept his eyes upon her, as she moved from the table towards his bed.

On — on; slowly — slowly, till she came to the bed; upon which she laid down, whispering Elvino's name, and then in a minute was sleeping peacefully.

He stepped lightly to the window, saw how she had entered, closed and fastened the sashes, returned to the bed — hesitated for a moment, then turning towards the door, he retired.

The woman Liza, immediately he had left, came from behind the bed, where she had remained, gave one earnest look at the unconscious Amina, and quickly left the room.

Now was the time for revenge. Now Amina should feel what it was to have a rival; now she should suffer for alienating Elvino from her. And Elvino, too, should weep, and be sorry for having slighted her. She would tell him he had cruelly dismissed her, and she would add that in revenge she would point at the Amina he believed so good and pure.

Now, the villagers instead of soberly going to bed, got up a demonstration of delight in honor of the count's return, and a score or so of the principal people in the place entered the inn to congratulate the count just as he left his room. The deputation grandly demanding of Liza to be shown into the count's apartment, Mademoiselle Liza, with all the simplicity in the world, said she would head them, and so the procession entered the haunted room to congratulate the count — but to find whom? The poor girl still sleeping soundly, and little dreaming of what was coming.

"Amina!" they all cried, as with one voice.

And they looked towards Elvino, who formed one of the deputation.

They made room for him, falling away on each side. He ran up to the bed side, and there she still lay asleep, breathing peacefully.

He uttered a loud cry, and with a start she awoke.

As she saw the crowd about her, she shrunk back with

alarm, and covered her eyes, thinking possibly 'twas some terrible dream. Then, as they all stood silent about her, she again looked.

Too terrified now to shut out the sight, she remained for a moment or two gazing before her.

Suddenly she spoke. "Where am I? Where am I?"

Bounding from the bed, she looked from right to left, still dimly seeing the faces, and again cried, "Where am I? Where am I?"

"Ask thine own unhappy self!" said a voice she knew, and turned towards it.

"Ah, Elvino!" and she put out her arms to him.

But he flung her from him to the ground, and there she knelt gazing at him with her arms clasped upon her breast, wondering what her fault was.

Not yet comprehending either her position or his words, she looked to the nearest woman; but she turned her back upon the girl, as did the next to whom the poor girl moved her eyes.

Then, panic-struck, she ran round the room from one to the other, still not knowing what her fault was.

They all drew back from her as though she were a plague; so she moved quite naturally to Elvino again — her husband as she thought him.

But he showed the greatest repugnance to her.

Then, as she felt herself deserted, they told her her crime.

Vainly she declared her innocence; vainly she wept, flinging herself upon her knees; vainly she spoke of her past life; vainly she said she could not tell how she came there; vainly she turned to Liza, whose heart was stone, who turned from her with the rest; vainly she clung to her Elvino's very feet: he shook her from him and strode towards the door.

As he was leaving the haunted room, Amina's adopted mother came past the threshhold, and though they all told her what they believed of the village queen, this mother, the only one amongst all these simple, honest village folk, went up to her daughter, and put her arms about her neck.

So at last the iciness of despair gave way before this

one touch of sympathy, and the poor girl with her mother's arms about her, wept bitterly, and so gave relief to her young heart.

CHAPTER III.

THE village generally condemned her; especially Liza. Not a single voice was heard in her favor but her mother's.

Ah, yes, there was one voice in her favor — honest Alesso's, the good-tempered fool's. He would not believe in Amina's guilt, which determination of his thoroughly stamped him a fool in the eyes of all. Her guilt was so palpable; doubt her guilt! you might as well doubt the light of the sun.

Liza, as before said, was especially severe, and doubted whether she ought to be allowed to remain in the village. But nobody supported such a doubt; they were not quite so virtuous themselves as to come to *that* conclusion. Alesso, indeed, spite of his belief in Amina's innocence, admired Liza more than ever for her stern virtue, and sighed as he thought that man would be happy who should call Liza wife.

Alesso had long thought he should be happy to be that man, but though Liza had never given him much hope, he had never given it up in despair, therefore it may be imagined with what grief he heard only the next morning after the catastrophe, that Elvino had made up his mind, and told somebody, who had told somebody else, who had told it to Alesso, that Elvino meant to make proposals to Liza; and before three hours had elapsed this was confirmed throughout the village.

As for the poor girl Amina, she wept most piteously.

Towards the afternoon of the unhappy day which came after the catastrophe, she sought him out, helped by her stout-hearted mother, and made another effort to regain his old love for her. She was no heroine — only a simple village maid; so she did not upbraid him, she only entreated and protested.

He would not listen to her: when she again left him, he

had got back the betrothal ring he had placed upon her finger — the dear ring his mother had worn.

By that night he had asked for and gained Liza's consent to take her to wife, and poor little Amina's remaining hopes (nursed by her mother) were all dead.

When evening came upon the village, the greater part of the villagers were in their tiny cots, and a score or so, together with Liza, Elvino, and Alesso, were seated before the inn door, behind which stood the cottage, within which was the unhappy little woman, now fallen asleep, and sobbing as she slept.

What made Elvino suddenly start — what made him run forward with his fists clenched, and his breath convulsive?

The Count, the Count Rudolpho, who had been missing since the unhappy affair, now came forward to speak out the truth, and upon whose silence the cowardly Liza had relied.

It is a comfort to know that a libertine need not necessarily be a liar though he very frequently is: and in this especial case Count Rudolpho spoke the truth. He declared the whole tale from beginning to end, and, doubtless, he would have appealed to Liza for corroboration, but that, that discreet person got out of the way.

As for the lover, who still so deeply loved, that he was actually going to marry a woman for whom he cared naught as a revenge, he would believe nothing that the count said. Indeed, how could the girl have entered the inn, if not with the count's aid.

The noble pointed to the unused bridge, but Elvino scouted the idea; why it would fall at the least touch, how then could she have passed over it?

The count was turning away in despair, when a noise a little distance off arrested his steps; the villagers turned and saw the village phantom, and they saw at once who it was.

Again, Amina was walking in her sleep; again she was moving towards the old ruined bridge; again she carried a flickering light in her hand.

As Elvino saw her, all his old love returning, he ran forward and would have shouted to her, but that the count sped after him, laid a hand upon his mouth, and softly, yet imperatively, bade him be silent.

The lover flung himself upon his knees, stretched out his arms towards his pure wife, and with straining eyes watched her coming.

Nearer to the old bridge — which was rotten, and below which was a roaring torrent. Nearer still, then one foot was upon it.

All silent with fear they drew back a pace, as though each had stepped upon the tottering wood, or as though he could prevent her second step by the act.

Again a step forward, and she was fairly on the bridge, the angry water roaring beneath.

Suddenly there was a crackling sound, and as they heard it, they flung themselves down upon their knees, and hid their faces in their hands.

When they stood up again they expected to see her and the bridge no longer before them. But the brave old bridge had only cracked; there was a great flaw in it, and there also stood Amina as though in doubt, as though cautious of her next step. The hand which had held the light was still held out, but the lamp was gone, the rupture of the stones had shaken it from her hold.

If now she sees her way by the lighted lamp; if now she stands undecided, because she can no longer see where to make her steps, she is lost, for no one can dare step on to the rotten bridge to save her, and she will fall over the low parapet, and so be lost.

But no; again she steps on — feeling carefully with her foot; again she hesitates, as her sliding foot comes against an unaccustomed projection, caused by the fracture of the stone-work.

Then again she moves on — a step; another; yet another — and she is safe.

Then they all fell on their knees, and so gained pardon for having wrongfully accused the poor girl.

For had she been guilty, she would not have had the courage to try and cheat the villagers. Yes, she was really asleep, and had no idea of the danger she had run.

She came close to the spot upon which knelt her Elvino, whom she had now gained back to her whilst she slept; and then she went through the motion of setting down the lamp, now rolling at the bottom of the torrent.

Soon she began talking of the lost ring — the ring he had given her, and had torn from her.

And she broke up into atoms the score of roses he had also given her on that happy night, and which she now took from her bosom. Then again she wept for the ring, and felt on her hand for it.

He still had the ring, for he had not hardened his heart enough to put it on Liza's hand; and, under the direction of the count, he quietly slipped it on the sleeping girl's finger.

'Twas enough.

Feeling the ring once again, she awoke. But ah! to how much joy? The whole village crowding around her, sorry for their unjust suspicions, and more desirous of getting a kind look from her than ever; her Elvino, proud and happy, near her; her dear old adopted mother, proud and self-satisfied. Was it not better as it was — that that happiness should come after such deep trouble (which is ofttimes a short cut to years of joy,) than that the two young people should have dropped into wedlock after a happy, unclouded childhood and love, without having had a pang to teach them the sweetness of peace and innocence.

As for Liza, the less that is said of that lady the better. That scarf of hers told terribly against her; and though poor Alesso felt the blow terribly, he could hardly show the remains of any bruise whatever to his new love when Liza left the village.

L'ELISIR D'AMORE. (Donizetti.)

THE ELIXIR OF LOVE

CHAPTER I.

It is pleasant to see the reapers resting after their work, in the shadows of the trees. Indeed, it may be pleasant to be a reaper reposing. Yet a disappointed, wretched lover can find no pleasure in anything but being miserable; and lovers, disappointed in love, do so indulge in misery, that it *must* be a pleasure.

Nemorino, the poor young farmer, was a disappointed lover, and on one particular autumn evening, when the reapers were sitting in the shadow of the trees, he took no notice of *them*, but kept his eyes fixed upon Adina, who, on her part, kept her eyes fixed upon her book, like St. Dunstan of old.

The fact is, Adina was a coquette, and no one likes your unalterably attached man more than a thorough coquette. A coquette — that is, a thorough coquette — never does marry an unalterably attached man. She usually marries a man who thinks just a little more of himself than he does of his bride, and a coquette is happy ever after in consequence.

Well Adina, who, by the way, was by no means poor, lived in a farm-house, in the exact centre of her farm, and did nothing but what she pleased. And Adina ran very considerable risk of marrying Sergeant Belcore, of the attractive chasseurs; and she quite laughed at the attentions of Nemorino. Handsome; yes, certainly handsome, but *so* stupid, so different to Sergeant Belcore.

See you, in her heart of hearts, a coquette knows her own inestimable little worth, and so, consequently, she cannot help despising a man who thoroughly believes in her.

On this particular evening she was more contemptuous with respect to Nemorino than she had ever shown herself, and truth to tell, sitting under a tree reading, she looked, and was, very pert indeed.

She made him jealous of her very book; it was such an interesting book. Suddenly, when the poor fellow ceased looking for an instant —

" Ah, ah! capital! Just listen : ' The beautiful Tristano quite burned away with love for the cruel Isotta, who SCORNED him (here she looked scornfully at Nemorino). At last, he found a sage, who gave him a love-philtre, and after that, the lovely Isotta was continually following the handsome Tristano.' Nonsense! that only proves that the lovely Isotta was as stupid as somebody else I know. Hark! there are the drums; oh, delight, here comes *the sergeant ;*" and then she looked wickedly at the disconsolate Nemorino.

Who was certainly very different to "*the sergeant.*" Nemorino was tall, comely-looking, flaxen-haired, and ingenuous; Sergeant Belcore was equally tall, but he was more than comely-looking. Such a figure had Sergeant Belcore! And Sergeant Belcore's moustache, a long, sweeping moustache, which stood out straight on each side of his face, in the mathematical manner, and was as bright as his splendid boots. His handsome black hair, too, was clipped short to the pole of his neck; and altogether, Sergeant Belcore was very spruce indeed; and Sergeant Belcore knew it.

He thought he was in love with Adina, but he certainly was not; whereof, in proof of which, witness the nosegay. No lover — really a lover — comes up as cool as a cucumber to offer his bouquet? No, he suggests the flowers, so to speak, with many doubts; and if it be accepted, he don't twirl his moustaches (if he has any), as though he had done a very admirable thing.

All of which conduct was Sergeant Belcore's, when he stepped cavalierly up to the maiden. As for Nemorino, poor fellow, he looked more lone, dismal, and ridiculous than before.

"O, country nymph, I present this nosegay to you, as Paris did the apple, because you are the loveliest."

"Ah, ah, ah! very good."

Nemorino sighs.

"And I see clearly I've carried your heart by storm. Well, well, no girl can withstand a red coat."

"Ah, ah, ah! very good, sergeant."

"Ah, me!" sighed the love-born swain.

"Well, pretty one, if your love equals mine, let's ground arms — capitulate; on what day will you marry me?"

"Ah, ah, ah! very good, Sergeant Belcore."

"Come — come — come — here's the conqueror."

"Sergeant, sergeant, you storm too soon. Who should cry victory before the battle has begun? And besides, *I* am Adina."

"I wish," thought the poor stricken lover, "*I* could talk as bravely as the sergeant."

"Well well, as sure as I've a military moustache, I'll not desert the post."

"Spoken like a brave sergeant. But, in the meantime, may I offer you something to eat?"

"I'm one of the family already," thought the sergeant; so he said, "If *you* sit at the same table."

"Ah, ah, ah! *very* good, Sergeant Belcore. Go in, go in."

She saw Nemorino was coming up to speak to her.

"One little word, Adina."

"Oh, *two* little words for Nemorino. The usual sighs, though he had much better go and see his uncle, who is ill — they say *very* ill."

"He is not so sick as I am, Adina."

"And, then, if his uncle dies, he'll make somebody else his heir."

"What does that matter to me, Adina?"

"And then he'll die of hunger and misery;" addressed generally to the surrounding landscape.

"Either of hunger or love, what matters it, Adina?"

"Well, well. He *is* modest, which Sergeant Belcore certainly is NOT. This Nemorino don't presume, and I never shall love him."

"But why — why, Adina?"

"He might as well ask the wind why it loveth to go this way or that, over brook or field."

" Then I ought ? "

" Then he ought to think no more about me."

" But I cannot, Adina."

" But why ? "

" You might as well ask the river why it flows to the sea."

" Ah, I see; because he *must!* "

" Even as the river floweth onwards to the sea, I'll follow Adina."

" Ah, ah, ah ! "

And with this general winding up of her interviews with the luckless youth, she ran in, and clapped to the little door.

CHAPTER II.

ONE hour later and everybody in the market place was opening his or her eyes, as widely open he or she could. For with a great blowing of trumpets, and other unusual sounds, came *such* a visitor !

In a carriage, too — not an ordinary carriage, but a gilt carriage. Not a mean covered-in carriage, like a van, but a fine open carriage, with *such* a gentleman sitting within it. One had to look twice before he could comprehend him — he was *so* grand. His waistcoat was a fair field, and his forehead a great plain. But as for his legs, to what shall they be compared ? The legs of Jupiter himself, or perhaps Hercules ! Yet he had a benignant face, this new comer, and he seemed to know he should be welcome.

Who was he — a lord, a prince ?

And who was his trumpeter behind, blowing a triumphal march ?

All the people gathered round this wonderful being with open-mouthed respect. Then this great man condescended to step from his grand carriage and address the villagers, as his carriage and his trumpeter stopped together.

"Listen, listen, listen — oh ! oh ! you rustics all
    Listen, listen, listen, or great and small.
    I am, I am, I am the greatest of great men !
    For I can fright away the greatest oldest wen !
    I, present now,
    Who make a bow,
    Am Doctor Dulcamara.
    In France I'm known,
    The French will own,
    In Venice and Ferrara.
    Such things I've done,
    That more than one
    Have said I am — no matter ;
    But this I know,
    Where'er I go,
    I make no little clatter.

"Listen, listen, listen every one that's here.
    If amongst you any's dying, let him no longer fear.
    I'll cure her, or I'll cure him, with physic quite divine —
    In fact, you wouldn't know it from very nice sweet wine.
    Apoplexy
    Need not vex ye,
    If unto Dulcamara,
    With rapid run,
    You straightway come.
    And as for those with asthma,
    If they but drink,
    I'm sure they'll think
    They need not drink much longer
    If they're too weak
    Almost to speak,
Quick — presto — they'll be stronger.

" Oh ! listen, listen, listen.   If any one has gout,
    Oh ! let him buy a bottle, and let him drink it out.
    As for tooth-ache,
    But one sip take,
    You'd think no more of that tooth.
    And as to age,
    I do engage,
    Two sips will bring back your youth
    Oh ! yes I am,
    Your'e sure I am,
    Great Doctor Dulcamara
    In France he's known,
    His fame has grown
    In Venice and Ferrara.

"Oh ! listen, listen, listen.   No donht you think 'tis dear.
Oh ! rustics, rustics, rustics, of that now have no fear.
A hundred pounds !
A hundred crowns !
A bottle I don't ask you !
Oh ! yes — oh ! yes,
The price now guess.
To guess high, I don't ask you.
Well, half-a-crown,
Just lay it down.
Ah ! ah ? my friend, health bless you.
All doctors pale,
Before me fail,
I only can redress you.
Come buy, come buy — oh ! rustics, that's if you'd be well ;
Your duty is to purchase — my duty is to — sell."

Now amongst the "rustics" who had heard this very eulogistic patter, was Nemorino; and this youth, biting the rim of his rustic hat, struck himself with the idea that the doctor could cure people of want of love.

"Sir doctor, pardon me, do you know many secrets?"

"Secrets, rustic, I'm *all* secrets."

"My faith!   Well, have you, by chance, the love drink of Queen Isotta?"

"Hu-u-m.   Well, well, well, rustic."

"The real love-drink that awakens love?"

'Ah! I'm the only brewer of it."

"And — and do you *sell* it?"

"To those who can afford to buy it, rustic."

"Good doctor, and what is the charge?"

"Well — hum — well!"

"I've half-a-dozen crowns."

"I' faith, you've hit it."

Then the doctor went to his gilt carriage, and brought out something singularly like a small wine-bottle.

"I' faith," said the stout doctor, taking the crowns, "you will be cured if you drink that."

"I' faith (this to himself,) fools there are 'neath the sun;
A fool, yet none the less a brother — this one."

"Oh, but doctor, how am I to manage?"

"Ah, I forgot, young rustic.

5*

> " Now with great care,
>   In weather fair,
>   The bottle must be taken ;
>   Then up and down,
>   Mind, *do not frown,*
>   The bottle must be shaken !
>   Pulled out the cork
>   Per screw or fork,
>   The bottle to your lips, oh,
>   You then must place,
>   And — no grimace,
>   The potion drink in sips, oh.''

" Yes, yes, young man, this is the *real* elixir of love ! "
(And perhaps it was, for 'twas good Bordeaux.) ·

" And young rustic, don't take it till to-morrow. (By that time I shall be gone.)"

" Oh, good doctor ! "

" I' faith (to himself again,) fools there are 'neath the sun ;

A fool, yet none the less a brother — this one. And mind, young rustic. A word in your ear. Silence, *silence!* 'Tis dangerous to sell love-potions now-a-days. I don't speak for myself, young rustic, for *I*'m the great Dulca-mara, famed in Venice and Ferrara ; but for *your* sake, young rustic — ah! ah! all the women in the place will be dying for you. To-morrow, mind. Good bye young rustic, good bye."

And the worthy doctor vanished through the doorway of ·the village inn.

" Faith," said the lover to himself, no longer in a disconsolate tone, " a good thing is a good thing to-day as well as to-morrow. And 'tis fair weather, for am I not sitting down here with my elixir of love ? And the bright sky above me. Good ! I will ! " Pop ! 'tis the cork. " Ah, ah ! good ! another sip. Good ! — another."

" La, la, la, la, la, ra, ra."

" Good ! Good ! yet another ; and another sip."

" La, la, la, la, la, ra, ree."

" Can I believe my eyes ; why 'tis Nemorino singing Actually Nemorino singing. Ah, ah ! "

" 'Tis she ! I shall go to her ! No ; why should *I* go to her ? Let her come to me. La, la, la. La, la, la. For to-morrow; yes to-morrow. They'll be sighing at my feet!"

"He doesn't even look at me! ah, ah!" Rather a louder "ah, ah!" than the first.

"La, la, la, re, ra, ra, ra. Aie, aie, aie, eie, ah!"

"'Tis all put on!"

"She's very clearly not in love with me *yet*. La, la, la, re, ra, ra, ra. Aie, aie, eie, ah!"

"It MUST be put on! Good *evening*, Nemorino. *Very* good. You're taking my advice. You're, you're quite *merry!*"

"True; I like this new life."

"Then your sighs, and your sobs, and your tears!"

"La, la, la."

"Silence, sir."

"Re, ra, ra, ra,"

"How dare you!"

"Aie, aie, aie, eie, a, a, le."

"*Very* good."

"Oh! I shall be heart-whole to-morrow."

"Indeed! we shall see! We shall see!" The second "we shall see" very low and confidential.

Then came a voice from the inn, which cried,

> "Tran, tran, tran,
> In love or in war;
> Tran, tran, tran,
> You ne'er saw before;
> Tran, tran, tran,
> A Sergeant Belcore;
> Tran, tran, tran,
> A Sergeant Belcore."

"Ah! here comes that *admirable* sergeant. Ah, sergeant; is that you?"

"Yes; dear heart of stone!"

"Stone! oh no."

"Sound to the assault, sergeant. Now, tell me; when shall we be married?"

"We-e-e-l-l-l — Perhaps s-o-o-o-o-n."

"Ah!"

"He started," said Adina in a low voice. "Don't pull your moustaches, sergeant," said she in a louder voice.

" Always obey orders ; well, in six days ? "

" Wel-l-l-l — Per-hap-p-p-s."

" Victory, victory. As sure as I'm a sergeant ! "

" Ah, ah, ah, ah, ah ! " laughed Nemorino.

" Oh, oh ! he's actually laughing." And somebody was almost crying.

" What's that donkey laughing at ? " shouted the sergeant. " If he don't retreat I shall charge him."

" Oh, I — could — bite — my — fingers — off — with — rage — he — don't — seem — to — care — in — the — *least*."

" Ah, ah ! " thought the donkey ; " wait till to-morrow, brave sergeant ; wait till to-morrow ! "

" Tr-r-r-m, Tr-r-r-m, Tr-r-r-m."

" Hallo ! hallo ! What's that ? "

" Sergeant ; " here there was a military salute from a soldier. " Despatch."

With a fierce twirl of his moustaches, " sergeant " opened the paper. " Hum ! we march to-morrow."

" Oh, *dear !* " cried several young girls together. And there was a general impression that a shifting garrison was a national wrong.

" Con-n-nfound it," said the sergeant ; " and my marriage"

" Yes, yes ! to-morrow, my friend," again thought Nemorino.

" Oh ! I shall not forget you, sergeant ! "

" Forget ! Peste ! Hu-m-u-m, Adina — why can't we be married to-day ? "

" He — seems — moved — now ; in — fact — he — seems — quite — frightened ; " thought the little coquette.

" To-day ; " thought rustic Nemorino, " to-day — if they're married to-day there will be no to-morrow — and the elixir of love — will be useless ! "

" We-l-l-l sergeant. Y-y-y-es ; to-day ! "

" Oh, no, no, no ; Adina. Wait till to-morrow."

" Ah, ah ! "

" You cannot marry him ; because, I — I — I — know why ! "

" Co-r-r-r-rpodi Bacco "

" You can't, Adina. You'll be sorry if you do. Don't, don't marry him till to-morrow."

"Begone, booby; or I strangle you!"

"Sergeant, pray take no notice of the poor fellow. Half-witted, sergeant. He thought; ah, ah! thought I should — should *love* him. Oh — the — ridiculous — creature. *He* thought! I'll be revenged on him," she said to herself. "How *dared* he to sing before me. He shall fall at my feet in penitence before I'll have a word to say to him."

And all the girls about said, " the *idea !* a common husbandman to dare to be the rival of a sergeant in the army; the *idea !* "

"Come, sergeant."

"The notary; corpo di Bacco; the notary."

"Yes, yes; sergeant, come."

"Doctor, doctor," shrieked out Nemorino. "Doctor, help! quick! help, doctor!"

"Now, then; all of you there; fall in; march."

And away they all went to see sergeant Belcore married to Adina the coquette.

Leaving Nemorino the rustic to call for the doctor at his leisure.

CHAPTER III.

WHEN they all got to the great room in Adina's farmhouse, they quite filled it. Well, there they were, looking out for the notary. Adina, too, was looking out for Nemorino, for she had a faint fear she had gone a little too far.

Even an invitation from Doctor Dulcamara, who was there, to sing a song, did not cheer her; and not even the song itself, though she sang it very well, gave her any consolation.

"Here comes the NOTARY."

"Bravo, bravo, bravo," said the doctor.

Out of respect to the notary, all the neighbors withdrew to the lawn outside. And also out of respect to the notary, he was shown into the best room; so only the doctor remained in the hall. And only for a moment too, for Nemorino came rushing in.

"Oh, doctor; here you are. Nay, don't run away, doctor." For that stout man was certainly trying to effect an escape.

"Doctor, I must be loved now, at once; to-morrow will be no good."

"I 'faith, fools there are, 'neath the sun, a fool, yet none the less a brother — this one. By Bacchus, he's mad! Take the elixir, sir."

"Sir, I have."

"Then take another dose."

"Give me another bottle."

"Good; but first give me your money."

"Money — money,— I have none."

"Well, well, well, my young rustic. Come to-morrow, or, get some; and ask for me at the inn as soon as you like. Good night, good night." And the doctor seemed rather glad to shuffle off, losing thereby, the feast to which he had been bidden.

"Ah, me!" sighed the youth, flinging down on a seat.

"Heigho! women are an awkward lot, as sure as my name's Belcore," said the sergeant, sauntering in. "Of course she loves me, and yet she will wait till this evening for the marriage. Hullo! hullo! rustic, what's the matter?"

"I want money, and it seems I *may* want it."

"Well, you're a fine fellow; enlist, and you'll have twenty crowns."

"*Twenty!* did you say twenty crowns, Mr. Sergeant?"

"Look! here — jingle, jingle — here they are. And glory, and honor — and love — the soldier need never sigh."

"*Twenty* crowns?"

"Tw-w-wenty crowns!"

"Done!"

"Here, just sign this paper. Good; take your money. You'll soon be a corporal, if you look up to me."

"Ha! ha! oh! oh!" laughed the sergeant, "I've enlisted my rival; oh! oh! a good tale to tell."

And he swaggered off, while Nemorino rushed away to buy bottle number two.

CHAPTER IV.

EVERY woman then and there in the market-place was full of it, and crowded about each other to hear and receive the news. "Did you ever!"—"Oh! *quite* true!"—"Who *would* have thought it, you know?"—"Yes but who told you?"—"Hush! not so *loud*."—"It's a secret."—"Oh, of course!"—cried twenty voices at least. "Because, *I* heard it from the young grocer (She *always* hears every thing from the young grocer) who heard it from the mercer, who had it from the lawyer himself; and so you know *then* it is."—"Oh, of course; well, I'm sure *I* should never have thought it."—"And such a fortune."—"Why, he's the richest man in the parish."—"I wish *I* had a rich old uncle."—"Yes, and he never went to see him."—"All through *that* Adina."—"Eugh!"—"There he is!" (Twenty voices again.)

"He" was Nemorino. "He" had run to the doctor, who again fraudulently appropriated the crowns; again "he" had imbibed the elixir of love, and this time he really hoped the elixir would have some effect.

"How humble he looks."

"He don't know his good fortune *yet*."

"Good evening to your curls, Nemorino," said one.

"Good evening, and a curtsey to your heart, Nemorino," cried another.

"Good evening, and a smile, Nemorino," exclaimed a third.

"Your humble servant, signor," said a mean fourth.

"THE ELIXIR!"

"You'll forget your old playmates now, signor."

"Oh! no, Nemorino is too *amiable*."

"Your humble servant, signor."

"THE ELIXIR."

Here two persons coming stopped in the utmost wonder to see Nemorino, the rustic, in the midst of a group of girls. One person was the enormous Doctor Dulcamara, and the other person was the far from enormous Adina.

"Bless *me!*" said Adina to herself.

Nemorino ran up to the doctor, and whispered — "You were right, the elixir this time was *stronger*."

"Can . . . I . . . believe . . . my . . . senses?" exclaimed Dulcamara. Then he said to the women — "Does he please you?"

"The insolence of that doctor!" all the girls seemed to say with their little noses in the air.

"Can — I — believe. *Am* I the proprietor of the love philtre?" For we may tell lies till we actually believe them ourselves.

"Well," thought the rustic to himself, "if every girl loves me, she ought."

"And I thought to find him in tears, and if he still loved me, he *would* be," thought Adina.

"You'll dance, Nemorino."

"Yes, Gianetta, with you."

"With me, your humble obedient servant, signor, too."

"Yes, yes."

"With *you*, indeed! Ah, ah. *Very* good." And here the pretty noses were brought into action again.

"Can — I — bel —. I DON'T."

"Ne—ne—ne—ne—mo—ri—no!"

"THE ELIXIR. She comes!"

"Can — I — I CAN'T," said the doctor.

"So, for a few poor crowns, you've become soldier, Nemorino. I must speak to you," said Adina.

"Nemorino!"

"Well, Gianetta."

"Hark! there's the music. And you know you promised me."

"True, true, I'm coming. I'll hear you presently, Adina. Coming, Gianetta, coming."

Scene — a despairing little woman pressing her little hands one within the other. And whether anybody is there she cares not, as she says in a whisper, "I love him, I do love him."

Says Doctor Dulcamara. "Can — I — no believe my senses. "Ah, ah! I'm a gold mine. I'm a Crœsus!"

"Ah, ah, ah!" cried a quick, sharp voice, the personal property of Gianetta in fact. And as she went off to the dance, audacious with Nemorino. "Ah, ah, ah, *she* thinks

she's to have the homage of all the men in the village, but
she WONT."

" *She* " heard the remark, but it did not make her angry.

"How cruel, how cruel!"

" Ah! all my doings."

" Yours, doctor."

" Yes, I have Queen Isotta's love secret!"

" Queen—n—*Isotta's!* I won't believe it. And you
gave it to Nemorino!"

"Oh, yes. To try it on some cruel fair, who would
have naught to say to him."

" Ah, then he *was* in love with — some one,"

" Yes, the poor fellow; and to get money for Queen
Isotta's secret, he enlisted."

" The poor youth!"

" 'Tis my impression she would buy elixir herself," said
the doctor to himself.

" And now, Nemorino is fortunate in love?"

"There's not a girl but — here, just look at them. This
way!"

" And who is he in love with?"

" Faith, I know not, but they are all in love with *him.*"

" And once I *know* he only loved *me.*"

" The elixir is not dear. Think! you might have a hundred lovers at your feet!"

" I'd not know what to do with them. I — I only wish
but *one.*"

" And every woman in the place would hate you."

" What are they to me!"

"Or if you'd marry a rich man."

"I'm rich enough already."

" A count, a marquis."

" Good, if named Nemorino."

" And my philtre!"

" You may swallow it yourself."

" I rather think Adina knows a good deal more than I.
But I also think Adina for all girls don't reply."

"He *shall* come back to me," said the little woman to
herself, "he shall, he shall! A look, a smile, a little frown,
and he is at my feet. For I *have* the elixir, here, in my
face, here, in my eyes."

And away she went to find Nemorino. If she had only
looked behind her now. For there he was; and as she
fluttered away, he came a few steps forward.

As a clear evidence how fond he was of her in this, that
he was sorry he had gone away with Gianetta, perchance
the mercenary. Indeed, he thought he had marked a fur-
tive tear or so in Adina's eyes; and, very softly, he thought
to —

"O, Nemorino! what, left the dancing?"

"Yes, I was tired."

"What, and left Gianetta?"

"Yes; for I was tired of her, too. You see, when a
poor youth is loved by *all* the girls, he need not care for
one only. Heigho! they all want to marry."

"Well, they can't all marry you; and what do you
say?"

"*I* don't know."

"Now listen to me," said the maiden, coming up close
to him.

"Well, Adina (she's going to confess.)"

"Why — why are you going to leave us? Why are
you going away for a soldier?"

"Going to seek my fortune, Adina."

"But — but we *all* like you here. And — and we should
all be *so* sorry to part with you. And — and" (here the
little right hand went to the little natty apron-pocket, and
brought out a paper.) "And — and *I've bought your discharge.*"

"Ha! you love me!"

"Love you? We *all* love you — like you. There,
take the paper. And pray keep amongst us. I dare say
*you will find somebody you can fall head over ears in love
with;* for I'm sure we *all* like you. *Good* bye."

"But this isn't confessing!"

"*Good* bye, Nemorino."

"But — but you're not going like that!"

"Why, what more can you want? you have your discharge. *Good* bye, Nemorino."

"Oh, good bye; only you have forgotten something."

"Indeed — what?"

"The discharge. Take it. I shall remain a soldier.

For the doctor has deceived me; and — and — God bless you, and good bye, Adina."

"Oh, no, no, no, no. He has not deceived you. I — I want to make you as happy as I have made you wretched. I — I *know* you love me, and — and I LOVE YOU WITH ALL MY HEART!"

"THE ELIXIR!"

"Hi! hi! hi! what's this? what's this? Can Sergeant Belcore believe his handsome eyes!"

"If he can't, he must believe Adina's tongue. My husband, Sergeant Belcore."

"Your husband, ma'am; your husband! Keep him. Sergeant Belcore won't break his heart for *one* woman."

"Ah! but one Sergeant Belcore would break the hearts of a thousand women. Let him buy the elixir of love, ten crowns a bottle. I, Doctor Dulcamara, only sell it. Who subdued the sweet Adina? I, Doctor Dulcamara, did!"

"Cursed mountebank! may you and your coach fall into the next ditch."

"He! he! he! she only marries him because his rich uncle is dead." This was the malicious remark of Gianetta.

For one moment Adina drew away.

The next moment Nemorino drew closer to Adina.

Adina did not withdraw.

"And pray, who made him die?"

"Why, rustics all, 'twas I."

"Oh! listen, rustics, listen, if either has an uncle,
  Almost dead with — say lumbago, phthisics, or carbuncle,
  I'll kill him, or I'll cure him, precisely as you say;
  But this way, or the other, my friends, you'll have to pay,

"I, present, now,
  Who make this bow,
  Am Doctor Dulcamara.
  In France I'm known,
  I'm famed alone,
  In Venice and Ferrara.
  Such things I've done,
  That more than one,
  Have said I am — no matter;
  But this I know,
  Where'er I go,
  I make no little clatter.

" Oh ! rustics, rustics, rustics, if e'er you would grow fat,
   To purchase these my bottles 'tis the best thing to be at,
   Women — ye maidens who'd in the waist be thin,
   Try one bottle; 'tis far better than lacing yourselves in.

         You soldiers, there,
         Who court the fair,
         I pray you make one trial.
         Why, sure as fate,
         Sure as I'm great,
         You'll ignore the word denial
         Thank you; and you,
         Four crowns, 'twill do.
         I am great Dulcamara,
         But two? take three !
         Cash hand to me !
         I'm famed in Carrara.

" Oh, every one, or old, or young, or you of middle age,
   To do all things — I don't care what — I doctor do engage.
   Grow rich, grow poor, grow young, grow old, I'm Doctor Dulcamara,
   Famed north, famed south, and as I've said, I think, in far Carrara.

         " You want a head ;
         No sooner said,
         Than done — if I'm your doctor.
         Your skin, I ween,
         I'll color green
         Or make you look a Chocktaw.
         But mind you all,
         Both great and small,
         Don't draw away afraid, oh !
         The money bring
         For every thing,
         Dulcamara must be paid, oh ! ' "

And after this happy conclusion, who shall say there is
not *some* virtue in the ELIXIR OF LOVE.

IL BARBIERE DI SIVIGLIA. (Rossini).

THE BARBER OF SEVILLE.

CHAPTER I.

The barber, Figaro, was, in his way, a blessing.

I don't mean to say for one moment that he was at all equal to any one benison uttered by any one ecclesiastic in the quaint old city of Seville; yet I do assert, and plainly, he was a blessing — Figaro, barber and bleeder of Seville.

For, besides being a barber, a Spanish barber, Figaro *was* a bleeder; and in Figaro's days, barbers were of infinitely more importance than they are now.

Ah! and Figaro was also a postman; but, I grieve to say, he never delivered letters with double knocks; indeed, the only percussions at all in *these* matters arose between the hearts and the ribs of those to whom the billets d'amour were delicately addressed.

On the whole, however, I do NOT think Figaro was the pattern of a moral man. But, dear me, you must pick up your bread where you can find it in Seville, and Seville never was, and never will be, a highly moral centre.

Well, then, you will please to understand that Figaro was ubiquitous (so to speak,) clever, ready-witted, a good barber, a good bleeder, a good musician, and a not over scrupulous Spaniard.

But, in the affair of the Count Almaviva, everything was strictly moral and proper. The count was madly in love with Rosina, and desired her for his countess; but, alas! Rosina was an imprisoned flower, and she spelt her jailor's name thus : — g-u-a-r-d-i-a-n. ·

Well, well; the count adored Rosina, though where he first made her acquaintance, tradition sayeth not.

But this is certain, he came one night, as usual, to serenade this dark beauty, who was close shut up in her guardian's dark old house. *Her* darkness was delicious, but
the darkness of that old house was abominable. There
was, however, a balcony to it, and to that balcony the
poor Rosina would fly whenever she could.

On this night, too, the count did not serenade alone;
he had with him quite a crowd of serenaders, delighted to
serve a man of *his* quality. And, truth to tell, he and his
crowd played their best music, and not a sign was there
from the house. But the day itself advancing, the crowd
was dismissed, and the count stood alone, happily unhappy, near the door of the enchantress's guardian's horrid
house.

He was still pensively watching, when by came Figaro.
Never mind upon what errand he had been — 'tis no business of ours; he had his guitar in his hand, and on his
guitar he was playing; singing, too, rather egotistically,
but never mind.

La ran, la lera, la ran, la la.

There's no time for the city's factotum here,
He must off to his shop, for dawn is quite near.
La ran, la lera, la ran, la la.

What merrier life, whose pleasures more gay,
Than those of this barber, good people say,
Ah ! brave Figaro, bravo, bravissimo,
Is there a better one? oh dear, dear me, no !
La ran, la lera, la ran, la la.

Ready at call, both by day and by night,
No one more active, and no one more light.
What better cheer, or happier lot,
Have any men, pray, than barbers have got?
La ran, la lera, la ran, la la.

Lancet, and scizzors, and razor, and comb,
Your Figaro sells when he's at home.
But when he's *from* home, his trade's billets-doux,
Which he'll carry for that man, or this man, or you.
La ran, la lera, la ran, la la.

How I am looked for — wherever I go,
On this side a belle — on that side a beau.

Whore is my wig, you stupid pig,
Just take this packet, under your jacket
Figaro — Figaro — here, sir, here,
Figaro up — Figaro down,
Figaro, presto, all over town.
Oh yes ; I'm as quick as lightning's bright flash,
And what's best of all, I earn plenty of cash.
Oh brave Figaro — bravo bravissimo,
Is there no better one — oh dear, dear me no.
    La ran, la lera, la ran, la la.

This contented personage was rushing off to his shop
wnen he went crash up against the count himself. "Good
master ! "

"What — Figaro ! Hush, be silent ! I'm not known
here."

"Surely — surely — surely — Senor."

It would be hardly within the bounds of possibility to
believe that the grand count actually set to work, then
and there, in the dark, to tell Figaro of his loves; but
then it was Figaro — and the barber was a father confess-
or in all affairs of the heart. The count stated that he
had fallen in love with a lady whom he took to be the
daughter of an old physician — and he, count as he was,
called himself Lindoro, and was, night and day, watching
that balcony.

"*That* window ! Senor — you are lucky." Then the
barber set him right. Her name was Rosina — she was
not the doctor's daughter, but his ward — and she hated
him; and he was jealous of her — and she was wretched,
and he was wretched, and a very pretty house it was. As
for him, Figaro, in that said house he was everything —
barber, hairdresser, and surgeon too.

He was in the full tide of chatter when the count started. Barber knew, without looking, that the window
opened — and *she* was in the balcony.

Rosina — lovely as the night — stood in the balcony,
holding a letter in her hand. She was wondering where
somebody was.

Crack ! — she had barely got into the balcony than the
old doctor was after her.

"A fine morning, child. What letter's that ? "

As she answered, she saw the proposed owner of the

letter. "A letter — no — a piece of music. Oh, dear, it has fallen into the street — pray go and pick it up."

He required no recommendation. He trundled his jealous old legs to the street door, but the letter was delivered. He looked sharply about, while the young lady deplored that the wind had carried it away.

"I'll surely have that balcony walled up," said the old doctor — "I surely will."

And he went in and barred the door.

As for the letter — opened and read by Figaro — it stated that the lady had a laudible curiosity to know who and what was the serenader, and why he came there — that she was touched by his attentions; that she was wretched; that she hated her guardian; and that her name was Rosina.

After reading the letter, said Figaro — "And a sad old fellow is that same guardian — a miser, a monster, a wretch.

Again the barber was brought up short — the doctor had left his house again — going to see a patient. And he left strict injunctions to let no one enter while he was away; though, if Don Basilio came — let him wait outside.

A stream of condemnation for Don Basilio — who, truth to say, was a rival of Figaro's. "A match-maker by trade," said Figaro; "a penniless, know-nothing rapscallion, who had recently set up as a music master. A long, lank, lean man, with a nose like a hook; and he taught Rosina music too!"

"Chink — chink." This speaking sound was the passage of gold from count to barber. Barber engaged upon *that* argument to do all things.

Clearly the first thing to do was to get into the house. One second, and the barber had it. A regiment had just arrived — the count must disguise himself as a soldier and present a billet. The count was charmed with the idea; and the barber was charmed with himself. "Chink — chink," from the barber's purse. Another thought. He must be drunk — 'twould put the guardian off his guard — what *gentleman* would be drunk!

So, on the very best terms with each other, the count and the barber walked off to put their plans into execution.

CHAPTER II.

IT is, I hope, no imputation upon Rosina's character to say she *watched* the count and the barber as they chatted; and it is to be hoped no one will accuse her of impropriety, if, in that hour, she fairly made up her mind that the count would make an admirable husband! And —and after a time she wrote another letter — a delicious lover's relief—and wondered how *he* was to get it; and she was just thinking that perhaps Figaro could ——

When Figaro came into the room.

" Good day, Senorita."

" Good day, Senor Figaro; I am dying of weariness."

" Then look in the glass, and you'll be charmed."

" Charmed in a tomb, Figaro? This house *is* a tomb."

" Dear, dear — hist! — he's coming."

Figaro slid to the other end of the room — Rosina whisked from it, and the barber was a most unconscious person — when Dr. Bartolo and Don Basilio — humbug and music-master (vide Figaro), made their appearance.

Figaro was ordered out for the present.

Terror for Rosini — what says her guardian to the other? — that either by love or force he will be married to her, and that too, within twenty-four hours.

" Ah! Count Almaviva has arrived." Here the informant, Don Basilio, serpentized all his fingers.

" What — what — that same unknown lover of Rosina's ? "

" The very same — but softly — softly —let's paint him black — as black as paint may be."

The doctor shook his head, beckoned his friend aside, for this was a thing which should be discussed in a closet — not in a room.

Hardly had they left the apartment than it lighted up with the presence of Figaro and Rosina.

It was the duty of Figaro to hear — " chink — chink " — he had been paid for it. But it was not the duty of Rosina to listen; so she had not heard.

" Wedding cake, Senorita!"

" Not here, Senor."

" Yes — yours ;. your guardian intends to marry you."

" La, la."

" On the faith of a barber — he and the music-master are at this moment arranging the matter."

" Indeed ; but Figaro, who was it that I saw you talking with a few hours since in the streets ? "

" My cousin — a fine fellow — with the best of heads and hearts. He has come here to study, and make his fortune."

" Fortune — and he'll make it, Figaro ? "

" He has one defect — he's over head and ears in love ! "

" *Indeed* — how interested I am ! Where does *she* live ? "

" Not far off."

" *Indeed* ; handsome ? "

" Hum — yes ; here's her portrait. A pretty graceful figure — such jetty ringlets — a rosy cheek — eyes too that sparkle — and . . . . . "

" And her name ? "

" Rosina ! "

" What ! *I* the poor Lindoro's flame ? "

' As sure Rosina is your name ! "

" And I shall see him, and speak to him ? "

" You will — and soon — and here. But he, poor fellow, fain would have some token — just two lines ; come — quick — a note."

" A note — oh — here's one ready."

> " Ah ! In love I plainly see,
> She's taken her degree,
> What man knows woman's art ?
> Faith — what man knows a part ? "

And he was gone.

She wore a very pleased expression of feature for two minutes after Figaro had departed. But then she justifiably pouted, for Dr. Bartolo came into the room, feeble in all his parts but his eyes, which were glancing about like sharp knives. Figaro. He was doubtful of Figaro. And he was sure of Rosina's simplicity.

> " What man knows woman's art ?
> Faith — what man knows a part ? "

So he thought he would question her.

"Pray what brought the barber here so early — he spoke to you?"

"He always does! And chatted of a thousand things — the latest fashions from Paris — and — and other things."

"And the answer of your note! No quibbling — the note, the piece of music you dropped this morning from the balcony? You blush — how came that finger marked with ink?"

"A burn — I used the ink to cure it!"

"That paper — where's the sixth — there are but five sheets here."

"I wrapped some sweetmeats in it, that I sent to Figaro's little niece."

"And this pen — why 'tis yet wet."

"Yes — I designed a flower."

"A flower indeed!"

Finding she had the worst of the battle, she flounced away and out of the room, the doctor following her, and positively breathing jealousy.

*   *   *   *   *

There was such a knocking at the street door, that the whole house shook in alarm; and old Bertha, the housekeeper, thought it was coming down about her ears. Hence she opened the door with greater speed than she had used for years, and she stood a ghost as there, upon the door step, she saw a soldier — and, moreover, a drunken soldier. She would have banged to the door again — but in so doing she must have crushed the intruder, for he was coolly leaning against the post.

The old housekeeper came steaming back into the room, her arms wide open, and, so to speak — full of the subject — the soldier — the drunken soldier!

"Tramp — tramp — tramp — tramp." Two steps and a stagger on the part of the soldier.

Dr. Bartolo heard the noise, and came in at a sharp trot at one. door, as the drunken soldier came stumbling in at the other.

"Here you — are you — are you — well ARE you he?"
"He — he — what he?"
"Doctor Berteldo — Balordo — whatever it is ——?"
'Go to the deuce, sir — *my* name is Bartolo!"
"Well — well — Dr. Barbaro —it *don't* matter —how
are you, Dr. Barbaro? Let us embrace, doctor."
"Stand back, sir."
"I WILL embrace thee. Ah, how good that is!

> "The marshal of regiment I,
> A doctor, too, of full degrees —
> A billet on your house I hold
> Pray look at it — dear doctor — **please**."

As the doctor took the paper in a sightless rage, little
Rosina came tripping in.

> "Methought I overheard just now,
> A most unusual clamor here,
> A soldier — and my guardian — too,
> There's something much amiss I fear."

"I am Lindoro." Thus the drunken soldier, in a soft,
delicate voice, suited to — love-making.
"Oh," she cried, which caused the old guardian to
start, and look up. At her he ran like a mad bull.
"Go along — girl — go along!"
"And, faith I, marshall, aye, and doctor too, will e'en
go with her."
"Indeed you wont."
"My quarters, sir, are here."
"He reeled towards her, but his voice was far from
thick, in fact, deliciously soft, as he whispered, "Dearest,
dearest!"
"Help," she screamed, but her glance was quite kind,
nevertheless.
Meanwhile, the guardian was spluttering wildly —
"Zounds, sir, stand off."
"Quick — quick— your handkerchief— let it fall," he
again softly whispered; and as the old doctor had his
eyes on him, he drew forth his sword and made a dreadful lunge at Bertha, who, with a squeal, shot away with
all the speed she could muster.
As for the guardian — he thought he should burst with

rage. But the next moment he had to scamper too, for
the drunken wretch made a lunge at *him*.

"Sir — sir — I'm exempt from billeting."

"Quick — quick — Rosina — take this letter;" and with
a remarkably steady hand the soldier held her out a delicate little billet.

But she saw the eyes upon her, so she could not take it.

Still with his eyes on her, the old doctor thrust his
hand into a desk, and brought forward a paper — an ex-
emption from billeting.

Said the soldier, "Don't pull that paper out, old man
— unnecessary pain. I've taken up my quarters here —
and here I will remain."

"You will — not if there are cudgels in Seville."

"You'd fight — then let's begin. A charming thing a
battle — truly. I'll show you how to fight. Now mark
me — let this be the trench — and *you* the enemy. Now
pray you mark me, sir,— (drop your handkerchief) —
now — but look the other way."

Here the drunken soldier let fall a something like a
note, and immediately something like a lace handkerchief
fell over it.

The doctor saw it, though he did not see whence it
came; and he made straight for the contraband property.
But the soldier stopped him.

"'Tis nought but a prescription, sir; I told you I was a
doctor, well degreed. The writing's bad, I fain would
have you see it not."

"And I myself would just fain see it."

"Ah! 'tis a little love affair, perhaps of hers. Pardon."
Here he picked up the note and lace, and handed them to
Rosina.

The doctor deserted the soldier directly, and fell upon
his little ward. "Quick, quick, the paper!"

"If I could but change it," thought she; and she did. In
a pretended little fright she leant against the table, covered a paper with her hand, and the deceptive deed was
done.

'Twas but a list of groceries!

"A fool — a fool — a very fool am I," thought the old
doctor. But he did not say so.

Here there was the sound of weeping on the part of a young lady, who was heard to remark, in a tearful voice, that such oppression was intolerable, and such a life quite unendurable. These remarks, unusual in the sprightly Rosina — for she loved to defy the doctor — caused inexpressible pain to the drunken soldier, who was still reeling about; and perhaps somebody knew the little stabs these same remarks would give.

> " What man knows woman's art,
>   Faith — what man knows a part ? "

Suddenly the soldier lunged forward with his long sword again, and did so fly and lay about him, that old Bertha took more exercise than she had taken since her hair turned white. As for the old doctor, he flew about till his respectable black legs looked like a dozen at least.

" Help, help ! " shrieked the doctor.

" Murder, murder ! " quavered the old lady, getting over the ground more quickly than ever.

" Oh ! oh ! oh ! " said the young lady, in great fear of the drunken soldier. " Pray be still, soldier ! "

Suddenly, and with a bound, rushed in barber.

> " What's the matter — what's the clatter ?
>   About a quiet house 'tis pity.
>   I pray you, doctor, gaze below,
>   What's this to-do, the crowd would know."

>> " This is a rogue."
>> " Then you're another."
>> " This is a knave."
>> " Then you're my brother."

Then the barber:

> " Good Mr. Soldier, have a care,
>   Or, as sure as you stand there,
>   This basin here, at one fell smack,
>   ' Gainst your sconce it shall go crack."

" Bang — bang — bang ! " at the street door.

" Bang — bang — bang ! "

The old guardian hesitated for a moment; but then, thinking he couldn't make matters worse, he went and opened the door; and in came the watch, and part of the crowd, and tramped all over the place.

Said the officer:

> " I ne'er heard such a noise before,
> Whence springs this horrible uproar?"

The drunken soldier, and the indignant guardian, and the rapid Figaro, and the pert Rosina, and even the flushed old Bertha herself, hastened to give their evidence in chorus; but, with a stern wave of the hand, the captain of the watch bade one speak at a time.

The doctor's grey hair carried it. He deposed that the soldier was a scoundrel, a coward, and a scamp, who had sought his life and drawn his sword — and that, too, without the least provocation.

Here the barber could not help striking in, "Yes, Senor, and *I* came in, and *I* parted the sanguiuary combatants."

"Oh dear, oh dear!" This was the voice of a frightened little maiden who began to think a certain drunken soldier was in trouble.

"You are arrested," said the captain of the watch to the drunken soldier.

Who, thereupon, thinking that the farce had been played long enough, tore open the breast of his coat and showed the Order of the Grandees of Spain.

We are bound to set forth the particulars of the Spanish chronicle, whence we learn that the effect of this "Order" was order indeed. The officer, with unpardonable partiality, immediately un-arrested (to coin a word) the drunken soldier, and everybody was respectfully astonished. Then, everybody went peacefully home, and (bed time arriving) went possibly, to bed.

CHAPTER III.

NEXT day, Dr. Bartolo sat him down to discuss the drunken soldier. The aged gentleman had sent out streams of inquiry in every direction, and he had ascer-

tained that no such person as the drunken visitor was
known in the regiment. Then who was he? Suspicion
gave birth to acuteness, and this jealous old gentleman
soon made up his mind that the stranger was in the
employ of his ward's — the unknown — lover, the detest-
ed Count Almaviva.

He was in the midst of a deep plan of retribution and
revenge, when a thwacking at the outer door jerked him,
as it were, from his reverie. Before old Bertha could
open that door the knocks were repeated again and again,
and the doctor had just risen to open himself (that is the
door) when a visitor appeared.

A youngish looking, fairly handsome man, whom partial eyes would have declared to be very much like the
drunken soldier, alias Lindoro, alias Count Almaviva,
stood just within the room, dressed sedately in black, and
making the profoundest of bows.

"May heaven send you peace and joy." A profound
bow.

"Thank you; they'll be new gifts of heaven, but don't
trouble yourself. Who are you?"

"May peace and joy be yours for years, and years by
thousands." Another profound bow.

"Thank you; but don't trouble yourself. Who is
he? I think I know that face, h-u-u-u-u-m! But yet
the countenance is changed, and certainly the dress,
h-u-u-u-u-m!"

"Yes, joy and peace, and peace and joy, and joy and
peace together." Here the stranger bowed lower than
ever.

"Well — well — well — well — well!"

"Yes, joy and peace I think — I said with all my heart.
He nearly laid his nose upon the doctor's instep. And
the new comer rather thought this last disguise was perfect, and panted for the moment when he and his Rosina
should sweetest converse hold.

"And pray, sir, who *are* you?"

"I'm Don Alonzo — and I am of music a professor,
and I am, as well, dear sir, a pupil of Basilio's — I mean
good *Don* Basilio's. Poor man, he's very ill, so in his
stead —"

"What, *very* ill — then I must run and see him."

"No, no, pray don't run and see him, 'tis no dangerous illness."

"Hu—u—u—um. Come, let's go."

"But, sir!"

"Hu—u—u—m."

"Now hear me."

"Hu—u—um."

"I'm Don Alonzo truly — but — but as the truth you'll have — I come as well from Almaviva — count."

"Softly, softly, my *good* sir."

"The count."

"Yes — yes — yes — but softly, softly!"

"This morning to my lodging came, and in my hands, by chance, there fell this note, directed by your ward to him."

"Her very hand."

"You see, good doctor, busied with a lawyer, Basilio could not come, and so sent me, but he knows nothing of this letter, trust me. Well now, for I am mightily desirous, good sir, of your favor, if now I could speak a word to her?"

"Speak, speak with her!"

"I might induce the senorita to think I had this letter from—"

"Well, well."

"A mistress of the count's. And then you see."

"Good, good. She'd hate him. Softly, good! a calumny. Ah, ah! a worthy scholar you of Don Basilio's. Well, well, I'll call the chit, and since you are so interested in me, why, I'll e'en repose great confidence in you."

The old man shakily going out of the room to hunt up his unfortunate little ward, the music master sat musing the most delicious thoughts. If now she would only consent to his plan, then they would be completely happy.

When the doctor came back, leading the opposing and indignant Rosina into the room, his jealousy was awake in a moment; for how should Rosina know that the Don Alonzo was somebody else at the same time? Hence, when she looked up haughtily at the music master, behold her face changed its expression directly, and to a little scream she added a little start.

The doctor saw the first, heard the second, and felt the third.

"Well — well — well!"

"Oh dear me, Senor, the *cramp!*"

"Hu — u — u — u — m."

Meanwhile, the music master was again making the profoundest of bows. Then he profoundly placed a music stool before an old piano, and profoundly proposed to the young lady that she should sit down.

Perhaps not unwillingly, she sat down, and perhaps not unwillingly, she poured forth a delightful song.

Arriving at the end of it, and even the most delicious songs *will* come to an end, the new music master was most enthusiastic in his praises.

The doctor would qualify *his* praise. The voice was good — granted. But the airs — why the airs of the present day — what were they? Contemptible. Now, for instance, when the wonderful Cafariello sang, and when he sang that wonderful 'la, la, la' of his, why there was an air to which none could object. In fact he would sing it. It began —

> "When thou art near, Rosina dear."

To be sure the song said Giannina — but never mind.

> "When thou art ne-e-e-ar, Rosina de-e-e-ar,
> With joy and fe-e-e-ar, there falls a te-e-e-ar."

This delicious romance the old doctor pointed by means of his right foot and toes. He also elaborated the accent by means, first of his right hand and arm, and then of his left hand and arm; and getting to te-e-a-r, he laid both his hands on his heart, looked sentimental, and fell into a rage; for he caught sight of Figaro behind him, mimicking him.

Meanwhile, the professor of music was diligently explaining (perhaps the ground-work of music), to the young lady, who was as diligently listening.

The barber was horrified at the doctor's discovery, and immediately flourished about his razors.

"Well — well — well."

"Excuse me, Senor — I come to shave you.'

"I'll not be shaved to-day."

"Then not to-morrow. I'm engaged to-morrow."

"I say I'll not be shaved to-*day*."

"What, doctor — think you I'm a *country shaver!* So please you find another barber — I am off."

"Well — well — have your way. Go to my room and — no — no, I'll go myself."

I have forgotten to say that the old doctor had locked up the balcony, and carried the key in his pocket — with all the other keys — a mighty bunch. The doctor locked up everything.

Amongst other things and places, the doctor always locked up his own room. Now, therefore, he hauled forth the mighty bunch, and turned his legs towards the door. Suddenly his suspicion was all awake again. What, leave the stranger and the barber there! No — no. "Here, Figaro — take the keys; be careful, and break nothing!"

As Figaro passed the young lady she looked up, and said rapidly — "The newest key there is."

With a jingle of triumph the barber ran off.

"Hu-u-u-m — that Senor, music-master, was the rascal who brought her the letter from the count."

"Indeed!"

At this moment there was heard a horrible crash, which sounded like a canonnade with china bowls.

Away flew the doctor after the barber; again the explanation of the "ground-work" went on; and was only interrupted by Figaro's flying entrance — a bright new little key between his fore-finger and thumb.

Victory — in fact!

But he showed a very doleful countenance as the doctor came deploringly in the room.

> "Six plates — eight basins — one tureen !
> Was such damage ever seen ? "

But, in spite of plates and dishes, the time of a town barber was not to be wasted; so Figaro, flourishing his instruments of torture about, the doctor sat down, and the barber was preparing to dash at him, brush in hand, when his arm remained suspended in the air; for Marplot, in the shape of Don Basilio, stood in the doorway!

For an instant the barber was disconcerted, but recovering his presence of mind, he prepared to assault the doctor. But the latter, struggling to his feet, called out, "Basilio! 'tis Basilio!"

Don Basilio made a lean bow, taking off his shovel hat with his long fingers. "Good day to you; good day to all."

As for the young people at the piano, they could only wonder what could come next.

"And pray, Basilio, how are you?" asked the doctor, earnestly.

"How am I; as well as ever."

"Excuse me Senor, but that confounded beard of yours; a town barber cannot wait all day!"

"Yes, yes; directly. And the lawyer, Don Basilio?"

"The lawyer?"

The professor of music deserted his post and fled up to the doctor. "Of the affair, Senor, of the letter, recollect he nothing knows."

The barber turned to Don Basilio, who was elevating his eyebrows, and all the wrinkles in his forehead, wondering what all this might mean. "Oh heavens, Don Basilio, this is fever."

Said Figaro,

> "Yes, I swear it by my post;
> You're as chalky as a ghost
> Fever! ghost!
> Don Basilio — go to bed,
> 'Tis the fever called the red

The professor of music made that "chink, chink" chorus already alluded to; and when he performed it he was standing near the barber. Thereupon said Figaro, still in his quality of surgeon, and still to Don Basilio.

> "And as you'll want a nurse,
> Let me recommend — this purse;
> Yes; you are very bad indeed,
> In such cases one must — bleed."

The music-master, the barber, and the young lady too,
were all *so* interested in Don Basilio's health, and they
did so crowd about him, that the doctor could neither put
in a word nor get near his friend, whose fingers went
twisting about, trying to discover the most profitable line
of conduct to pursue.

At last : —

> " Good day to all — with all my heart,
> I make my bow, and so depart.''

The town barber was immediately himself again with
his implements. He turned even his handsome body to
account; for he made of it a screen, and so hid the piano
and the two young people from the doctor's green eyes.

" Do, re, me, fa."

" We have the keys of the balcony; at midnight be
you there."

" Yes ; Sol, la, si, do-o-o-o-o."

" Now pray don't forget the hour."

" No.   D-o-o-o-o, si, la, sol-l-l-l."

" At twelve you will be mine."

" Yes.   Fa-a-a, me, re, d-o-o-o-o."

" And now you trust yourself to me Rosi —."

" A-h-h-h," shrieked the doctor, his head coming round
the human screen, and noticing the whispers.   He evaded
the quivering razor and rushed at the music-people, one
of whom, to wit the master, looked the picture of innocent consternation ; while the other was quite astonished.

Cried Figaro : —

> " When thus a man doth rage and rave,
> The thing to do 's his head to shave.''

" I think I'd better go," said the music-master,
tremblingly.

" I think you had," said Figaro.

" Alas ! Why, before he went, did he not tell Rosina
of his giving her letter to the doctor. Alas ! Why did
this necessity escape the attention of the all-seeing
Figaro ? They both departed — the barber flippantly, the
professor profoundly. And neither thought of the for-

getfulness up to the time when they were both fixing a
ladder against the locked up balcony.

Meanwhile, little Rosina had been converted into a
little tigress.

For not an hour had the count and barber been gone,
when Don Basilio had persuaded himself *his* line of profitable conduct was to come creeping back after a little
more money. This time he knew not a purse full, for the
doctor was old and his purse low. He came in with his
low bow.

" Noble doctor, do you know who this Alonzo was ? "

" No, no ; sent by the count, perhaps."

" It was the count himself. Some scheme is sure
afoot."

" Good ; and I'll scheme too. Now, haste, Basilio, to
the notary, and bid him come. This very night I'll marry her."

" But, noble doctor ; fetch the notary ! And it rains in
torrents. Again, most noble doctor, the notary is engaged ; this very night the barber Figaro gives his niece
in marriage."

" The barber Figaro *has* no niece ! Another plot —
another plot. Now, go, and call the notary ! Go — go —
go ! Here, take the street door key, and go — go — go !"

Then he cried out for Rosina ; and that young beauty
appearing, he very quickly turned her into a young
tigress.

" A pretty pitfall, Senorita ! "

" Indeed ! "

" I've some news from your *new* lover."

" Lover, indeed ! "

" Indeed ! most nobly you've bestowed your young
affections, truly. Why, with another he makes sport of
you."

" He dares ! "

" (I'm right.) Yes, Senorita ; as you say, 'he dares.'
Behold this letter ; it formed for them a comedy."

" My very note."

" (A pretty plot.) Why, this Alonzo and the barber
are but tools, whose master is Count Almaviva."

" Oh, Lindoro,"

("Lindoro, is it!")

"Vengeance! Did you not say you'd marry me? You did; then let us married be. And now, at once (stamp of the foot), at once, at once! At midnight he'll be here, and with him, Senor, barber Figaro. It all was settled I should fly and marry him."

"Ah! I run to bar the door."

"'Tis useless, Senor, you'd better bar the window."

"The window!"

"Yes — yes — they have the key!"

"The key! I'll not stir from the spot. Yet, should they come with arms! I'd better call the watch, and call them thieves. Go, shut yourself within your room, and double lock the door!"

And out into the pelting rain he rushed, while the little tigress, somewhat accusing herself of hastiness, went slowly to her room.

At first there was nothing heard but the rain; then "click, click," the turning of a key in a lock. Then the window opened slowly, and with light jumps, in came the count and the barber.

And at this very moment, Don Basilio, drenched to his very fingers' ends, was stalking along the street, towards the doctor's, and with him was a notary, who with reluctance had left his house.

And at this very moment, also, Dr. Bartolo was full three streets off, laying a complaint before the Alcade.

"Rosina — Rosina!" cried Figaro.

"Rosina — Rosina!" cried the count.

No answer.

"Why, where can she be?" cried both together.

She had not, of course, meant to come; but hope is strong, and so at this precise moment she came softly into the room.

"Dear Rosina!"

"Stand back, Senor,—I but come here to tell you, you have lost me."

"Can I believe my precious senses!" exclaimed the barber.

"Rosina!"

"Peace, Senor. Did you not pretend to love me, that you might betray me?"

" And to whom ? "

" The Count Almaviva."

" Ah — good ! " said Figaro to himself.

" Then thou didst love Lindoro ? "

" Too well."

" Then thou didst love the count ? "

" The count ! "

" Rosina — yes — the count is thy Lindoro.

" And Lindoro is the count," said Figaro.

The bliss of these young people was soon ended — for alas! Figaro, who, as a general precaution, was looking on all sides and on all levels, saw from the balcony one lantern and two persons down below at the door!

" Quick — the ladder," shouted he, and instinctively he felt for it. Gone — vanished. Even Figaro was disconcerted.

Footsteps !

The one lantern and the two persons. Don Basilio and the notary.

" Noble Dr. Bartolo," whispered the gaunt man.

Figaro slipped quickly round the new comers, and then said softly to the count — " 'Tis the scamp Basilio and our notary. Cheer up, leave all to me." Then aloud he added, " Good evening, gentlemen, — I pray you place the lantern on the table here. Senor notary! this evening at my house you were to see a contract signed between the Count Almaviva and my niece. — Well, here are you and I, the count, and also, here's my niece."

" But where's the doctor? " said Basilio, to whom Figaro, handing him a ring from the count's hand,

> " Put this ring upon your hand,
> And let no more be said,
> Or the next report may be,
> You're shot clean through the head."

Don Basilio saw the force of the argument, and accepted the ring.

" Then there was the scratching of pens, and the signing of names, and in less time than it takes to record the fact, Rosina was a wife !

And at this moment arrived Doctor Bartolo, with a

posse of people — the Alcade, and one, two, three — a whole regiment of alguazils.

"Arrest them, arrest them all."

"What me. Figaro — arrest me!"

"I say arrest them all, they all are thieves."

It is reported that the alcade marched up to the count with great dignity, but when he saw who it was — a real living count — he fell back without any show of dignity whatever.

And to a certain question that the doctor put to Figaro, this was all the reply: —"Chink, chink." The question — simply how it was that Figaro could turn against him and betray him: "Chink, chink." An argument without reply.

The doctor was not a bad doctor — and as he could do himself no good by being angry — and as the bridegroom was a count — why he forgave them.

And as this chronicle is all about the loves of two people who are now happily married, and about a guardian who is a guardian no longer, why, obviously, this chronicle is ended.

RIGOLETTO. (Verdi.)

This tells of a hunch-back only, who wears two masks,
The one is mocking jest — the second godlike love,
And if he wears them both too mixedly — chide not —
But dole him and his woes some pity.
                                        Now fall to.

CHAPTER I.

In the sixteenth century, kings and dukes still kept
their fools. The Duke of Mantua had his — a poor hunchback, whom they called Rigoletto. He was as witty as any
fool in France or Italy; and he was an honest man in this
— that he despised the courtiers, who bowed low before
the tyranny of the duke, who broke up their families as a
child would toys, and quite as fearlessly. And if, as the
tale goes on, you find he had some human love in him,
remember he is a hunchback, and give him double praise.

The duke, whose whole life was a panorama of gallant-
ry, despised his conquests; and, being handsome, believed
no woman could withstand him. He was as heartless as
he was handsome, and he had no affection for a living
soul, unless, indeed, for Rigoletto, whom he loved for his
power of satirizing the courtiers, who loved Rigoletto
accordingly.

This fool, Rigoletto, was superstitious; moreover, he
had a secret, which it was the hope of his life to keep
from that terrible court; for a fool, a jester, a hunchback,
may have loves and secrets like other men.

The duke had discovered a beautiful girl, whom he followed daily as she went to prayers. For weeks he
followed her each day, and yet all he learned was that she
lived in a mean house in a mean street, and that every
day the same unknown man visited her.

He still knew no more; when, on a certain night, he gave a grand ball at his palace. A happy, happy ball, where each man trembled as the giver of the feast turned eyes upon his wife or daughter! A happy, happy, fête! He was paying the Countess Ceprano great attention, when Rigoletto entered the hall, and saw the husband of the lady jealously watching them.

"What troubles you count?" said the fool, smiling maliciously.

Rigoletto turned away gibing at the courtiers, crossed the hall, and was gone.

Hardly had he left, than the Lord Marcello stepped quickly up to a group, declaring he had great news to tell them. They crowded about him, wondering what he had to say. 'Twas of Rigoletto. "What, had he lost his hump?" cried one. "Had *he* become straight?" cried another.

"No, no," replied the lord. "Rigoletto, Rigoletto has a mistress!"

They all laughed merrily, perhaps a little cruelly, for men and women love to return blow for blow. "What a change, from a hunchback to a cupid." They were yet laughing, when the fool passed near them with the duke, who was still thinking of the Ceprano's wife.

"Steal her away!" said the fool.

"Easily conceived, but not easily performed," replied the duke.

"This very evening. Have you no prisons, great duke? Can you not banish him? Or take his head?"

"What, Ceprano's head?" asked the duke aloud, and turning to that noble.

"Yes — what is it good for?"

The count drew his sword as the duke smiled, and the fool affected to be overcome with fear.

"Ah! ah! he is very amusing to night." But the fool did not see how menacingly the courtiers drew together, and frowned at him.

The duke lightly warned the fool that he might jest too deeply, and that the count's sword might end his jokes.

"Bah! who shall be brave enough to touch the duke's favorite?"

And he imitated the duke, and turned away from the group of nobles, not noticing their angry looks and gestures.

At this moment an aged lord appeared at the door, and violently thrust himself into the hall, though the servants tried all they could to hold him back. His hair was white, his limbs trembling — his was another family the duke had dishonored.

The guests started with surprise.

"I *will* see the duke, and even here blazon forth his crimes."

"I *will* see the duke — and even here blazon forth his crimes," exclaimed the fool, mockingly, and, as well as he could, imitating the grand posture of the aged noble.

"Poor wretch!"—— Then, turning to the duke, the lord again exclaimed that he spoke in the name of his dishonored family, and called for justice.

"Justice — justice!" continued the fool.

"Let him be arrested," said the duke, as he frowned upon this new comer.

"He is mad," said the fool, solemnly.

"He is mad," repeated the courtiers.

"Be both accursed," cried the old lord to the fool.

The soldiers seized him —"thou and thy shameful master — who can laugh at a father's grief — be both accursed."

The fool, as the curse was uttered, drew on one side, put his hands together affrightedly, and said to himself, his superstition all dominant, "He cursed me — he cursed me."

Meanwhile, the cowardly courtiers merely looked after the doomed lord as he was led away.

*   *   *   *   *   *

That same night, when the weary dancing was over, and the duke no more required his fool, Rigoletto stole out, and went quickly to an obscure part of the city, to a high thick wall, in which was a small retiring door.

He had almost reached it, his head drooping at the thought of the terrible curse, when a ruffianly man jostled him. "Who are you? Go; I need you not."

" Signor, I am a man who has a dagger at your service, ready at a word ! "

" You are a thief."

" No; but a man who for money will rid you of your rival. You have a rival."

" Who is he ? "

" Is not your mistress near at hand ? "

The fool trembled violently for a little; but recovering, he hurriedly asked how much the fellow would charge to kill a man ? How he would be sure to slay him ?

The brigand said he struck his victims in the street, or in his own house.

His own house ? How was that ?

Said the brigand — his sister danced in the streets, she decoyed the man who was to fall, and, by his faith, the matter was at an end. And how did he kill ? By his faith, noiselessly, with the sword which he then carried.

The fool hurriedly asked where he could meet him again, if he might want him — was told here, at that very spot, on any night. Rigoletto gave some money, and the ruffian slouched away.

Instead of opening the door, the fool stood looking after the brigand, and thinking what difference was there much between them ? If the brigand wounded with his steel, he, the fool, thrust and wounded with his tongue. Then again he thought of the terrible curse, and turned towards a gloomy house at hand — the house of the very man who had but now cursed him. Then he thought that if he were bad, 'twas not his will, but the wills of nature and of men. To be deformed, to be a fool, to be condemned to laugh against his will, never to be pitied, never to gain tears ! Then he frowned as he thought of the cowardly and hateful courtiers, and then again he was thinking of the awful curse — for surely a curse by one condemned to death might live — might live ! He trembled as he asked himself why this thought so clung to him ? Then warily he opened the door and crept in — into a courtyard, a jealous courtyard, which hid what it held from the common gaze by great high walls.

To him ran a beautiful girl, who kissed and embraced him. A mistress ? No! no! His daughter — his daughter, whom he so loved, who made him human, who made him fear the curse! The mother of that girl had married him for pity's sake, and the poor fool's daughter knew not what her father was. She often wondered; and now, on this very night, she no sooner saw him than she began asking him gaily to tell her the long promised secret. She prayed him to tell her who had been her mother, what he himself, her father, was.

He confusedly parried her questions, and told her hurriedly that she must never leave the house — never except to prayers. She answered that for now three months he had ever spoken so; should she never, never. see the city? Again he only warned her never to leave the house, and trembled as he thought that if he lost her they would only laugh at a poor fool's loss.

Giovanna was his daughter's companion and servant through the weary days, and as she now came from the house into the courtyard he ran to her, and nervously bade her guard his Gilda — his only child. Truth to tell, the memory of the curse sat heavily on him, and he trembled greatly.

Suddenly he thought he heard a noise at the gate; in the dark, thick night he rashly opened it, and ran two or three steps forward. Before he could return, a figure had glided into his stronghold and reached the shelter of a tree. Is there nothing that will warn him of the thief — the thief that came in that night to steal away his treasure? Is there nothing to prompt him to stay at home that night — near her to guard her? He has come to the house but for a few blest moments in which to see her; he hastens to creep back to the palace to play the fool again. This is one of the desolate nights when he may not creep to her door, and watch like a faithful dog till morning. He must return to the weary palace prison. "Good night, dear Gilda," he says. The girl pouts, but the father kisses her frowns away, and says again, "Good night, dear daughter," and unwisely turns away, and pulls to the creaking door.

"His daughter," thought the thief, who had stolen through the doorway. "His daughter," thought the duke, for it is he — "The fool, then, has a daughter."

So, while the father crept back to court, the duke was trying to gain the love of his innocent daughter, whispering that he was a poor student who thought only of her — "Gilda."

At last the noble liar stole away again, and then, Gilda, thinking more of the supposed student than of her father, turned from the gate to which she had walked with the duke, and moved towards the house. She had to ascend a score of steps to reach a terrace, past which was the house, and as she arrived on the highest of those steps, she was seen from the dark street by several men, who said amongst each other, "See, that is she. How beautiful she is. That is Rigoletto's mistress!"

At this moment the poor fool returned to his gate. "Why do I return? Alas! the curse, the curse!"

As he stood, the men in the street came near to Rigoletto, and so drew his attention to them. They knew him in a moment — the hunch showed plain. They were lords of the court; and amongst them was Ceprano, the count, who had drawn his sword upon the jester, and who now again drew it. "Softly," whispered one to him; " if he is killed where will be our laughter to-morrow!" Then the speaker turned and told Rigoletto — who started as he spoke — they were there to steal from Ceprano his countess — that the fool must help them. They had the keys of the house, they said. See, the speaker handed to the trembling fool the keys.

The curse — he still thought of the curse as he took the keys. What if they had come to steal his treasure? For a moment he held these keys listlessly; then suddenly he swept a trembling fore-finger over the loop of one of them — and as he did so he half knelt and nearly wept aloud — for on the friendly steel he felt the count's heraldic crest. So they were not deceiving him — they had come not to the house where lived his Gilda — but to the other — the other. Then, full of thanks, he had to laugh and make a sorry jest — because of their adventure.

"Come," said the same speaker, "aid us," and he placed on the fool's face a mask, and bound it about his head with a handkerchief — and the next moment the poor creature was holding the ladder by which they climbed to steal his daughter.

Standing there, he heard the crash of wood as they forced a window. ("Why, if they had the keys," he thought, "did they want a ladder? why break into the house?") Then for a few moments there was silence. Then a door opened, feet trampled near him, he heard even a smothered cry. Still he remained holding the ladder, still he saw nothing, for a handkerchief, unknown to himself, was hanging over his eyes. Then the steps sounded more distant, and at last were lost altogether.

He waited a little, and was then startled as his wandering hand found the handkerchief hanging loosely over his eyes. He flung it from him, and oh! by the faint light, he saw, the whole terrible truth. The open garden gate, — a scarf that had fallen from her shoulders as she was carried away — the desolate home!

He ran in — round the garden like a chased rat — up the steps, till he reached the house — into it — tore at the serving-woman — dragged her forth silently and without a word — then at last, finding his voice, he cried, "The curse — the curse," and fell upon the ground, mercifully insensible.

CHAPTER II.

Oh! the weary, weary hours till daylight; till he could search through the city for his daughter. The age of fear, with but a faint poor hope to bear him through it. See the poor fool who has mocked the aged lord — see him wandering up and down the house; then out into the streets; and then back again into the house, afraid to leave it! The house — how changed! And when he sees anything dearly associated with her, he touches it, kisses it — as though she were dead, and for her sake he loved it! Wearily, wearily dragging on life, till the crowd of courtiers met to receive the duke, on his rising for the day. Then the fool's gay dress was donned again, covering his breaking heart, and the cap and bells mocking his deep, loving sighs.

"Good morning, Rigoletto — what news?"

"News? you are nearer hell to-day than yesterday, by a score of hours. (Oh! my child! where art thou, oh! my child!)"

"See," they whispered to each other, "see how his eyes search for her. Mark how hardly he draws his breath!"

Then turning to them, he went on lightly, "You look well, gentlemen. Last night's cold air, then, did you no harm?"

"Last night," said one, "I slept well through the night."

For an instant he thought perhaps it was all a dream; but the next moment he saw a mask and a handkerchief lying on a table. "See," they said to one another, as he walked negligently to the table, "see how he marks all things!"

Then he saw the handkerchief was not hers, and still wondering if she were in the palace, he asked jauntily, "Is the duke still asleep?"

As he spoke, a page entered, and said the duchess desired to see the duke.

Said a courtier, "He is asleep."

"But," said the page, "he was awake not a minute since."

"Canst thou not understand? He would not now be questioned."

The fool heard this conversation, and guessed its meaning. "Ah! then she is here!"

"She — who?"

"The poor girl you stole from under my roof."

"You are mad. If you have lost your mistress, 'tis not within these walls you will find her."

For a moment he stood before them, jauntily and smiling as ever; then the revengeful lords might have surely been satisfied, for the mocked fool was at their feet.

"This is a new jest for thee, Rigoletto."

All the small silver bells upon his head-dress rang as he clasped his hands together. "She is my daughter, she is my daughter. If, if I have offended you, you are great lords, and will not be revenged on a poor fool."

Then he started to his feet as several courtiers looked

7

meaningly towards a door, and ran towards it. But they pressed upon him, and drove him back. He battled with them hard, he threatened, yelled, overthrew them. All to no purpose; he was still far, far from the door. Then he wept, and in his wretchedness flattered them, and said he knew they had feeling hearts, and again asked them where was his daughter. And then again he fell upon his knees before them, before them who had so often flinched from him, and lowered his head humbly.

He was still kneeling when the door opened, and through it came his daughter — white, trembling, frightened.

She saw and ran to him, as he sprang from the ground.

"My daughter, my daughter! See you, my lords, she is my child, my only child! Oh, be not afraid, daughter, these are all noble lords; it was only in jest, only in jest. Why even I wept, but you see I am laughing now! But why dost thou weep, why dost thou weep?"

She made no answer, only hid her face lower and lower.

Then he flung himself down in a chair, half in mad jest, half in real madness, and in a pompous voice, cried out, "Begone, ye people, and bid the duke not approach while I remain here."

They began to laugh, for the vengeance was complete; there was no more need to bar the door. Saying, fools and children must be humored, these great lords departed.

Then she confessed to him how each day going to church she saw a handsome stranger; how this stranger had come only the night before and told her he was poor and loved her. Then the men who had just left them tore her from her home; and the rest of her history was miserable silence.

A moment he held her from him; then he laid her head upon his breast and caressed her, and absolved himself of his sins by bitter, bitter tears. So then, heaven did not hear his prayer, that the curse should fall on him alone; it had, indeed, fallen on her. He stooped down, and kissed her as she lay in his arms; then he bade her look up, and told her that they would leave that place for ever.

Still she was weeping, and hiding her eyes from him, her father, when the door opened, and there stood the aged count, who on the day before had cursed him. He was surrounded by soldiers — had been condemned, and was now being led off to prison.

He did not see the fool; but as he came near to the fool he muttered, "So my curse was vain; this duke still lives. Is there no hand to be found to slay him?"

"Here, here," whispered the fool, "here." And though he rocked with fear he came a step forward, his daughter still in his encircling arms.

The next moment the one father had passed from the room, while the other again bent his head, wept over, and kissed his lost, and yet found, daughter.

CHAPTER III.

A stormy angry night; the wind weeping and whistling high up in the sky, and a thick stifling vapor crawling over the earth — over the whispering muddy river; winding in and out the gay palace like a poisonous serpent. Near to this sickening river was a cracked ruined house through the crevices in the walls of which might be observed a flickering light.

No house was near this wretched hut, which was called an inn. Within this place lived the ruffian who had accosted Rigoletto on the night when his daughter was stolen away. He was cleaning a leathern belt and singing softly at his work.

Who are these wayfarers, toiling along the dark road to the ruined inn? They are the fool and his daughter.

She still loved the duke; and the fool, hoping to kill the awful passion, had brought her to this lonely spot. He told her to creep softly to the house, and look in through the broken door. As she did so, the duke himself, now in a new disguise, came quickly along, and up to the door. She shrank back from him, and he passed into the inn, ordering a room and wine.

Then as she and her father stood shivering near the

door, he began singing in dispraise of woman. They saw the brigand lay upon the table some bottles and glasses. That done, he struck the low ceiling several times, and immediately a girl came running into the room — a gipsey girl who danced about the streets. The duke ran to her as she avoided him, and the brigand came cautiously out upon the road.

"Shall he live, Signor Rigoletto?" whispered the ruffian.

"Wait — wait," replied the father. And both men spoke so softly, that Gilda did not hear. She did not care to hear, as she looked once more on him whom she had so dearly loved when she thought him a poor student.

"Good," said the bandit, and went out slowly into the darkness.

Then as the two stood there miserably, the duke began laughing and chatting with the gipsey girl. Soon Gilda was weeping, as was also her father. Yet still within the hut continued the laughter and the singing.

"Thou art sure now, he loves thee not — thou art sure now. Hear me: we will leave this country at once. Go thou home, dress thyself in the clothing of a nobleman, my child, and fly to Verona. Thou knowest where to go when thou art there. I will come to thee to-morrow."

"Now — come with me now."

"Now? No, not now." He spoke with terrible hesitation.

The girl kissed her father and went towards their house. Through the gloom he watched her and saw her pass the garden gate. Then he searched about for the bravo. The assassin was lounging at the corner of the house, and at a motion from the fool he came forward.

Eagerly Rigoletto put money into his hand, saying the rest should be his when the man was dead. Then he turned away, saying that at midnight he would return.

The bravo carelessly replied that he had no need of help, he could, alone, cast the body into the river.

"No," said the fool, suddenly stopping; "let that be my portion of the work."

"Good," said the assassin, carelessly; "who is he?"

"His name is Crime and mine is Punishment."

The bravo shrugged his shoulders, and then carelessly opened the door of the hut, and entered, while the fool turned, and with downcast head, moved slowly away, afraid to go home till the vengeance was completed.

Loud roared the storm; the lightnings lit up the hovel, and the wavering thunder rolled incessantly. Yet had the assassin no fear.

The duke said he should remain all night, and bade the new comer leave them. But the gipsey girl prayed the young duke to depart. Said the bravo, he should be glad to place his room at the stranger's disposal, and he hid the golden money the fool had given him.

The duke attended by the bravo, ascended a ricketty flight of stairs to a room, more dilapidated, if possible, than the one below.

Saying it was like sleeping in the open air, the noble flung down his hat and sword, fell upon the bed, and was soon asleep.

The ruffian by that time was drinking the wine the duke had left. At last he said slowly — "Go up, and if he sleeps, bring away his sword."

The gipsey girl obeyed sorrowingly, for the stranger was so handsome that she had grown to feel some pity for him.

As she stole up the stairs another girl was near at hand — the wretched Gilda; who, disguised in the clothes of a page, came creeping towards the inn.

Nearer and nearer till she was close to the door and pressing it. Looking through the crevice, she saw the girl coming down with the sword glittering in her hand.

"Do not kill him — do not kill him," cried the gipsey girl.

"Kill him!" cried the fool's daughter.

There, still listening, she heard the gipsey tempt him, saying, that when the fool came back he could take his money and kill him. But the bravo angrily cried that his honor was dear to him; he would not kill the fool, he would slay the stranger. Rigoletto had paid him well.

Gilda shuddered as she listened; so her father had paid the bravo to kill the duke.

Again the gipsey girl prayed for the stranger's life.

Again the assassin refused. At last he said quickly that if a traveller came past he would slay him in his place — the fool could not tell who might be in the sack.

Then the gipsey wept as she said there was no hope of a traveller passing while the storm raged so fiercely.

Why does she tremble and draw back from the crevice? What? shall this woman, this dancing gipsey, weep and pray for him? And shall she, Gilda, do nothing to save him? Who is this woman that she should weep for him? Will she — this gipsey — die for his sake? Yet she, Gilda, could. Again she looked, and saw the gipsey still kneeling and weeping. Then she would die for his sake. Thus her love and jealousy had lost her.

The next moment she had entered — the storm raging more fiercely than before.

Walking proudly and fearlessly through the night air, came the fool, sure that by this time his vengeance was complete — the vengeance for which he had waited an age of grief.

Forth from the hut came the bandit, dragging a heavy sack. There he lay, then — dead; there was the chinking of money over the still burden, and there the bravo had left the fool alone with the destroyer. "So then," thought Rigoletto, "here was the great duke, lying dead at his, the poor fool's feet." Then he thought he should like to see the face of his enemy, before he cast him into the black waters.

Yet no, he would not like to see his face; so he began drawing away the sack, when — merciful powers! — he heard the voice of the duke singing gaily, as he moved away, saved, in the distance.

"But then whose body lay at his feet? Whose?"

With a might of horror, he tore open the mouth of the sack; and there, within it, lay — his daughter!

"My daughter! Heaven! my Gilda! Yet no, she is now on her way to Verona. Is this a dream? Oh, no! no dream. My daughter! oh, my daughter!"

In an agony of grief he ran to the door of the hut, and beat at it, when he heard a voice — *her* voice — calling to him.

"SHE LIVES — SHE LIVES! OH! SHE LIVES!"

He was down at her side again, tearing her from the shameful sack with his trembling hands.

"My father! oh, my father!"

"'Tis thou, and they have stricken thee."

"They have stabbed me — here — here."

And wearily she pressed her hands about her heart, as the wretched man drew back, saying to himself, that he — he himself had killed her.

She was silent for a moment, still wearily pressing her breast.

"Speak — speak to me! oh, daughter!"

"I am almost too weak to speak, dear father. Lay thy hand upon my head, and bless me. If I may always think of thee, I will. Near my mother, I will pray for thee — near my mother."

What is this with which he is suddenly stricken; what conviction is growing on his mind as his eyes grow yet wilder, and he grasps his throat with his trembling hand?

"My child, do not leave me. Have pity on me, tarry yet a little longer — leave me not in the world alone — oh I — and I am thy father — bid thee stay!"

She does not answer. He bends over her, as the dread conviction forces itself upon him.

"DEAD! DEAD! DEAD!"

He wraps his hands round his head, looks wildly to the lowering sky, and cries: —

"THE CURSE — THE UNDYING CURSE!"

Then he speaks no more.

Mercy for him as his breath grows thick — mercy for him as he clasps his helpless hands together prayerfully. Mercy — mercy!

His faults are not all his own. He hath but mocked the world as it hath mocked him! Who would not hate where he is scorned? Oh — many are forgiven who have sinned more deeply.

See the clasped hands — the bloodless lips. Mercy — mercy!

So at last it hath fallen on him — the grace of forgiveness.

I PURITANI. (Bellini.)

THE PURITANS.

CHAPTER I.

Immediately succeeding the execution of Charles I., General Walton was in command of a fortress, then standing not far from Plymouth. One of his officers was his brother, Colonel George Walton. This man loved his brother's daughter, as many an unmarried uncle will love nephews and nieces, and with an affection almost equal to that of the best of fathers!

And it is also true that this daughter, Elvira, loved her uncle even more than she loved her own father, the general. This young lady was promised in marriage, to a puritan officer, Captain Richard Forth, but it may be stated that she herself had favored the pretentions of Lord Arthur Talbot, a strong, unyielding royalist.

Just after the death of Charles the First, a lady arrived at the fortress, and was received by General Walton as the friend of his daughter — the friend of his daughter only in this, that a dear friend had recommended the unknown lady to his care.

She called herself Madame Henrietta, and no more. They thought her a French lady — and indeed her slightly imperfect English proved her to be a foreigner. But they asked no questions. She was franked by the dear friend, and so she was made welcome.

She soon became the companion of Elvira, who, young and light-headed, would kiss, torment, and delight this unknown lady, all within a minute. And thus things were when the General gave way to the united entreaties of his brother and Madame Henrietta, and recalled the promise of his daughter's hand to the Puritan Colonel.

Imagine the curtain of our story drawn up, and what do you see? A platform of the fortress, the solemn sentries walking to and fro. The sun rises, and then these honest, straightforward religious puritans, sing their usual morning hymn.

This service over, the gates of the fortress are opened to the market girls, with their fresh, demure faces, and their neat, almost sombre, garments.

There is much talking about the young lady Elvira, the governor's daughter, and how she was going to be married, and who to, and what he was like — but all this little tittle-tattle was carried on gravely, and with a demure air.

But pacing apart is Captain Richard Forth — his puritan heart strongly beating against the governor's injustice in recalling his promise, and the shame that a puritan leader should marry his daughter to one of the godless cavaliers.

Nay — he speaks his complaints out aloud — whereon Robertson, a fellow officer, tells him to wear a fair face — there are his country and his soul to live for yet. "Open thy heart to me."

"'Tis not a righteous act, I say. He hath promised me the maiden — and now I have returned, he doth recall his word."

"Heaven is a bride who never turneth away from the true lover."

"Death were welcome."

"I would fain death passed over thee if thou art in that frame, Richard Forth."

"I have lost her — I have lost her!"

And thereby perchance thou hast gained much. Heaven is merciful and all-seeing. Hark! dost hear the good march — embrace thy good sword —'twill not fail thee."

"But my weak arm may, my friend."

"Shame on thee, Richard Forth — methinks thou art a coward."

"No, friend, no! not a coward, but weak."

And the two friends turned towards the castle.

CHAPTER II.

THAT same day Colonel George Walton was sitting with his niece, Elvira, and chatting with her about the marriage. The leaven of puritanism was not so severely bitter in high as in low life. Among the latter there was still left something like cheerfulness and blithe talk.

Sitting down near his niece, the uncle asked why she looked so sad?

"I am thinking, second father."

"And of what, Elvira?"

"Daughter, always call me daughter, second father."

"Well then, daughter. So, to-day, you are to be a bride!"

The uncle then playfully supposed that 'twas the puritan lover who was to be the bridegroom; whereat the young lady protested, but the uncle soon uttered the talismanic name, Arthur.

They were still talking when a trumpet call was heard without the fortress.

A happy sound, for it announced the arrival of the bridegroom — Lord Arthur Talbot, in reality, but plain Master Arthur Talbot in those puritan times.

Soon the young lord was within the room where were waiting for him the gentle Elvira and her good uncle Colonel George — not the plain little room where they had been chatting, but in the chief hall of the castle, where armor glistened on the walls, and from the windows of which could be seen the bristling fortifications.

He met her, proud of himself and of her, and dressed gaily, in defiance of popular taste. And, truth to tell, but few in the great room could compare in demeanor or good looks, with Lord Arthur, or rather Master Talbot.

Among the ladies present was Madame Henrietta, bustling about from place to place like a careful housekeeper. She did not notice that a messenger came rapidly to the general with a letter, nor did she mark that as he read it he started and then looked up at her. Nor did she hear the order he gave to let no female pass from the castle without an order from himself — except, of course, the marriage party. For the marriage was to take place at the neighboring village church. The messenger bowed low and left the room, and still Madame Henrietta was bustling about, busy and cheerful.

Turning to his daughter and Arthur, the general said, he should not be able to attend the ceremony. And he was presently in deep conversation with several of his gentlemen. Suddenly he turned to madame.

"Lady — a parliamentary order compels me to depart with you for London — have no fear."

Those about her saw Madame Henrietta start and turn pale, but they did not think much of the matter; and, being bidden to the feast, were soon moving from the room.

Arthur heard the intimation given by the general, and said, naturally enough, to the colonel, "Is she a friend of the Stuarts?"

"She is, I believe, suspected," replied the discreet colonel, turning away.

The young bridegroom looked pityingly at Madame, and she saw that he did so. As the company were leaving the room Arthur came up to the lady, and began talking idly to her, but when the room was empty of all but themselves — when the little bride had flown to her room, and the general had gone to consult with his officers — she said in answer to some question of his, "Cavalier!"

Quickly he answered, "You may trust me, lady. Speak, speak."

"May I speak, even if my head is in danger?"

"You shudder. Be not afraid. Speak, whoever you are; I will save you. Speak softly, or thou mayest be heard."

"Save me! too late. The fate of Charles will be the fate of his wife."

"The queen, the queen!" the young lord whispered, half in respect, half in fear, and he sank upon his knee."

"'Tis a mockery to kneel to me."

"I swear to save your majesty, or be lost myself"

"My lord, my lord, you speak vainly. Leave me. You cannot save me, and would involve yourself in ruin. Rise, sir, rise!"

He immediately obeyed, and stood humbly before her.

"Well, my lord?"

"I will save your majesty."

She turned hopelessly away, but the next moment she was smiling cheerfully, as Elvira, holding a white lace veil in her hand, came running up to her companion of so many pleasant weeks.

"Am I not charming? Am I not as white as snow? Am I not like a lily? Ah, ah! This is my wedding dress; and my hair, Signor Arthur, is perfumed with the roses thou hast brought me; and on my neck are the pearls thou gavest me."

They both praised her and her dress, but the young coquette kept her eyes upon the veil.

"Madame Henrietta, dost love me?"

"Does a mother love her child?"

"Ah, well, then I would know how this long veil of mine will look on me, by seeing how 'twill look on thy dear head. Now stoop — stoop — stoop — madame, as though I were a queen, and you were to be dubbed a knight."

"Nay," said the young lord, as the lady was about to kneel.

"But I say I will," said the bride.

"I would I could as easily assure thee lasting happiness, fair girl," said the lady, gravely. And kneeling, her head was soon enveloped in the beautiful lace veil.

The bridegroom looked on helplessly, and seemed troubled at this act.

"Charming — charming," cried the laughing Elvira. "Who can see your blushes now? You look like a bride yourself. Pray now, who could tell you from me?"

The young lord suddenly started, and his grave face lighted up with hope.

"Nay, wear it — wear it," said Elvira. "I must leave you for a little, young bride and bridegroom; for I have yet to put on my diamonds. Stay here — stay here." And she ran laughing from the room.

"Thou art saved — thou art saved!"

It was the young lord who spoke, and, as he did so, the imperilled queen for one moment hoped, but the next she was deep sunk in despair, and only breathed the air of liberty again when the colonel entered the room, and coming up to her, said: "The fairy Elvira should not hide her face beneath that envious mantle — let me raise it."

"Nay, nay," said Arthur."

"No? Surely! May Heaven bless thee, niece — daughter! May good Heaven bless thee, and keep thee as happy as thou art now I hope — thou dost not speak?"

"She hath vowed neither to speak nor show her face till we are one."

"So — so: but 'tis time we had set out — so follow me — follow me!"

And he left the room.

The queen was about taking off the veil.

"Stay — stay, your majesty; — 'tis a miracle! Who shall know you? And have I not a pass from the castle?"

"Nay — I fear for thy life, my lord."

"Nay, queen; to refuse would be to cast from thee Heaven's gift. Come — come." And he led her respectfully towards the door. But there stood a wild-looking puritan — Captain Richard Forth to wit — his sword drawn, and his eyes flashing.

"Thou shalt draw steel for her," and he stood immovable in the doorway.

In a moment the lord's sword was out of its sheath, but the queen ran between the thirsty weapons, and in so doing her veil was deranged, and her face seen.

"I forbid thee, my lord, and thou — man of blood."

"'Tis not she, 'tis Madame Henrietta," murmured the puritan, and lowered his sword.

The lord's sword, however, was still raised.

"Thou canst go, Arthur Talbot; thou mayest take her with thee. Go, both of ye, in peace. Go, and I prophecy that thou shalt weep bitter tears — that thou shalt sit apart and lonely, that thou shalt yearn for thy distant country, that thou shalt float in a sea of misfortunes. Begone! thou wanderer."

Then the young lord trembled as he thought of his bride whom he was about to desert. But the loyalty of a cavalier was his honor; so he turned to the door and led Madame Henrietta over its threshold.

The puritan stood erect and motionless in the room waiting for retribution. He — he the rejected, the insulted, would triumph.

Through the window he saw them reach the bridge, pass it, pass the gate, to horse and away, away!

Still he waited.

Then came footsteps towards the room, those of the bride, her father, and several attendants.

"Arthur — Arthur," said the young bride coming in laughingly for the crowning veil. "Ah captain! good day! Master Talbot — is he here?"

"He was but an instant since."

"And — and now?"

"He hath fled, he hath deserted thee!"

Then there was a great cry and a start.

"And the lady — Madame Henrietta — gone also?"

Soon horsemen were flying from the castle — the rattle of drums calling to arms spread over the place — every soul about the castle was hurried and frightened. All but Captain Richard Forth, who stood cold and gratified, nursing his vengeance, and saying it was a judgment.

But as he hears the alarm bell, he hears mixed with it a strange wild cry — near him — almost at his ear.

Still the call to arms was repeated — still the alarm-bell rang out its dismal warning, and again the dull appealing cry was heard.

This time he knew whence it came. It was uttered by Elvira.

Wildly she was looking before her, and tearing the bridal flowers she wore to shreds, and breaking into bits the lace about her dress.

"She — she wears the white veil! He looks on her, he smiles, and whispers that she is *his* bride. And I, whom now am I? Elvira is his bride — am not *I?* Elvira? why is he not here?"

Then wanderingly she placed her trembling right hand upon her head. "No, no," she cried, and dropped the hand to her side.

"Elvira — dear daughter — speak to me."

"No — no — NO — I am not Elvira,"

"How pale thou art, Elvira."

" And — and thy eyes are fixed and staring."

"The judgment is heavy," said the Captain, implacable. "Thus heaven punishes perfidy. SHE IS MAD.

And yet the captain stood calmly as the general fell despairingly at his feet.

"But thou wilt return — mine Arthur — thou wilt return. I will faithfully wait for thee — wait — wait! And thou wilt come, Arthur. I will weep, I will weep for thee."

"Tears, tears," said Captain Richard Forth; "tears for such as he — heaven's tears. MAIDEN, I WILL AVENGE."

"Oh! how my heart throbs; and before my eyes is a great rain of blood. Arthur, Arthur, help me — help — help!"

Then all those puritans there standing cursed him, and "the woman."

"Let not house, nor shore, harbor these accursed. Let their heads be free to the scorn of the wind and the storm, and may the dogs bark wrathfully at them. Let the whole earth war with them through life, and cast them from her bosom when dead. Let them live wishing for death. Let heaven be unapproached by them."

CHAPTER III.

So she remained, day after day, ever waiting for the bridegroom's return, and dismally decking herself in what she took for marriage garments. Sometimes she would take a soldier walking on the ramparts for him she had lost. But she would soon discover her mistake, and then she would sit patiently waiting and gazing from the window.

When, too, the sound of drum or trumpet reached her ears, she would imagine herself again going through the terrible scene when she discovered Arthur's flight.

Meanwhile, Captain Richard Forth held fast by his vow of vengeance; and, like a soldier, calmly waited for the hour of the fight.

The doctors who were called in to Elvira could give no hope; but one said that perhaps a sudden joy or grief might restore the lost reason.

On one of many days, the colonel was conversing with the captain, when the luckless girl wandered near them.

Her uncle addressed her kindly.

"Prithee, who art thou?" she made answer to the uncle she had loved so well.

"What!" said he, assuming a heart-breaking cheerfulness; "dost not know me Elvira?"

"Ah! truly, truly. He is waiting for me. Quick, quick! Thou wouldst not surely keep a bridegroom waiting. Quick — quick — quick."

Then she perceived the stern puritan, Richard Forth, who was now weeping.

"Verily, 'tis a tear on thy face. Ah, thou, too, hast loved, and art forgotten. I love thee for thy lost love."

It was on this occasion, after the lady had been induced to return to her apartment, that the colonel took the captain into his confidence.

"Thou must save this man."

"How? — whom?"

"Lord Arthur Talbot."

"Save Arthur Talbot? And again? It is not in my power to do so."

"If thou couldst save him wouldst thou?"

"'Twould be by death."

"The flight was not Talbot's fault alone; at least, 'twas as much the fault of his loyalty, for she was a royalist."

"The arm that striketh him shall go unpunished. He is outlawed; he that will may kill him. He shall die."

"Is thy vengeance justice, man? or is it jealousy? Again, the hand that shall slay him will also slay Elvira. Then thou shalt hear remorse whispering in the storm, and thy life will be a burden to thee. Forget this hate; forgive — mercy!"

For a little while the stern puritan held up his head. Then it fell.

"I will forget this hate — I will save him."

"'Tis the proof of thy patriotism, Richard."

"If his heart be open — not if he cometh armed. Not if he bear arms against his country."

"No, no — then no mercy, Richard, no mercy."

"What if he were among the cavaliers now encamped near us, who, it is rumored, will attack us at daybreak?"

"His blood be on his own head. Let him perish."

CHAPTER IV.

Not two hours after that conversation, Lord Arthur Talbot came rapidly towards the house which the general, now encamped at some distance from his fortress, occupied. It was a large house near the camp. Surrounded by an enclosure of tall trees, and high walls, this house stood, and in its old weed-filled garden, the witless lady sometimes wandered. Some of the windows of the house opened down to the grounds, and to a wide terrace.

Arthur reached the wall, soon clambered to the top, and was just dropping to the ground when a sentinel espied him and fired. But he missed his aim, and the next moment the lord was on the grounds of the house.

"Safe," he muttered thankfully, and looking about him he thought how sweet it was to see the house and garden once again, to see his dear native land, which he quitted three months before to save a queen, who was now in safety and comparatively happy. What joy he thought it would be to tell his Elvira the glorious truth—that he had saved a queen from death—and had restored a mother to her children. His heart beat as he thought of her joy when he had told his tale, and proved his honor and his love for her. He was loyal too, even though a royalist, and had never thought of bearing arms against his country.

As he moved hesitatingly towards the house, the lost lady passed the open windows, singing a ballad her lover had taught her.

He started, and turned towards the spot whence came the welcome sound.

So gently he began singing the ballad. Nay—he sang it quite through, and yet no answer was made.

As he concluded, there were heard the sounds of steps near him. He fled into the shadow of some friendly trees, as his beating heart told him of the coming of the puritans.

Nearer and nearer came the sound. Surely, 'twas a picket of soldiers. They passed on, and their steps were lost in the distance. He stood again beneath the windows, and once more chanted the ballad she so loved.

She came to one of the casements — slowly — slowly — dreamily.

"It has ceased — the loved wind, which sings his song."

She stepped through the open window on to the terrace.

"Ah, my Arthur, where art thou?"

"Here, dearest, by thy side — at thy feet."

"Thou! is't thou?" And she put her arms about him. "Thou dost not deceive me?"

"I deceive thee! never, Elvira."

"I tremble; why? Is misfortune near?

"No — no; be joyful. Love smiles beneficently upon us."

"How — how long is it since I saw thee?"

"Three weary months."

"No, no; three centuries of sighs and agony. And have I not called to thee — Arthur — Arthur — return!"

"But she was in danger, and I saved her."

"And — and thou lovdst her?"

"I? — her?"

"Is she not thy wife?'

"Nay —"

"Nay, but *is* she?"

"I love her whom I have ever loved — whom I shall love till death is with me — and 'tis *thee*."

"Ah! then he did *not* love her. Then I will love him better than ever — better than ever. Yet tell me, if thou didst not love her, why didst thou follow her?"

"Her life was in danger."

"Whose life, love? Whose?"

"The queen's; she was the queen."

"The queen!"

"A moment more, and she would have been doomed to the scaffold."

"Then — then thou dost love me?"

"Art thou not in my arms? Doth not my heart tell thee how I love thee? I would rather die than part from thee. Each waking moment since we parted I have thought of Elvira, and dreamt of her each minute that I slept; and when I was on the sea, I said my love was as boundless as the waves."

"I am dying with joy — dying; and yet — yet I am afraid; I am quite afraid. Put your hand upon my heart. Now, *doth* it beat?"

As she laid his hand upon her breast, there was heard the sound of a drum-roll. Immediately it destroyed the partial sense with which she had been blessed while speaking to her lover.

"Hark!" she said, hurriedly and terribly, "I know the sound, but now I fear it no longer. Yes, I tore her veil from off her head, and trampled on it. I did — I did. And — and thou wilt not leave me?"

"Great powers?" he cried, looking into her dreamy eyes; and in a great whirl of fear, he fell back from her.

There came floating on the air the exchange of the watchword, "England and Cromwell."

"Come," he said, moving towards the house: "let us go in."

Then she was seized with a violent paroxysm. Calling out that he wished to leave her — to go back to her for whom she had been deserted. She poured forth shriek upon shriek till the air was all astir.

Alarmed at the sudden discovery he had made, he tried to fly from her, but she clung to him — still shrieking that he would leave her, and that he was going to the woman with whom he had fled.

"Be silent."

"He would fly me—"

"Oh — be silent."

"Help — help — for pity's sake!"

"Ah!"

Then came the alarmed puritans, running in from all sides. From the house — from the garden — over the walls they streamed — nearer and nearer, till they surrounded the lover and his mad bride.

While he, all his fear merged in overwhelming sorrow, stood gazing at her who was then his ruin; for had she not called his dread enemies about him?

Amongst the rest came Captain Richard Forth. And

as he saw his enemy in his power — his enemy wearing his sword, and come secretly in the night-time from the puritan camp — he saw he was unworthy to live, and he cried, "The ungodly shall perish from off the face of the earth. Thou hast crept to death, Arthur Talbot; thou hast crept here to death!"

The dreadful word made a dreadful impression on the lady. She trembled violently, pressed her hands about her head, and uttered the word over and over again. Was this the great terror that might save her? The learned doctor had said a sudden joy or terror might restore her.

"Arthur," she cried at last, in a tone far different from that in which she had spoken to him but a minute since, and fell upon his breast. She was saved! So he had returned to restore her to reason, and she — she had destroyed him.

Even in the one word, "Arthur," she betrayed him.

"Arthur Talbot," they cried aloud; and each man drew his breath hard, and grasped his sword.

"Let the unrighteous perish; let no hand be stretched forth to save him."

Said the captain, "Thou art brave enough not to fear death, Arthur Talbot. Be prepared — thou art of the camp of the lost — thou shalt surely die."

"He die? and have I caused his death? I who love him better than I love my life?"

The stern puritan, as he watched the effect of his hasty speech upon the poor lady's countenance, was sorry he had spoken.

Said the puritans among themselves — "Behold a judgment. Is he not delivered into our hands? Then he must surely die!"

"Fear not," said the lost man to his destroyer — she whom he loved so well. "Fear not, death is easy to the brave, and I am brave, or thou wouldst have never loved me."

The captain and the colonel looked hesitatingly one at the other, and then at the cavalier. The puritans murmured and cried aloud.

"What! shall not the sword fall when the Lord hath bidden it to destroy?"

"I have killed him, I have killed him," she exclaimed, now miserably sane.

"Fear not, my own Elvira."

Again the puritans cried out —

"Wherefore shall we not destroy the enemy?"

Suddenly a trumpet sounded.

A moment, and the face of the colonel was full of joy, and yet wet with new-born tears. The message was a pardon signed by Cromwell, for all cavaliers who should lay down arms before the action.

Said Lord Arthur Talbot. "I have never borne arms against the nation. I have belonged to no camp. I have arrived in England but this evening, and came hither from the vessel."

The puritans forgot themselves, for they gave a shout of joy.

And even the bitter Captain Richard Forth was heartily glad to find that Arthur Talbot's blood had not been shed.

So the young bridegroom did not die, and the bride did not therefore destroy him, and his marriage at last took place, sanctified by the glorious truth that he, the bridegroom, had saved a human life. Not only the life of a queen, but the life of a loving mother.

LA FIGLIA DEL REGGIMENTO.   (Donizetti.)

THE DAUGHTER OF THE REGIMENT.

CHAPTER I.

TAKE any young creature of warm, generous disposition, put a military coat on her fair young shoulders, a
smart military hat on her head, and hang a little brandy
keg over her right hip, and then you have a delightful
vivandiere of the grand army — a very honest, decent
kind of girl.

Our vivandiere was called the daughter of the regiment, for she knew no other parents than the rough, but
warm-hearted soldiers.   They found a little child on the
field of battle; they nurtured her, and called her "Marie."

Many units of her collective father were knocked over
before Marie grew to be a very pretty girl; but, spite of
continual arrivals, seeing their daughter for the first time,
there were many who remembered Marie being found, and
with her a letter, and nobody better than Sergeant Sulpice — who always kept the letter, and who, in fact, had
picked it and Marie up when he was a full private, and
quite a new recruit.

Well, they taught Marie to tap her drum at a very early
early age, and she tapped it till she was nearly seventeen;
and on her birthday, and all other social festivals, she
tapped it very loud and fast.

The French were scudding all over Switzerland, and
nobody was more frightened, then and there, than the
Marquise de Berkenfelt.   As a rule, the Swiss opposed
the French bravely, but the marquise was a disgrace to
her title.

She stood among the villagers of her particular village
trembling far more than the young girls.   As for the
marquise — fifty, if a day!

She could not return to the castle, and yet she could not stay where she was,—and then, the enemy might be down on them in a moment.

"Plan — plan — rataplan," away in the distance.

The marquise's steward immediately assured her that the men were retreating, and the marquise was immensely glad to hear it. She would not, however, go back to that castle of hers, but chose to sit on a secluded rock, while the steward went to reconnoitre. Barely was she left to herself than Sergeant Sulpice was walking rapidly past her.

"By the lock of a musket, if they could fight as they can run, we should be sent back to France in a week. Aye, run — run — as though peace was not proclaimed. Hallo! here comes Marie — Marie of the 11th."

"Oh' é — é — é — Salute, Sulpice."

"Here comes the heart of the regiment."

"Well — I think I begin to do you credit."

"Angel."

"Pooh — nonsense. Soldier! Born in a camp — the roll of the drum my only lullaby — a drum my only toy — except you — you grizzly old father, you."

"The regiment is lucky to have a Marie."

"Marie is lucky to have a regiment, you mean. Why, each man was her carriage when she was a child — her rations were better than any one's; — yes she ate and drank to the trun — trun — trun of the drum. And now — now I'm grown up — every man touches his shako to me."

"They revere you."

"Revere, nonsense — they love me. Don't I too have all the pleasure of the camp!"

"Yes, and who takes care of the camp? — who has a kind word and hand for a wounded man, while she gives the other hand to him who comes to help her?"

"Yes — and who is it fills your glasses — and sings you songs?"

"Yes — and who makes us happy?"

"Why, *not* the daughter of the regiment!"

"Oh — of course not!"

"Now — now — now — Sergeant — attention. Right about face. Ma-a-a-r-r-rch!"——

"Tum — tum — tum — Ra-ra-ra-ra."

And so — drilling her drum — she and the sergeant march off to the camp.

Barely had they marched off from the neighborhood of the marquise, when following them or rather her, with his eyes, came a young Swiss — as handsome as you would have him, ladies — perfection.

Truth to tell, Tony *was* handsome.

Also truth to tell, he had fallen in love with Marie. And love, the conqueror, had even whispered to him to turn traitor to his country, and enlist in the ranks of the army, and, it need not be said, the ranks of the glorious 11th. Then he would be near *her* — then, perhaps, he should some day marry her. And he *might* become a general. And she — she would be the general's lady. "Why not?" He was honest (except in the matter of patriotism), good-humored, and handsome — why should she *not* fall in love with him?"

But seeing the sergeant and Marie returning, he ran to shelter and to shadow immediately.

"Well, but Sulpice, — why not say it as we walked along? What need to come to this quiet spot as you call it?"

"Because I want to speak to you in private."

"Attention!"

"You are a fine tall girl, and you are handsome."

"Is *that* what you want to tell me in private. Why I'm told so *fifty* times a day."

"And ——"

"Oh there's an end!"

"And — and you ought to look out for a husband."

"You mean a husband ought to look out for me. Plenty of time — plenty of time."

"Plenty of time? Then who was that you were talking to at our last encampment?"

"Who — who? Let me see; ah, the Tyrolese youth who saved my life, you know!"

"Your life? How?"

"Attention! but what's that noise?"

For there was a great disturbance as though somebody was being pushed about, and as though somebody was rather objecting to it.

"A spy — a spy — a spy."

And the next moment Tony was being lugged before the sergeant by as many of the brave 11th as could conveniently keep a hold on him at one and the same moment. He butting, kicking, and struggling all the while.

"Spy — no spy — I want to be a soldier.

" 'Tis he — 'tis he."

" What the young Tyrolese, Marie ? "

"Of course it is, Sulpice ; who else could it be ? Your servant, Tyrolese — what brings you here ? "

" Hang him — hang him — a spy ! " shrieked out a full dozen of the brave 11th.

" What — hang him — who saved my life ? "

" Cre-é-é-é-é —' tis another affair that — he shall live," decided also at least a dozen of the brave 11th.

" But for him I should have been at this moment at the bottom of a frightful precipice. Yes ; and he nearly lost his own life."

" Brother — he's a brother — he shall be one of us !" was the dictum of the men of the brave 11th. Give him a welcome. Marie — a glass of brandy."

Briskly Marie poured it out.

"Long live the French — my new friends," said the new recruit, raising his glass.

" Hurrah — hurrah."

Then was heard a roll of the drum — the call to camp in fact.

" Come — come — comrade," said they to Tony. But Tony showed a desire to stay ; and so also did Marie. So she called out, " Leave him with me. I'll answer for him. You know — he's my prisoner."

But they wouldn't part with him, and hurried him away.

She was preparing to follow the soldiers — when with a run he was at her side, quite out of breath. She did not care about following the soldiers now. Truth to tell, she sat down on a bank and began chatting.

" Here I am, you see."

" What already ? "

" La — when I gave them the slip — the sergeant roared like a bull."

" Ah — my father ! "

" (Confound it.)   No — one near him."

" Well — *he's* my father.

" I mean the old man."

" And *he's* my father too ! "

" Why, the whole regiment ? "

" Exactly so.   The whole regiment is my father."

" Ah ! I see."

" But now tell me, why have you followed the regiment?   I thought when I said good bye to you that I should never, never see you again."

" I don't think you did think so, because you must have known I couldn't live away from you, because you must have known I loved you, and I *do* love you."

" Ha, ha ! "

" Will you not believe me ? "

" Well — I don't know."

" From the moment I saved you — I have known no rest."

" Ah — then you had better not have saved me.   But want of rest don't prove you love me ! "

" But I have left my friends and my country to follow you ! "

" Such desertion I can't pardon ! " —

" And I would die for you — and I will ! "

" Oh nonsense — why die ?   When a youth loves a girl he should live for her."

" Marie ! "

" Ah — well.   Here's the decision of the court martial : — I think you *do* love me.   And — and *I* don't feel so free as I did."

" Then you do not hate me."

" Hate ! — no — no.   Here am I," she thought, " who always hated the enemy,— here am I — talking with one of them — and — and not disliking to talk !   And — and Tony, she said," slyly, " that flower you gave me — I have it now."

Whereupon and thereupon he clasped her to his heart like a man.

" Ho — ho — ho — by the look of a musket," said Sergeant Sulpice, coming up in time to witness this delightful embrace.   " The Tyrolese, who just now escaped ! "

" Sergeant — I'm Marie's husband's self."

" Traitor ! "

" Tut — tut — tut — sergeant," said the little vivandiere, coming before Marie's husband's self — like a bastion
— " qui-i-i-iet."

" I say Marie is already promised to the bravest in
our ranks."

" Pooh! a girl can't marry her own father, you know.
Besides, your own words prove Tony's right. You say
I'm promised to the bravest man in the regiment,— well,
he's of the regiment — and was either of *you* so brave as
to save my life ? "

" Good — Marie — good ! "

" Si-i-i-i-ilence — private ! "

" I may speak, sergeant."

" I say she shall marry one of us."

" Shall — sergeant ? Then here it is. I will marry
Tony, and I will marry nobody else but Tony."

" Gone over to the enemy bag and baggage. But as
for you, my man, I'll break your bones."

" Attention — march — Tony." And away the two
went, leaving Sergeant Sulpice boiling with rage.

He was walking away, when the marquis's steward
approached very respectfully.

" Captain — pardon."

" By Bacchus — if she marries him."

" Him — captain — pardon. "

" Hullo ! there, don't be afraid."

" Captain."

" Ser-r-rgeant."

" Surely, surely, sergeant, this lady would ask a favor."

" Oh, Sir! I'm terribly frightened. I was endeavoring
— I am still terribly frightened — but your men stopped
me. I was endeavoring to reach my castle — my castle
of Berkenfelt."

" Berkenfelt."

" Berkenfelt. Do you know my castle of Berkenfelt ? "

" Now, what connexion can there be between Captain
Bazancourt and that name." The grizzly sergeant said
this amusingly, but it had a strange effect on the aristo-
crat.

" Captain Bazancourt, did you say Captain Bazancourt ? "

" Yes, you know him perhaps ! "

" Know him — yes — my sister — I think — was secretly married to him — and their daughter."

" Marie ?   She is the pearl of the regiment."

" Does she live ? "

" She does if *I* do.   Steady, lady, steady."

For the lady had to lean against the bank on which Marie had been sitting.

" I' faith, Marie's fortune is made."

" But the proof, the proof."

" The proof — this letter, then ! "

And from his stout breast the sergeant pulled forth a tough old pocket book, and from the book he took a letter.

This letter had been written just before the battle in which the captain fell.   He had confided it and the child to a servant, who was unluckily knocked over by a stray shot.   The child was found sitting by the dead servant, and there being no clue beyond the letter, which simply named the castle of Berkenfelt, the child was then and there adopted by the regiment, and taught to carry a brandy keg, be good-humored and brisk, and beat a drum, as, indeed, has already been explained.

The lady took the letter I discovered with some emotion, but in the midst of it, she contrived to say, " I hope she has been well brought up."

" Brought up, marquise, in the most genteel and polite manner ! "

" I'm sure her aunt — I am, of course, her aunt — I'm sure I'm very glad to hear it."

" Par-r-r-r-bleu! Par-r-r-r-bleu ! Here you are, Sulpice, and there you are wanted.— Par-r-r-r-bleu ! "

" Great impossibles — can that be her," asked the marquise of herself.   And the steward opened his eyes at this terrible talking young woman."

" ' Tis she," said the sergeant to the lady.

" Co-r-r-r-bleu ! " again commended Marie, marching up to the sergeant.   " Cor-r-r-r-bleu, do you call this duty, Sergeant Sulpice ? "

"Why, she's positively pulling his moustache," said the marquise, so far forgetting her dignity as to speak familiarly with her own house-steward. "What an education."

The steward was dolefully and properly shocked.

"Come — come — old grumbler, come along, or I'll pull you by your grizzly upper-lip."

"Order — order."

"Come — come along, then; the whole family is waiting for you."

"Marie — we've lost one of the family."

"When — how — where — what — whom?"

"You!"

"Parbleu! What do you mean?"

"The owner of the old letter is found."

"Co-r-r-r-bleu! Where is he?"

"She."

"Well, where is she?"

"Here — here — dear girl! I am your — aunt."

"Niece — you my aunt? Cor-r-r-par-r-r-bleu. Exchange for another regiment — no!"

"Your soldier's life is over now, Marie."

"Not till my life is —"

"NIECE!"

"Oh."

"Read the letter, Marie — I, your father Sulpice, bid you read the letter."

She took the old letter, which she had never much thought of — for, whereas, somebody belonging to it had deserted her — she had found scores of fathers. She took the letter. Read it through. Let it fall. Covered her face with her hands. And the little daughter of the regiment quite wept again.

"Come, niece, come away. I have a pass, elegant, I presume, to my castle — my Castle of Berkenfelt."

"Surely, marquise, I — I — dare say you will be happy, Marie."

"Come, niece, come." Then turning to the steward, "Order our carriage."

Our carriage. The vivandiere's carriage.

The marquise marched up in great state to her niece. But at that moment there was a tremendous to-do on the

drums, and the next moment a score or so of stout soldiers, Tony among them, came forward. By this time
they were quite friendly with Tony, and had somehow
cause to perceive what an admirable arrangement his
marrying their daughter, the vivandiere, would be.

" Ah, there you are, Marie."

" Pray, *who* is this young man ? "

" Pardon, lady — Marie's husband. Her fathers have
said so.

" Fall back, private — fall back. There's a general of
division has stopped the match."

" What ? "

" Yes, comrade — Marie leaves us. The letter has
done its work. This is Marie's aunt."

Perhaps many of the brave eleventh would have disputed this position with the butt end of a musket or so,
but respect for their daughter stopped such a frightful
proceeding; yet with one mighty voice they cried out,

" Marie going to leave us. No, no, she won't leave us."

" Leave us — no, no, Marie. Leave us — leave me,
Tony ? "

" I must, I must." She was a very different being now
from the brisk vivandiere. Before, she was all smiles,
now she was all tears. " I must go. For shame, do not
make me worse than I am."

Tony took off his hat, which was decorated with the
gay French cockade, and looked upon the innocent little
fluttering ribbons with horror, for they told him he was
bound to the regiment, and could not follow her.

" Pray is our carriage ready."

" Good-bye, oh ! good-bye all — all of you; and dear,
dear Tony."

The soldiers were rude enough to push the marquise
aside, that they might shake the hands of Marie, and
some actually kissed her.

" Men ! " was the only remark the marquise could make.
" Men ! "

" Good-bye, oh ! good-bye all — all of you; and dear,
dear Tony."

" When *will* that carriage be ready ? "

The carriage was ready at last, but as she stepped into
it, she turned her head to her then old companions.

They had hoped she was going to run away to them, under which evidence of preference they would have defied the marquise, but the next moment she was seated, and "our carriage" rolled away.

Her eyes were upon her old friends till she could see no more for tears and distance.

And there poor Tony stood despairingly watching the carriage, his hat pressed with both hands to his heart, and the cruel, triumphant little ribbons fluttering about in the breeze.

CHAPTER II.

At home in the grand castle, dressed, no longer like a vivandiere, but like a real young lady, sat Marie. She was not happy, but she cannot be said to have been utterly miserable — that sparkling young girl could not be utterly miserable; but she was half way on the journey to utter misery, and she, erst vivandiere, did not like the road.

To be dressed in the fashion — to learn lessons — to make curtseys to grand folks — all these things want an early apprenticeship. If you go into the business after you have gone out of pinafores, you are pretty sure to fail.

And Marie failed signally. Every day there arose a series of contentions between Marie and the marquise; and when the young lady was seated amongst the grand people of an evening, listening to vapid songs about Venus, and Phillis, and all the rest of the delicately-finger-topped crowd, she longed to get up, bang a drum, sing the rataplan, and show them all how they marched in the brave eleventh. But she did not at any time carry such a wish into practice, or the young duke, whose name it is perfectly needless to know, would certainly not have proposed for her hand and heart, as the young duke certainly did, to Marie's great concern.

When, some little time after, Marie had become a lady, the war broke out again — when again the old regiment was near "my Castle of Berkenfelt."—and when the grizzly Serjeant Sulpice was wounded, the marquise could not refuse Marie's request that the sergeant should remain at the castle till he could again fight in the field. So, rash with mild gratitude, the marquise let this tempter into her fold.

Tempter he was—for, from the day he made his appearance, pale as to his face, and his arm in a sling, he never lost an opportunity of praising up the regiment camped not half-a-score of miles away, and depreciating the value of the castle.

But at no time did he so asperse the castle, the marquise, and all their surroundings, as on that terrible day when it was understood that at 6 P. M., the duke, the duke's mother, the duke's brother, and all the duke's noble friends would come to assist at the signing of the marriage contract.

On that particular morning the sergeant was more indignant than ever; for, from the great drawing-room, where he had to sit, per command, he looked into an adjoining room, and saw the little vivandiere, who could trip you a measure so that you could hardly see her feet, the little vivandiere trying to slide through a solemn minuet and signally failing in the attempt.

For four mortal hours did the indignant sergeant mark this saltatory misery, and he was meditating an assault and crash upon the extorting dancing-master, when that unlucky professional withdrew, and Marie came running in to Sulpice.

"Oh, I could have slipped about no more, if I had died for it; like a dead march, only not so brisk."

"Patience, patience, daughter."

"Patience, indeed—how's the arm by this time?"

"O! a great deal better."

"Well—I'm very glad to hear *that*—still you need not leave us directly."

"What—what? A vivandiere counsel a sergeant of the grand army to desert!"

"Oh—no—no, leave of absence, sergeant."

"Ah, it seems *you* have leave of absence from your aunt."

"Not for long, she's coming here. Now the dancing is over, the word is "singing." Such slow singing, I want to dash my hands down on the keys to make just a little stir, you know. And she says I shall sing to-night before the company, but he is wrong. I won't, I won't, I won't."

"Or-r-r-r-der."

"I say I won't — I won't — I won't! And I won't marry the duke, and I won't marry anybody but Tony."

"Ah, Marie, how can you help yourself?"

"If I don't help myself, I'm sure nobody else will, not even Sergeant Sulpice."

"Hush! — here she comes — full dress parade."

"And in stalked the marquise."

"Thank the chances I have found it — this superb romance. Hem — hem! —'Tis a beautiful romance. Come, Marie — there you stand like a simpleton. Come to the piano this moment."

"Yes — aunt."

"There — now begin."

"Ve-e-e-nus."

"Very good."

"Venus — the goddess of love."

"Enchanting, my dear — go on. I will play slowly."

"Venus — Venus — descends fr-r-ra-rom above."

"Quite admirable — now, go on."

"Marie!" this was the sergeant, creeping up behind the chaste back of the marquise, and whispering to the vivandiere. "Marie — rata —"

"Rataplan — rataplan — rataplan. Rataplan — plan — plan — plan — plan — plan-n-n. Rub-a-dub. Dub-a-rub."

"My DEAR — what are you singing there?"

"Oh — certainly — aunt."

"Ve-e-enus — Venus — comes down to dark earth."

"Ve-*he-he*-nus appears — to light she gives birth."

"Ra-ta — PLAN — Marie!"

"Each soldier says it — each soldier vows."

"MADEMOISELLE! I *beg*. Now pray begin all over again — and when you come down at the end of the sixth line — to 'sigh'— mind you sigh just like Venus."

"Oh — I can't. Oh — I won't. I like the sound of the drum better. There! Rub-a-dub-dub-dub — Rataplan — rataplan."

" How dare you ? "

" Rataplan — rataplan — rataplan."

Useless was it that the marquise stepped with dignity
after the vivandiere at this declaration of war.

" Now, fall in there. Right about face. Ma-r-r-rch."

" Girl ! "

" Rataplan — rataplan ! "

Tramp, tramp, up and down the room went the soldier
and the girl, the marquise continually following and
expostulating.

At last she could bear it no longer, so she took advantage of marching right to the door-post with them, not
to wheel, but to keep straight on through the doorway,
and to fluster up to her own apartments.

And very apropos had she retreated, for barely had she
gone when the military manœuvres were brought to a
close by an announcement of the steward, as he stood
judiciously outside the door, prepared to run in case of
military assault — an announcement to the effect that one
of the brave eleventh was at the door.

Whereat the steward flew on one side to make room
for a charge on the part of both sergeant and lady, who
both rushed to the door to welcome the visitor.

And who was that visitor from the brave eleventh ?

Tony ! and a score more, who came storming the
place as though they had a right to do so. And when
they reached the grand drawing-room, where the duke
was to be received, they set up such a shout as almost
paralyzed the marquise, who, as she did not come to ascer-
tain the cause of the uproar was, perhaps, temporarily
deprived of the power of action or remonstrance.

" Hurrah ! Marie — Marie ! "

And there was to be seen the spectacle of " a young
lady in fashionable attire," shaking the hands of a score
of common soldiers, and giving to special favorites a
friendly dig in the ribs with her fair little fingers.

Common soldiers, all but one — Tony !

Hopeless despair is sometimes success. Tony, fighting
madly for welcome death, lived throughout all to be
Captain Tony, and to wear a cross of valor.

She immediately, after a few confidential words with

the captain, proposed comfort of an ardent kind to the soldiers. "Aye! Aye," said they "where's your keg, Marie?" And then and there the vivandiere's keg appeared in the person of the butler, who came to the door trembling.

And the next moment he was borne off in trembling triumph to the assault of his own cellars.

Marie was not the girl to give way to much sentiment, so the next moment or so she was talking briskly with her old comrades.

"So, here we three are again, eh!"

"Yes, Marie, as in the old days."

"How long ago they seem, Sulpice. And so you are a captain, Tony."

"Yes, and a very brave captain too." This was not the remark of the captain himself, but of his sergeant.

"Now Sulpice, sit down there. Good: now the captain will sit on one side of you and I will sit on the other. There. And now I must begin. Sergeant Sulpice, you must help us!"

"Help whom, Vivandiere?"

"Marie, and Marie's captain."

"How?"

"Speak to the marquise."

"I'd rather storm a fort."

"Sergeant Sulpice, you must help us. I say it — you must speak of our troth."

"Yes — and we did pledge our troth, Marie — did we not?"

"Surely; but I am speaking to the sergeant. You see, sergeant, the poor captain is deeply in love with me; and — yes — I think I am deeply in love with the captain. Well, sergeant, you must help us?"

"Yes, sergeant — I, your captain, tell you — you must help us."

"Confound you both."

And the sergeant moved his chair — but Marie moved hers, as also did the captain his.

"Yes — yes — yes," said the sergeant. And barely had he registered the promise in a strong bass voice, when the marquise entered the room. She was almost paralyzed again at the sight of the third party.

"Aunt — aunt — this is he who once saved my life; and — and I love him."

"Love! To use the word openly, like that!"

"But, marquise, this is Tony — her husband!"

"Silence, sir — the Duke of Krakentorp is Marie's husband. Love, indeed! A soldier — a common soldier!"

"Pardon me, marquise — but Tony is a captain now."

"Then, if he is an officer, he knows, I presume, the laws of good breeding; and when I tell him his presence is distasteful,"— here the grand lady curtseyed, for the captain, without another word, retired, but not without a certain look from Sulpice, who, having given the promise, was proceeding to keep it. He looked Tony from the presence of the marquise, and then he looked Marie also from her presence.

"Ah, I would speak to you alone, Sulpice."

"And I have a precisely similar desire, marquise."

"You know I am determined on her marrying the duke."

"Ah!"

"And I depend on *you* to bring Marie to reason."

"Ah!"

"And I think when you have heard me, you *will* bring Marie to reason. If you do not — no one will — for she loves you better than me — though I'm......her...... aunt."

"Ah!"

"Did you ever fall in love?"

"Par-r-r-rbleu."

"*I* have fallen in love. *I*, ridiculous and fantastic as you think me."

"Not at all, marquise — not at all."

"And I have been married — and to a soldier!"

"Cor-r-r-r-rbleu."

"And knowing the misery I suffered from that marriage — knowing the misery which *must* follow all such matches —"

"I don't see it."

"You don't see as the wife, sergeant — I would not wish such a marriage for my daughter — if I had a daughter."

" Ah ! "

" And — and I have a daughter."

" Par-r-r-rbleu ! — what's her name ? "

" Marie ! — Yes. She is my daughter. And now, sergeant — if you would oppose the aunt, you will not oppose the mother. I tell you a marriage with the captain would be misery. So you will persuade her to marry the duke — a man of high character, I assure you, sergeant."

" I — yes — certainly."

" Then go at once to her, for I hear a carriage at the door."

Away went the sergeant — as dejected as though the brave eleventh had been signally defeated and cut to shreds.

" Ting — ting "— went the castle bell. The visitors came pouring in, and amongst them the duke and his mother, the duchess; with the inevitable notary.

When Marie came in with the sergeant, she ran to the marquise, and embraced her with more warmth than she had ever shown. In one dismal word or two she promised to obey her newly-found mother.

Then the preparations went on for signing the unavoidable contract.

Meanwhile, the high-flown marquise was asking herself whether the duke was altogether so admirable a party, and she was beginning to see it more clearly than she had seen for many years, the joys of that early martial life of hers, and the happy, loving husband *her* captain made.

And while she sat recalling that old time there was a great whirr from without. The next moment twenty common soldiers of the brave eleventh had burst into the room, headed by the Captain Tony. For love *will* make cowards of us, as he will, at his capricious pleasure, make us heroes of bravery.

And then, and there, before all that fine company, they called out in a loud voice to the marquise's daughter, addressed her as Marie, reminded her of vivandiering days, and recommended her to desert.

The grand ladies were immensely shocked at this awful exposition ; for it is needless to say that the story of Marie's discovery had not, at any time, formed part of the marquise's aristocratic confidences; and, indeed, the marquise herself was ready to shrink into the ground; but when she remembered the old dare-devil time — the spirit which had prompted her to marry the dead captain, now rose against the shocked indignation of the grand people present; and then Marie's tears — and then a rather strong fear that the duke would cry off; why all those reasons were as good as a crack advocate speaking for Captain Tony. And the consequence was, that when the notary respectfully asked for the name of the bridegroom — as though he did not know it — the marquise gave judgment in Tony's favor, and surprised the notary, and the whole aristocratic company, by turning to the captain, and leading him up to a quill-pen dipped in ink.

And so Marie was given away before, at all events, a portion of the brave eleventh, and certainly with that portion's full approbation.

The aristocratic ladies were shocked; but the marquise, by the lightness of her own heart, and the brightness of Marie's eyes, knew she had judged wisely; and so she fearlessly looked the grand ladies full in the face.

Rataplan! Rataplan! Marie is the Daughter of the Regiment still!

NORMA. (Bellini.)

CHAPTER I.

Rome, all powerful, had thrown out her arms to the east and the west, to the north and to the south, and boasted of being mistress of the world. She had conquered all Germany and Spain, and overcome the Gauls; and not only the Gauls, but the Druids, that powerful and wonderful priesthood, the relics of whose mysterious rites yet remain in various parts of the world.

This priesthood rose several times against the Roman yoke, and proved over and over again that they were not wanting in bravery, daring, or hardihood.

At the conquest of Gaul, the Pro-Consul appointed to Cambria, was named Pollione. Near his palace was the sacred Druidic Forest, within which dwelt the mysterious priesthood.

The High Priest was Oroveso; but higher in the awe and veneration of the Gauls stood his daughter Norma. Proud, beautiful, and cold, she stood amongst them, uttering the decrees of their faith, and believed by all to be inspired of God. All bowed before the High Priestess — the spotless virgin.

But ah! was she spotless — pure? No! seen by the Roman Governor but to be loved by him, she had forgotten her state, her holiness — and soon she was his wife.

Yet she was the High Priestess before the people, and the priests trembled as she passed them; while she herself often trembled as she performed the mystic symbolic rites, and she thought of her children. For she had two children — this proud, reverenced, high priestess — children whom she loved when no eyes beheld her but their own; often she ran to their little bedsides when she feared they might have been discovered; but up to the time when their father changed towards her, no one but herself, their father, and the faithful Clotilda, knew of their existence.

For the Roman grew cold to her, and often as she stood high and grand at the altar, her heart was beating. Yet she knew not why he had forsaken her.

Hark to the pompous march! List to the solemn step of marching hundreds! Who are these coming grandly in the night through the sacred grove? These are the Druids, the pure priests dressed in heavy white garments, their holy beards flowing to their chests.

See!—some of them speed to the hill-side to hail the moon's up-rising, and they call their followers to prayers by the clashing of grave bells. When the moon, the emblem of their God, is throned in the boundless sky, Norma will come to gather the sacred miseltoe clinging to the holy oaks.

Hark, how they vow to destroy and sweep the Romans from the land! Grandly they pass away again, chanting till the still air is full of sound.

But who are these two, flitting from tree to tree?—they are not clothed in flowing white—there is the flash of metal from their limbs. They are not Gaul or Druids, they are Romans.

The one is Pollione—the other Flavio.

"Why comest thou to this sacred forest—has not Norma told thee death lies within?"

"Why hast thou uttered that dread name?"

Hark! he doth admit he loveth her no more; the mother of his children. His new love is a priestess too, and he calleth her Adalgisa; he hath entreated her to fly to Rome with him. Still he speaketh, when booming on the night air is heard the sound of bells, and behold the air is suffused with soft moonlight.

Then the Romans fled—for again the sacred march rippled through the air; louder and louder, as they came to the high altar. Norma—proud as ever; defying fear and walking grandly amidst them all.

On she comes to the sacred oak, bearing a golden reaping hook in her right hand. High she mounts the steps of the grand altar, as the sacred fires flicker in the breeze,

and as the stately march rolls on. She knows there have
been mutterings of hate against the Romans — fearlessly
she bids them live in peace till she tells them to raise
their arms. Terribly she threatens those who shall take
no heed of what she says; she stands there in power
unspeakable, and they tremble before her.

Then she cuts the sacred misletoe, and as it falls from
the trees it is caught in a pure white cloth. High does
the chief priestess cast her eyes to the placid moon, as
she prays for its blessing.

"Chaste goddess, whose silver beams deign to fall on our
sacred plant — let thy rays come to us unshadowed by a
cloud. Calm these rash men who thirst for war; calm
them; spread over our land the peace and quiet of thy
boundless sky."

See how they bow the head before their great high
priestess as she addresses the greatest emblem of their
faith.

Then she turns her face from the illuminating moon,
and high above them speaks the ordeal which they believe their god speaks to them through her. See how
they bow as she tells them she — she only will utter
the war-cry — let their swords rest till she bids them flash
from their scabbards.

The sacred rites are ended. Solemnly the reverend
men have moved away. The priestess is perhaps fondling
her two children. The sacred fires die out, and for a
little the altar stands deserted in the midst.

Then comes Adalgisa, trembling and prostrate. See
her kneeling before the altar, the sacred fires flickering
dimly here and there. What a contrast is she to Norma,
who walks proudly and fears naught! Adalgisa is bowing, trembling; no mighty prayer issues from her lips, but
a timid appeal. Yet she thinks of the Roman who loves
her and whom she loves. Then as she confesses this to
herself, she bows lowly before the altar of the temple she
has shamed; and yet heavily she trembles as she thinks
of the chief priestess and the decree, if she but discovers
that Adalgisa loves the enemy.

Still she is kneeling when the Roman comes creeping
softly towards her.

She cries affrightedly as he touches her, and clings to the altar. Yet he speaks.

Hark how he pleads!

"Thou art weeping."

"No, no; but I pray — thou durst not speak to me as I pray."

"'Tis a false God thou prayest to. Come with me — come with me — pray to the gods *I* love — the true gods!"

"Let me go — let me go."

"Where thou goest I follow, Adalgisa!"

"Thou mayest not follow me to the sacred Temple!"

"The Temple — hast thou not whispered that thou lovest me?"

"Yet do I offer myself to the service of the Temple."

"Ah! if thou wouldst sacrifice — let my blood be shed. Thou willest my destruction."

"Hast thou not willed mine? Didst thou not whisper to me as I knelt happy and innocent at the altar?"

"There are nobler altars in Rome, dearest. Wilt thou not kneel at them with me?"

"Rome — thou goest to Rome?"

"When the day dawns thou wilt go with me."

"No, no."

"To Rome and its pleasures. Doth not thy heart tell thee thou art willing to be with me?"

"Ah! I fear thee."

"Yet thou lovest me."

Hark, then — oh shame upon her priestly virgin robes; she promises to see him yet again, and then to fly with him.

See, she steals away, and she — her better nature rising — will to the arch-priestess go, and seek her assistance and advice.

CHAPTER II.

YES — the priestess — the proud priestess is now the happy, yet fearing, mother. See her clasping her children, and turning, affrightedly, to the mouth of their cavern-house at every sound, however slight.

The sound increases — 'tis a footstep! The children are hurried away, and the next moment Adalgisa is at the feet of the high priestess.

She tremblingly tells the story of her love. But the proud Norma is not angry — does not upbraid her! Why? Does she not think of the time when Pollione whispered loving vows to her?

At last she asks, "Who is he — thy lover?"

"Not a Gaul — a Roman."

"A Roman — and he is named — "

Again a footstep. This time a rapid, haughty one — 'tis that of Pollione. Well he knows the entrance to the house. He comes to see Norma. As he marks Adalgisa he starts. And she, the young maiden, says, "This is he — this is he who loves me."

"He — Pollione!" See Norma standing proudly, and yet as though turned to stone.

"The very one."

"He! — do I hear — do I see?"

O, the world of anger on her face as she looks upon the man before her. Now she knows why he has deserted her. Now she learns the meaning of his cold words and frequent absences. Then vengeance whispers her — she has but to call, and they shall both die — he, the traitor, and this weak, cruel girl! Then jealousy swept over her, and she eagerly looked at her rival. But Adalgisa coming trembling and kneeling near her, and standing far away from the Roman, she was full of pity, and she said: —

"I would that thou hadst died — I would that thou hadst died before thou hadst seen him."

Threateningly raising his hand, he turned to go his way, but she commanded him to stay; and in spite of himself he did remain. Again rage possessed her.

"I read thy thoughts — but is she not in my power — can I not destroy her?"

"Thou shalt not do this!"

"And shalt thou stay my hand?"

He ran to Adalgisa and implored her to fly with him — but the virgin drew back from him, and again clung to Norma. But the priestess, jealous to blindness, flung the maiden from her, and bade her follow her paramour.

" Ah! no — ah! no — Norma."

Suddenly she relented — bent down quickly and kissed the acolyte. Then she rose toweringly high and bade him depart.

" Begone — forget thy vows, thy vows — begone! I curse thee. My voice shall whisper to thee on the winds and in the waves. Go — alone! She shrinks from thee, she whom thou wouldst destroy — I defy thee. Go — alone."

He met her look at first — but soon quailed before her. Then with his eye down-cast, he moved towards Adalgisa — but Norma stood defyingly between them.

So conquered — he turned, and left the place.

Behold her before the kneeling girl — her face towards him as he creeps away ; firm, defying, protecting — she has conquered him — she, the sinning high priestess; she, but a woman; she, one of a conquered race — Norma! She has fought and beaten the powerful Roman. She stands proudly, defiantly; *he* creeps away abashed, his very life her gift, the gift of her whom he has deserted.

CHAPTER III.

WHO is this, creeping towards two sleeping children? Who is this with an uplifted dagger, and an awful frown upon her face? 'Tis Norma — mad with jealousy and hate, stealing in the dark to kill his children and her own.

Nearer and nearer the infants — nearer still; they are sleeping — they will not see the hand that strikes them — a loving hand — loving hand! "If — if I do not destroy them — if they live here, soon or late the flaming pyre will steal them. If — if in Rome, they would be slaves! No, no, never slaves! Let them die. Why can I not strike — are they not Pollione's children? What are they to me? He is dead to me — let *them* die also."

She raises the savage knife, high — higher still. Then she lets fall the blade. They are her sons — they are her sons! And fearing for herself, she calls to Clotilda, the faithful keeper of her secret, and bids her seek out and bring Adalgisa to the cavern — once a home !

"Adalgisa, I am sick to death. I will tell thee all my shame. Thou hast knelt to me — ah well! I now kneel to thee. Take them — my children, and guard them well — for no more have they a mother. Lead them to him — lead them to him — bid them kneel before him! Perchance to Adalgisa a kinder husband he may be than he has been to Norma! Take them; watch over them. I ask not for them fortune, honors. I only ask that they may not be slaves, abandoned and forgotten. Ah! remember, Adalgisa, 'twas for thee he did forget me."

"Ah! Norma — hope yet — hope ever. I'll to the Roman camp, and move his pity; and all may yet be well; hope on, hope ever."

High and proud yet, the priestess forbade the girl to seek Pollione; but, turning to her children, for their sake she faltered; and at last bade Adalgisa go.

So away to the Roman camp went the maiden; while sick at heart, the high priestess lay in the cavern, weeping.

Meanwhile, the Druids were planning a surprise and massacre of the Roman camp. In spite of the high priestess's commands, they had met to plot, and at their head stood Oroveso, her father. Angrily, and with heavy brows, they met; angrily, and with heavy brows, they separated — nerving themselves for the coming blow.

CHAPTER IV.

AGAIN she stands near the altar — this time the sacred spot where hangs the symbolic shield, which, being struck, gives forth the sound of thunder. None but Norma may raise this dreaded warning — none.

As she stood near the altar, she thought, would Adalgisa be successful? Would he return to her, repentant and loving? And as she asked herself these questions, behold the sun was overcast, and thunder muttered in the air.

Suddenly Clotilda ran in; her features had told her message of dismay — Adalgisa had wept and prayed in vain.

As she stood there, her first thought was her madness

in letting the virgin go; that she could have been so weak as to let him look upon her. Why — why if she prayed and knelt to him, she was but more beautiful, and more surely drew his love upon her. Then she thought that Adalgisa had planned the appeal to the Roman but to escape from her fury. Then suddenly she relents, for the messenger tells how Roman honor has overcome temptation. How the herald has been held sacred, and a free passage given her back to the sacred forest. Her face softens as Clotilda tells how the virgin humbly prays that she may take the vows, and dedicate herself to the service of the Temple. And now again her face is angered; 'tis at the last news the messenger has brought, that Pollione has vowed to tear Adalgisa from the very Temple — from the very altar.

"Let the blood of the base Romans flow," she cried. Then quickly she turned to the golden shield, the sound of which emulated the rolling thunder, and beat on it three times.

Then arose the sacred answering cry of the Druids, and from all sides came they running towards the sound — masses on masses — their weapons in their hands. On they came — in they rushed, till the whole temple was filled — a forest of angry steel ready to bathe in Roman blood.

"War!" she cried — "extermination — slaughter! Sing ye the hymn of battle."

Up rose the sacred hymn — high-sounding amidst the waving oaks — floating away on the winds, and threatening the southern invaders. Louder and louder spread the sacred war cry — death, destruction, extermination! — "Let the Romans fall! Let their legions be mown down like grass! — Let the wings of their eagles strike the ground. May our god descend on the rays of the sun to bless and rejoice in the triumph of his faithful children."

Then she trembles in her passion as she sees the high priest, her own father, prepare to ask the question she knows that he must ask.

"And the victim?"

The victim! When the stern, savage Druids warred, they called for a human victim, as a sacrifice to their gods

— as an offering and atonement for their sins — as a sacrifice worthy to propitiate their gods to grant them victory.

"AND THE VICTIM?"

Slowly she replies:—"The terrible altar never lacks a victim!"

Suddenly rose loud cries of anger; and through the thick throng of worshippers there ran several armed Gauls, bearing in their midst a man dressed in Roman garments.

"A Roman found in the sacred temple."

Who was this man — this Roman? She, Norma, trembled as she saw him; and she whispered the word Pollione!"

There was a suppressed cry of joy amongst the Druids — their gods had sent this sacrifice — this Roman, their enemy, who had dared to enter the sacred forest.

"Take thou the sacred sword and slay him."

He who spoke was Oroveso; she who heard — she who stretched forth her hand for the weapon — was Norma.

And as she took the sword, the Druids saw the Roman start and turn pale, and they said amongst themselves that he was afraid.

Slowly she came down from the altar, the shining weapon in her hand. Slowly she came near him — not a pitying look upon her face. Slowly she lifted the sword against him, as he raised his arm to receive the blow. And then — then she was weak; and she, the high priestess, let fall the point of the sacred weapon from before the enemy and the victim. In a mighty voice they called forth —"Slay him!"

But she said she must question him, and bade them retire for a little space.

Slowly and angrily they departed, and left her standing alone with him in the Temple.

"So at last thou art in my power. There is no hope for thee."

"I do not fear thee."

"Now swear — swear that from this hour thou wilt think no more of Adalgisa, and I will give thee life, and thou shalt go from before mine eyes."

"I will not swear."

"Dost thou know that my rage is terrible?"

"I fear not thy rage."

"And thy children?"

As she spoke he trembled, and with a cry of joy she cried out that he feared her at last.

"Spare them — spare them. Let me die alone."

"Thee alone? — all the Romans who are in Gaul shall die, and even Adalgisa shall perish in the flames."

"Pity! — pity!"

"What? Canst thou ask pity of Norma? Ah! she knows no more what pity is. See how I sate myself — how I glory in thy fear for her, and for yourself! Thou shalt suffer, as I have suffered."

Then she struck the sacred shield once more, and again the priests and the armed men came swarming to the Temple.

"Behold" she cried, "I have found another victim to your rage. A priestess forsworn; who hath forsworn her vows; who hath betrayed her country; who hath angered the god of her people!"

With one vast shout they asked for her name.

"Build the pile," she said.

Again they cried out for the name of the accursed.

Then over her heart swept a flood of pity for the maiden she was about to denounce. "What right had she, a guilty wretch, to revenge herself upon an innocent creature? Had not Adalgisa pitied her? had she done her any wrong? Could the poor girl save herself from loving the traitor? Had not she herself, she, Norma, fallen?"

As she hesitated, the crowd about her again demanded the offender's name.

Yet she hesitated. Then, turning to the trembling Roman, who each moment feared to hear her name the name of Adalgisa, the high priestess raised her right hand to her head, took from it the holy wreath, worn as the badge of purity; bent low her head, and said, "I—I am that guilty one!" So her better nature had conquered. All pride and anger gone! In her rage she would have denounced Adalgisa; but her sense of justice triumphed, and she denounced herself.

With a world of shame and repentance seething within him, the Roman cried, "No! believe her not, she speaketh knowing not what she sayeth!"

Still hiding her face, she said, "Norma speaketh the shameful truth!" And she saw her white-headed father draw away, degraded, from his brethren.

She crept up to her husband, and in her looks she told him what a loving wife he had destroyed. Then she whispered it was a destiny that they should die together, their ashes mingling on the same pile, and the same winds scatter them abroad.

All his old love for her returned in this sublime moment. Joy — a dying joy for her filled all his soul. She saw him look upon her as of old, with loving eyes, though they were now filled with pitying tears. "Pardon!" he cried — the most blessed words she could hear; for women will die that they may forgive men; "Pardon!"

But ere she could speak, her father crept up to her, and whispered that she had spoken falsely — that she was not so fallen — that she was yet pure. Then aloud he cried, "If the unyielding god who sees us holds back his angry thunder thou art guiltless!" Again he whispered, "Norma — my daughter — thou art guiltless."

What is it that she says which makes him start in horror? What is it that makes the blood redden his aged forehead? She has told him of her children — her living children.

He draws his robe from her, as though pollution were in her touch. His trembling feet bear him from her — his daughter — the once proud, magnificent high priestess.

But she follows him — prays to him to save them. Still his head is erect, and his eyes are tearless. She is his own flesh and blood. She bids him think of her own early days; she hoarsely cries that in a few minutes she shall be dead, and again she prays him to seek her children, who are with Clotilda, and to watch over them. Gradually his head falls lower and lower on his breast. At last, without fear of pollution, he lays his hand upon her head, and promises to fulfil her last desire.

The angry priests, muttering together, draw near —

9

fall upon her, fling over her the black veil of death, and
bear her away to the burning pile.

High blaze the flames, lapping about her — falls on the
body of the slain husband the flickering red light — the
Roman, who has died, pierced by scores of wounds.

The victim is sacrificed. Let them march on to victory. Their god is appeased! the sin which was amongst
them, which has drawn the favor of heaven from them,
is purged away by fire. Now, let the Romans fall — let
Gaul be free!

High blaze the flames, the red reflexions shimmering
from each white-robed priest, from the robes even of her
weeping father. Higher and higher till the victim is
turned to light ashes for the wind to drift whithersoever
it will!

ROBERTO IL DIAVOLO. (Meyerbeer.)

ROBERT THE DEVIL.

THE PROLOGUE.

Richard II., Duke of Normandy, who lived some forty years before the conquest of Great Britain by William, was without an heir to his dukedom. He prayed wearily for an heir — but never a child had he. At last he made a vow, in the presence of his courtiers, that if the demon's power could grant him a son, he would dedicate that son to the demon himself — sell him and his soul to the fallen angel!

The courtiers were breathless with astonishment.

Soon they remarked a change in the king, of which he himself was not aware. His face altered — his brow grew dark and heavy — his step slow, firm, and yet light. All color left his cheeks, and his lips grew pale and thin. The veins of his forehead could be traced — a deep blue color wandering beneath the skin; and his eyes grew mournful in their light. His hair fell about his head in deep waving folds — and he seemed the victim of utter despair. Yet he was known by all as the duke — the same as ever, and yet wholly changed. Nobody who had known him before this change came on but bowed to him as the duke; yet all who had so known him whispered that he was changed as never man changed who was not possessed of a devil.

Then great wonders began to be marked in Normandy. Storms would rise without warning and sweep over the land as though heaven was wrath. And while the storms lasted, moans were heard in the air — low, wailing, gentle moans — like the sighs of angels. Then, too, from the deep caverns came loud clattering laughs — peal on peal — like mocking thunder.

Soon it became known that an heir would be born to the duke. Then might be seen stretching across tho heavens a great flaming sword of fire, its edge ever trembling and surrounded by vaporous clouds.

At last, in a louder strain than any of that year — in the midst of shrieking winds such as had never before been heard by all who lived — the heir was born. Duke Richard was no longer childless!

Very beautiful was the child. But those who saw him, noticed that his features were like his father's, that his skin was colorless, and that his eyes lacked the sparkling brightness of infancy.

The attention of the courtiers being fully roused, they began to observe that the father regained his old looks and ways. His color came back; his eyes again flashed brightly, the sound of his foot was again heard, and once more he laughed. And they said among themselves that the change they had marked was caused by anxiety, and that now his son was born to him, he was himself again.

Yet a few years, and there was more strange court news. The child was as no other child; he would tear birds to pieces, screaming with joy the while; and waking in the night,— he would creep from his bed, open the shutters of his windows to the wind, and remain there with these same winds tearing about his head till the day came — when he would slink away to his bed. He did not love the light, and when night time came, then only was it that his eyes sparkled.

Yet a little — and then it was known that he only was gentle when both his mother, and his foster-sister, Alice, were with him. Then he was as child-like as any other child, and would lisp his prayers quite readily. But Alice away, and his mother distant, again he became the strange weird creature he was whispered to be.

Then came the rumor a few years later, of an old white-haired man being found dead, a child's jewelled dagger remaining in his breast.

Yet a few more years, and the whispers running through the court trickled out amongst the people, that the duke's son was a demon!

Sad grew the father, sadder and sadder. But it was

remarked that though his face grew grave and thoughtful, it was quite unlike the face he wore in that awful year before his son was born. And then it was whispered that if that time were referred to, the duke seemed lost, confused, and that then, and only then, something of that terrible look could be seen upon his countenance.

At last the heir was really grown a man; as handsome as any other in Normandy, as brave as any knight at court. But it was observed by many, that, handsome as he was, there was still a threat of the features which his father wore the year before he, Robert, was born.

Soon the people grew to detest the heir to the throne; for he swept through the land like a destroying angel. They abhorred him, and then it was they called him ROBERT THE DEVIL!

Then, broken-hearted, utterly cast down, but never wearing the old terrible look, the father, greyhaired and weary of the world, exiled his only son from Normandy, forbade him the land of his birth, and drove him from it.

Henceforth, till the old duke died, the people never felt the hand of "Robert the Devil." They heard of him, brave, fearless, terrible — ever conquering, never conquered, never even wounded. They heard of him, a monster — firing, destroying, waking up war wherever he placed his foot; and they trembled as they thought of the time when he should come to reign over them.

Meanwile the old duke and the sorrowing lady prayed hourly for their lost son; and joined in their prayers the lost son's foster-sister, ALICE.

THE LEGEND.

PART I. — THE TEMPTER.

A WORLD of tents — to the right, to the left — before or behind — a world of tents. And not dismal little canvas tents — but brave erections in cloths of gold and silver, and gay colors.

Truth to tell, all this was evidence of a tournament, given by the Duke of Messina.

Many knights intended to compete in this tournament.
Hence, that sea-shore near Palermo was gay as a garden
with colored tents, bright gold, shining armor, and brave
knights, sumptuously attired.

But no braver knight, more bravely attended, nor surrounded with more magnificence, was there than the
unknown, whose arrival had created such a stir in the
gorgeous camp.

This unknown knight, as he came from the tent erected
for him in the centre of his people's brilliant little encampment, was the observed of all observers.

" Dost know who he is ? "

" Wherefore comes he ? "

" I have heard that he will take part in the tournament."

Calmly the unknown knight came amongst the host of
gentlemen, bowing and smiling gravely.   They made
way for him — nay, some drew forward stools, and soon
the whole body of knights were seated about tables, more
or less magnificent, as the owner knight was rich and
brave, or brave only.

But he who drew on him as much attention as the
unknown knight himself, was his companion, a tall, solemn-
looking man.   His brow was heavy and dark, his step
slow, firm, and yet light; no color was in his face, his lips
were pale and thin, and the veins of his forehead could
be traced — a deep blue color wandering beneath his skin.
His eyes were mournful, his hair fell about his head in
deep, waving folds, and a kind of settled despair seemed
to hang upon him, and weigh him down.

This companion of the unknown knight was dressed
in garments of sombre hue, which hung in beautiful
sweeping folds about his person.   His hands were delicate
and white, and had in them a trembling motion, which
was at great variance with the close, firm mouth — little,
small, delicate hands, beautiful to look upon, and yet,
somehow, they looked like claws, the fingers seemed to
turn so naturally to the palms.

The knights commenced drinking and dicing at the
various tables.   Still the stranger knight and his companion sat by themselves at their table of bright metal, inlaid
with a winding pattern of jet.

Suddenly the companion whispered the knight, who thereupon, with a smiling face, turned to the body of gentlemen and saluted them, raising his goblet to them, and emptying it at a draught.

The knights readily responded to the appeal, and the next moment began conversing gaily with the two strangers.

The conversation, however, was soon interrupted by the arrival of two men, the one a squire of the stranger knight, the other a simple-looking country fellow, carrying his cap in his hand, and looking about him bashfully.

"Sire," said the squire, softly, "this pilgrim is a songster, and he cometh from Normandy."

"Normandy — dear, dear Normandy," said the young knight, and as he spoke the words he looked handsomer than before.

"*Dear* Normandy," said the grave, noiseless companion, as the hand lying on the table twitched. "*Dear* Normandy — I thought she had driven thee from her soil."

The young knight frowned the truth of these few words; and then turning to the pilgrim troubadour, gave him some money, and asked him what he could sing.

"Ho — ho!" said the minstrel, laughing and yet trembling in the presence of the splendid company. "Ho — ho! I can sing all songs; but, my faith, the best is the history of our young duke, whom they call Robert the Devil. He hath the evil eye on him, my masters."

Here he turned to the crowd of warriors who were drawing near, and did not mark the young knight place his right hand quickly upon his dagger.

"Sing of Robert, minstrel; sing of Robert the Devil."

Again the companion spoke. "'Tis but a poor minstrel."

The knight, obediently, it seemed, moved his hand from the weapon, and said, "True!" Then loudly he called to the minstrel, "Begin, thou."

"Oh, long ago, in Normandy,
 A valiant prince there chanced to reign;
He lived in peace — his wife he loved,
 And yet he lived a life of pain.

No child had he; for years and years
  He knelt at shrines — he knelt and **prayed**;
But all in vain — yes all in vain
  Was every sacrifice he made.

Then loud he swore, before the court,
  That if a son to him were born,
He would devote him to the fiend,
  And let his soul from Heaven be torn.

And then in time there came a son,
  Of all the land, the dread and shame —
Robert — Robert — the demon's own;
  And truly he deserves the name.

Not long ago — but at this day
  The valiant prince — if you'll believe —
He lives — he lives — as does the son,
  For whom the duke doth ever grieve."

As the gallants laughed at the ballad, and the earnestness with which it was sung, the minstrel stood with his back to the young knight. The next moment, the poor wanderer felt himself thrown to the ground; and, looking up, he saw a bright dagger high in the air above him. But restraining the holder of it, was a small white hand, the fingers of which seemed clawed about the other's wrist.

"'Tis but a poor minstrel!" he also heard a voice say.

Again the angry hand gave way, and fell to the young knight's side; but he bade some of his people seize the unlucky singer.

"I am Robert," he cried haughtily, and looking with defiance at the knights.

"The fiend!" cried the minstrel, falling on his knees.

"An hour for thy prayers, and the hour following thy purgatory! The next tree shall bear thee as its fruit."

"Good, my prince; verily we have come all the way to see thee, bearing a holy message."

"Message — we — who is your companion?"

"She who shall be my wife, if thou wilt let me live, master."

"A Normandienne, Bertram; a *Normandienne.* Are

there any women, think'st thou, their equals? Well, minstrel, thy wife's eyes have gained for thee a pardon. Send her hither."

"Good master."

"Thou art courageous!"

Some well-meaning man-at-arms here gruffly pulled the young minstrel away; and the last he saw of Robert was that he turned inquiringly to the knights, and that they all seemed eager to please him and be near him.

Yet quickly he turned from the knights, as he heard the footsteps of several men approaching, and with them the patter of a pair of light feet.

Then came in the midst of those rough, shaggy men-at-arms, a young, pure-looking girl. She had one of those faces not eminently beautiful, and yet at which you gaze with a kind of awe; holiness too proud to ask the aid of mere beauty! Men seemed to grow better as they looked upon this holy young face.

"Alice, dear Alice — my sister Alice!"

"My prince — my prince!" and the young creature flung herself upon the ground near Robert.

"'Tis my sister, gentlemen — our breath mingled on the same breast." And stooping he lifted Alice from the ground.

Strange — his face seemed much lighter than it was, and his very voice happier and freer.

As for his companion, whom he called Bertram, he rose from the table, kept his eyes from the girl, and moved away — farther away — farther away — till he was lost to sight in the midst of the tents.

The knights and gentlemen about seemed to know that she would speak to him privately, for they withdrew, and soon left a wide space between themselves and the girl Alice.

"Prince, Alice. Call me not prince. For I am to thee ever brother. So, thou hast come to see the exile? I have striven to die since last I saw dear Normandy; but I bear a charmed life, methinks. And now here, Alice, love itself is my enemy. But thou dost not say why thou hast come."

"My duty hath brought me hither."

9*

" Thou wast ever dutiful."

" The duty I owe to a dear mistress bringeth me to thee."

" Thou dost speak of my dear mother whom heaven bless."

" Then is she blessed in heaven."

" She — my mother !"

" And when thou shalt next see her, thou shalt be in heaven too."

" Dead — dead — my mother dead ! "

As he spoke Bertram glided from behind one of the tents, but the next moment was lost again. He turned his face angrily away as tears fell from the young knight's eyes.

" ' Go,' thy mother said, ' go, my Alice, to him, and say that, though he has made my heart bleed all his life, I love him heartily; that my last thoughts are for him; that I will pray for him and watch him through his dark hours of temptation. Tell him a terrible power enwraps him, but thou — thou,' and she laid her hands upon my head, O brother — ' thou shalt be his guardian spirit. I know that I may will it so. The hour must come when between me and the evil I have named my son must make his choice. Be thou near him then, O Alice, be thou near him, that he may pass surely on the narrow way to me!' Then she lay down, whispering that she would her son were by to close her eyes — and so thy mother died."

He hung his head and wept for pity and for love of that dear mother.

" You weep, my brother. I have yet more to tell thee. Before she spoke these last sad words, she placed a paper in my hands — her will — and she said, ' Bid him read it when he thinks he is worthy to read it.' "

" That is not now, Alice. Keep this will; something tells me 'tis best in thy hands. Read my mother's will now ! now that I am borne down with sorrow, against which I do rebel with all my strength. And, sister Alice — I love a lady who, I fear, doth dread me."

" Dread thee ? "

" She is the princess of Sicily. Her father looked on me with but a troubled eye — and so I strove to steal her.

But they fought bravely for their princess, and they saved her. I was down — down upon the ground, and I feared never more to see my own dear land — when a noble knight came to my rescue and delivered me. They fell before his arm as the blades of corn before the reaper. He saved me and he is my dear friend, my dear loving friend!"

As he spoke, Bertram was standing not far off, his face wearing a grave, almost a gracious smile, and his white right hand high above him playing with the folds of a flame-red tent.

"And the princess, brother — does she love thee?"

"Alas, sister — how should I know?"

"Nay — write to her."

"And who shall be my herald?"

"Who — I will be thy herald!"

He called quickly, and from his tent came a page. To this child he gave a rapid order, and the next minute he was writing a letter to the lady whom he would have stolen. When he had finished, he pressed the hilt of his dagger on the seal, as was the custom of the day.

"Go — sister of mine — fortune be with you!"

As she turned, she saw the knight, Bertram.

She was not afraid of him, but she seemed to know he was her enemy.

"Brother — who is that man?"

"Ah — Bertram! This is the noble friend I told thee of — wherefore dost thou regard him so strangely?"

"At home, in our village church, there is a picture which tells how the Archangel conquered Satan; and methinks I see in this man a resemblance to —"

"The Archangel?"

"No, verily, the other."

"Ha! — go, sister."

She obeyed him with a kind of fearless fear — a courage mixed with a desire to avoid this man.

"Thou art on good terms with thy conquest."

"Gratitude, Bertram."

"A good word — a *good* word."

"Were I bluntly candid, Bertram, I should say that near thee I never feel so honest as when thou art distant;

but now as I stood by Alice, I marvelled much how I
seemed to enjoy all things about me, and how much I
felt inclined to good."

" I love thee, Robert, as a father would his son — his
only son."

"Aye — but truly the advice of a father is ever godly."

"Is it likely I am the fiend? Tush! — drown your
cares; rejoin the knights and cavaliers — do as they do —
thou art no worse than they!"

" Verily! "

" *And thou art rich!* "

Diligently the white knight, as the knights began to
call the pallid Bertram — diligently the white knight
arranged the gaming tables, and when his friend took
the dice-box into his hand, he came and stood near him,
slightly smiling.

"Thou shouldst double the stakes, Robert," said the
white knight, after the youth had lost freely. "Fortune
hates the niggard hand. Double, friend, double." And
here the white hand gathered up the dice.

" Well, double the stakes! "

"Nay — if thou treblest, then thy chance is almost a
surety."

"Treble the stakes!"

Thrown, and lost.

"Fortune hates the niggard hand; hesitate not —
play!"

Again the rattle of the dice was heard, again the
knight lost.

Again, and yet again, he played and lost! Then he
even wagered the jewels from his robe; then his horses,
and his armor. Yet with fell purpose fortune turned her
back upon him.

" Fortune doth try thee, Robert. Still tempt her: she
loveth the brave."

Again he plays — again he loses.

" Gold is only a bauble — fling it, fling it, fling it away."

At last he had played away all — all! There was yet
the sword at his side, and the dagger with which he had
threatened the poor minstrel. Another moment and they
were lost too. He, Robert of Normandy, had disarmed
and beggared himself.

But in a moment his natural rage swept over him and he was frantic. With a threatening look at the knights about him, he wrested a battle-axe from a soldier near at hand, and was flying madly at the victorious group. Then indeed, Bertram showed himself a loving friend. He held the youth back, he entreated the gentlemen to pardon his ungracious anger. He shielded him. And all the while he trembled like a woman.

PART II. THE DECREE.

Not far from the camp stood the poor minstrel, waiting for his sweetheart Alice. While he was waiting, the knight Robert's catastrophe was achieved, and he was lying in the white knight's camp; lying with his face upon the ground, and the will to evil strong within him.

Raimbault the minstrel waited for some little time, and was beginning to think Alice would never come; when he heard a footstep, a light footstep, like but yet unlike the step of Alice. He turned, and before him stood the knight Bertram, his face more pallid than ever in the moonlight.

" Thou art Raimbault."

" Verily; whom the knight Robert would have hanged."

" He hath a strong will. Wherfore art thou here ? "

" To meet Alice, my good wife, so please thee."

" She is very poor."

" She hath a rich heart, and is no poorer than I."

" See, now, thou art richer than she is now."

" Verily, he hath given me gold ; real, real gold ! "

And the minstrel did not read contempt in the pale face; contempt that gold should make men happy.

" Thou art noble, and I will obey thee."

(Oh ! man, man, how weak art thou.) " So thou art to be married ? "

" Yes, now that the young prince has been discovered."

" Folly ! "

" Folly, nay, Alice is a good girl ! "

" Good ! Were I thee, I would wait, and be joyful.

Thou art rich; with gold man can do all things; and I have given thee gold."

"Verily."

"Be happy — feast — sin! Thou art young, there is time to repent — *time to repent!* (He smileth; his eyes brighten; he is lost.) Go, good Raimbault, Alice will follow thee; she may be thy slave. Go, go!"

The minstrel, weak and maimed with evil thoughts, went away stumbling in the darkness.

Then the smile passed away from Bertram's face — there was only to be read in it terrible despair battling with small hope! As a faint, warning, unearthly sound swept through the air, he trembled; and then he muttered that he had gained another soul! That he should have mercy shown him — mercy to him, the ambassador! Again the wild cry swept through the air, and Bertram's head fell. Clasping his hands together, he moved slowly into a deep lightless cavern, and was lost in the darkness.

Treading lightly through the moonlight then came Alice, to meet Raimbault, who was surely waiting for her — surely.

"Raimbault — Raimbault!"

No answer.

> "When I bade Normandy adieu,
>   Thus said a hermit sage to me,
> Damsel, to one beloved and true,
> Thou shalt e'er long united be.
>   Raimbault — Raimbault!"

The wild, wailing cry swept past her very lips as she ended her little ditty. As she heard it she trembled, and felt sure the very ground below her shook.

She began to run away, afraid, but a single word detained her — a single word, streaming through all the air — "Robert!"

"Robert!" She knew her duty was to watch over him till he had read his mother's will, so she stood still, trembling no longer. Then she thought the sound came from a dark corner near, and lightly walking to it, she peered in, and then drew back with mighty fear. She sped quickly to a rustic cross by the roadside; she fell at its feet, and lay senseless.

Forth from the cavern came the white knight. The doom, then, was irrevocable; unless Robert freely gave himself up — and before the morrow — they would be parted. Parted from Robert, whom he loved so much. "By his own will — by his own will, he must be won."

Suddenly he turned, as he heard a weak womanly cry, and he saw Alice lying at the foot of the cross.

"Thou here, Alice? What ailest thee? Thou dost draw away. Nearer — come nearer; nearer, I say. Dost fear me?"

Still she clung to the cross, the closer and more firmly as he approached.

"What didst thou hear?"

"Nothing."

"What didst thou see?"

"Nothing — nothing."

"Come near me."

With a loud cry, she crossed herself.

"Ah! thou knowest me!"

"I do not fear."

"Thou shalt surely perish, utterly — thou and thine! What hast thou seen? What hast thou heard?"

"Nothing — nothing."

"By a lie thou fallest."

As she flinched from him she saw Robert approaching, his head drooping, and his hands clasped.

"Speak not — fall away from the cross thou hast shadowed. Fall away, I say."

By the power of the untruth she had spoken, she was for a while conquered. Yet as Robert came near them, she felt her strength renewed. She ran to him to warn him. But yet again she was weak. The white knight raised high his glistening right hand, and she fled.

"What aileth her?"

"She is jealous of thee. Ah well — wilt thou not look upon thy best friend?"

"Best friend — thou art my only friend on earth!"

"Earth — what is earth? But thy fortune — Robert — thy fortune! I tell thee 'twas wrested from thee by unholy arts. Regain it by them. Where others have ventured fear not to venture thou!"

" What — can the demon have power on earth ? "

" Power! Power! There is but one power equal, or superior to his own. Power! Hast thou courage — is thy heart firm ? "

" Lay thy hand upon it . . . . ah, thou seemst to burn me with thy touch — take thy hand away."

" Thy heart is firm ; — e'en now firmer than before. Thou hast heard of the ruined abbey, whose inhabitants with itself were delivered to the powers of hell."

" I have heard, but not believed."

" Believe. In the midst stands the tomb of Bertha — why dost thou tremble ? "

" ' Twas my mother's name — 'twas my mother's name."

Think of thy fortune, Robert! Those who go to this tomb — speak not to the mysterious beings they see. But — over the marble effigy waves a branch of cypress. Who holdeth it holdeth power — POWER! wouldst thou be powerful ? "

" Feel my heart again — I fear not thy hand now ! "

PART III.— THE FALL.

A WILD spot: the accursed cloisters, where once lived sinning nuns. A wild spot, lighted now and then by the moon, when its light could flit down between the jagged, angry clouds which rushed floating by. The light showed a sombre square of burial-ground, covered with marble tombs, whereon lay effigies of the dead ; solemn white figures, still, still as death.

But something now moves in this accursed spot. Treading lightly through the moonlight comes a solemn-looking man, with small, white, claw-like hands. Arrived in the midst, he lifts these terrible hands above his head, and then he speaks — " O, ye impious women who sleep beneath these stones, shake from you your troubled slumber, and awake. 'Tis I condemned as you, who speak. But for an hour take life; move, breathe, and then sink to your weeping sleep again ! "

See — the white, sleeping figures move. The ground

breaks in long, ugly cracks. Stones are up-heaved, and trembling green lights flicker where once sacred altars stood. Slowly, forms, something like human, stand here and there, uncertain of themselves and each other, as with ghastly eyes they doubtingly peer into the darkness. Then, with noiseless steps, they approach and touch each other, stepping from side to side, as again and again a figure rises from the ground. At last, there are hundreds of these grim phantoms. Gradually, life seems to grow brighter in their faces. At last, they even smile; and then, behold, they are as human-looking as the pale, unyielding moon will let them look.

"Ye hopeless — hear me! A warrior whom I love shall come to pluck the weeping cypress; if he trembles, seduce his better soul from him, and with all your earthly charms, strive to destroy him. Rejoice — rejoice — for thou knowest whither I would lead him."

Again with his light, solemn step he passed away — his hands now clasped within each other.

Suddenly the weird figures seemed to shudder, as with evil eyes they marked the warrior's fearful coming. Hiding behind pillars and broken stones they watched him. He hesitated — then came forward. Then again he stopped. At last he stood near the cypress, which waved above the tomb of the abbess. But as he stretched his hand to pluck the fatal branch, he looked upon the statue of that abbess, and the face seemed as the face of his mother, wrathful and angry. He fell back stunned and speechless.

Then out trooped the living-dead — their features no longer ghastly, but full of wicked, sensuous life. They surrounded him; they tempted him; in a circling band they drew him to the fatal cypress. Yet he hesitated. Then they held to him a golden cup, brimming with delicious wine. Drinking it, again the evil look was in their faces. But when he returned the cup, they smiled again.

At last he plucked the branch, and held it in his hand.

Then the faces turned again to hopeless death. The figures screamed in their joy about him — loudly and more loud.

While he — his heart now failing him — shrank down

upon the ground and hid his eyes with his hands — one of which still clasped the terrible cypress branch.

PART IV.— THE CYPRESS BRANCH.

WHILE this horrible scene was being enacted — away in her father's palace was the lady whom Robert loved — the lady who also loved him — the princess.

The Princess Isabelle of Sicily sat watching the magnificence about her. It seemed to mock her sorrows. The King had decided upon marrying her to the Duke of Grenada, a Spanish noble.

Her solitude was broken by the entrance of a few young maidens, who, after the custom of the time, took advantage of the intended marriage to present petitions to the bride.

Among the girls who thus entered was one superior to the rest. She had a pure-looking, almost holy face — not more beautiful than any there, perhaps, but glowing in its purity and high resolve.

This young creature presented a letter to the princess. Isabelle took the paper languidly enough, but no sooner had she glanced at it than her face sparkled with joy.

'Twas the letter Robert had given Alice before the sun went down. 'Twas Alice who now gave the letter into the hands of the young princess.

Happily Isabelle read the letter; but her happiness was of short duration, for barely had she finished it than her tirewomen came forward to deck her for the bridal.

Then came grand lords and ladies of the court — a full procession — to accompany the bride to the palace chapel.

They stood without the great room and upon the wide staircase leading to the broad open doors. They were talking gaily and looking towards the princess, when suddenly the breath of death seemed to pass over and among them. Their words faltered on their lips — their hands fell listlessly to their sides; and though they could see and hear, they had no power to move. They saw no figure of a wild-looking, handsome man, waving on high a black, sweeping cypress branch. They saw the doors close of themselves, and remained motionless, like statues grouped about the marble stairs.

Slowly he came on, his face now almost the counterpart of Bertram's. On and on, to the spot where the princess sat, immovable like the people on the stairs. She saw no one before her eyes; she sat wondering what the sudden silence meant, when suddenly before her stood Robert—surely, and yet not with Robert's face.

He waved the branch over her fair head, and broke the spell.

"Robert! Robert!"

He looked upon her with a love so terrible that she cried—

"Save me—save me from him!"

"Thou art beautiful, and I love thee! Thinkest thou I would tamely leave thee to another? Look on me! Not the Robert thou didst once know. Look on me! Mark on my face the hellish joy I feel in seeing thee!" And he asked himself how he could look upon her fear and grief, and feel no pain?

"Robert, thy eyes are fire, and thou lookest on me as thou of all men least should look. What is thy power — and thy knightly oath — and thine honor? Hast thou forgotten them?"

"Hate knows no honor, Isabelle, and love is often hate."

"'Tis not too late, Robert! But now I saw thy old self again upon your face. Robert, be thyself. Fly, or they will kill thee!"

"I here am master; tremble—bow before me. None can see me—none can move but at my will. Thou art lost—*lost*—*lost!*"

The Princess fell on her knees and clasped her hands.

For a moment he trembled, · but then again his face was as Bertram's face, and he cried, "Thou art lost!"

Then, as she knelt to him—"Robert, Robert, thou whom I so love—to whom I gave my troth, look on me;

look on my terror! Mercy! For thyself, mercy! For me, also, mercy! Think of thy faith — thine honor! As you love me, mercy! See me, at thy feet. Robert, Robert, thou whom I so love, mercy — mercy!"

He doubts, he trembles, then his face changes to its old expression, as he stoops and lifts her from the ground. "Thou hast saved thyself."

"And thee, too, Robert."

"Nay, thou hast destroyed me."

"I — destroyed *thee!*"

"I cannot live away from thee; let me then die."

And, in a rage of agony and disappointment, he tore the branch to atoms.

As he did so the spell was broken. The lords and ladies on the stairs moved and spoke; and one of them, pushing open the great doors, saw the knight flinging from him the remains of the cypress, and saw, also, the princess stand apart, one hand trembling before her white lips.

A moment, and there was a violent and terrible noise of swords torn quickly from their scabbards.

The princess put out her hands beseechingly for him. But 'twas useless; fifty sword points were directed at his heart. Towards them he ran fearlessly, his warrior face — the old, good face — all-powerful now.

Suddenly, a knight was beside Robert, fighting for him. Steadily this new combatant beat a way for the beleaguered knight, and at last regained for him and for himself free air and liberty.

PART V.—THE REDEMPTION.

"BERTRAM, thou must come with me. See, here is the cathedral; wilt thou not enter? The sanctuary is sacred, and none will dare try to move me from it. Come."

"So, thou brokest the mystic branch; thy heart failed thee."

"Oh, it should not fail me again."

"There is yet a means!"

"Yet a means? Name it; I care not what—I will obey."

"Thou shalt sign a solemn pledge."

"Surely, Bertram, surely."

The white knight took a quivering paper, from his very bosom, as it seemed; dipped a reed in an ink horn at his side, and offered both to the young knight.

As he was about to take them his hand trembled — not from fear, but because of a soft hymn which welled forth from the cathedral — a hymn of praise, sung by reverend old monks and faithful nuns.

"What! dost thou again tremble?"

"'Tis the hymn my mother often sang to me in the days of my innocent childhood. Hark, again!"

Yet once more the sacred sounds swept through the air, "Holy, holy, holy."

The white knight turned away and frowned; but as the sound died out he said, "Come, let us go. What, again thou tremblest?"

"How gentle does this music make me. As I hear it I have no fear — feel no hate. Again, dear sounds, again."

Yet once more the hymn arose, "Holy, holy, holy!"

"He would be free! What, shall all my hope be destroyed? Never!"

"I am happy, I am happy!"

"Wherefore? That thy rival is blest; that they offer up prayers for him?"

"Again; again."

"Go also; kneel humbly — *humbly;* and pray for his welfare too! Go, coward."

The knight looked quickly at Bertram; gazed earnestly into his face; and, as the religious sounds again spread through the air, he cried out: —

"BERTRAM, THOU ART MY GREAT ENEMY!"

("Is there no mercy for me? I his enemy!) I thy enemy, Robert? Do I not love thee? Who supported thee in battle, whose arm hath been thine, who would lay all the riches of the world at thy feet? I, who am —"

"Thou who art —"

"Dost thou remember the whisperings in thy home? Thy living father, who was changed, and thy mother's woes? canst thou not guess my name?"

The youth looked on the white knight for a moment; then, with a flood of tears, he was on his knees before this strange being; his arms around the white knight's waist, and Bertram's small white hands resting on his head.

"Fear not; I will never leave thee!"

Then Robert saw the face above him change. He turned quickly, and found Alice standing there.

"Robert!"

The white knight stood before her toweringly; but, as she stepped forward, he, with all his power, was forced to give way.

"Robert, I bring thee a happy message. The duke of Grenada cannot pass the holy threshold of the cathedral."

"Come, my son, leave this woman."

"And the princess awaits thee."

"Come, let us depart, Robert."

"Thou darest not forget thy oath to her."

"Hasten, Robert, the clock is near the hour, the last hour of my stay. We may not part, my son — my only son — we may not part."

"My heart turns to thee — yet my vow!"

"But thy duty — thy duty!"

"Our duty," cried Alice. "Our duty is to him whom thou fearest." And without fear she stepped up to the white knight.

"My son — my only joy — thou wilt not hear her!"

"Let him hear me — I speak as I am bidden."

"See, Robert; here is the parchment. Turn from her, fix thine eyes upon me, and let us go, to be for ever near each other."

"And thy mother's will — O Robert." Quickly he turned from the tempter to the holy maiden, who held in her hand his mother's will.

"My son, turn thy face from her, and look on me."

"My mother's writing — my own mother!"

As he perused the paper Bertram stretched forth his hands towards the youth, placed them pleadingly together, and even wept.

The knight read the paper, and then, looking up from it, the white knight knew that his power was gone, for Robert drew away from him, and taking the hand of Alice, placed it on his own head.

As he did so, the clanging of the church-bell told them that midnight was come.

Then despair, horrible despair, crept over the face of the white knight. He came one step forward, placed his trembling claw-like hands above the head of the saved knight and vanished. Vanished in the black night, as a wailing cry filled all the air.

Saved! the good spirit had saved him—the good spirit working through a poor country girl!

See him creeping to the church he spurned till now. Saved — saved!

"Holy, holy, holy!" Behold the sanctuary, and the sacred priests, ready with open arms to receive the sinning, but now repentant Robert!

And so was the spell his father's wicked vow entwined about his life, for ever broken and destroyed. So was Robert the Devil transformed to Robert the Man, loving and beloved.

IL TROVATORE. (Verdi.)

THE MINSTREL.

PART I.—THE DUEL.

In the fifteenth century, and away in Spain, lived the
Count de Luna — he was as handsome as he was implacable, and folks said he was as implacable as death.

In the fifteenth century too, and in Spain, a great lord
was a petty king, and would as frequently make war
against his neighbor on his own account, as on account of
their common country.

But proud and implacable as he was, he had bowed to
the power of love, and weak and pliant in the presence
of the Lady Leonora.

His castle was always well defended — for attacks might
be made on it when least expected. Attached to his castle was a palace with superb grounds. On the approach
of danger both palace and grounds were deserted, and all
communication between them and the castle was cut off
by the up-heaving of heavy draw-bridges.

One night the guard-room of the palace was filled, as
usual, with soldiers off duty and various servants; but
both soldiers and servants were half asleep. This being
observed by Ferrando, he woke them up by saying it was
near the count's time for passing through the room.

Said a man, One had better sing or tell tales if he
would have " us " keep awake.

The proposal being generally approved of by the company, Ferrando settled himself easily in his seat, and told
them the old, old tale.

" Draw about me — all of ye. Thus it was. The old
count had two dear sons — the cares of his heart. Well
— they were sleeping peacefully — their good nurse near

them, when she awoke and saw — now, my comrades — what did she see?"

"Go to!" — and "go on!"

"A hag — of a verity, a hag! And, of a verity, she screamed aloud, which brought about her a score or so of frightened men, who bestruck themselves strong enough to drive forth the hag with many a blow. Well, what then, my comrades?"

"Aye — what then?"

The child dwindled till his flesh was as colorless as the white of thine eye, Gomez. Nay, start not, man. And he hath screamed, as child has never screamed before. Wherefore and thereupon, my comrades, they did search out the hag — fall upon her bravely, and fitly burn her. But, my faith, she had a daughter. By the rood, such a daughter! She hath sworn, my comrades, as I, man-at-arms, would never so beswear myself, she hath sworn to destroy the little one; and she hath done it; — for he is lost — gone — and there's an end, on't."

"And therefore hath the old count died?"

"He hath died o' heart-crack, a sore complaint, my comrades."

"And the living count —— ?"

"Interpose not thy remarks, youth. The living count hath sought for his brother, and hath not found him. And I will wager my chain here, which I won in honest fight, — that never shall human eyes see him again. But mark you this: — I could tell the thief — I could tell her — yea — marry, could I."

The castle bell began to toll, whereat a marvellous trembling came upon the men-at-arms. Then was heard the roll of a drum. The time to relieve guard had arrived, so the story-telling crowd dispersed.

————

Go we now to the gardens of the palace, where the moon looked down upon two female forms, the lady Leonora and Ines, her confidante. Leonora had been telling Ines of her love for some unknown knight. She had seen him at the last tournament — where he appeared in dark mysterious garments and carried a shield without armorial bearings. He gained the laurel; and she, — she placed that laurel crown upon his brow. But, alas! — almost immediately after, came news of a civil war, the assembly within a day dispersed, and with the rest went the unknown warrior. But — but a few nights since she heard, near her casement, the plaintive notes of a guitar and words of a plaintive song. Drawing near, she heard her own name sighed, — again and yet again; till the very air seemed to breathe forth the name of Leonora.

"'Twas he — by the pale moonlight she saw 'twas he."

"I would, lady, that you forgot him."

"Counsel easily given, Ines, but not kindly taken. Come, let us return to the palace."

Scarcely had they departed when the Count di Luna came softly towards the palace windows, that he might be near his beloved Leonora. The garden was bathed in the light of the virgin moon.

As he approached a window, from which streamed the rays of a taper, he started; for a voice he well knew began to carol forth a song — the voice of the troubadour, who had dared approach the palace windows, night after night, for many nights.

> " O'er the lands of the earth
>   He hath wandered from birth;
>   He hath much — wants no more,
>   Does this same troubadour.
>   He hath treasure, I'm told,
>   Quite surpassing all gold,
>   'Tis a lady — no more.
>   He's a rich troubadour."

Hardly had the last words floated away on the air than the window, behind which was the taper, opened on to the broad terrace. The next moment the Lady Leonora was softly coming down the broad steps to the green lawn.

As she reached the foot of the marble stairs, she saw a manly figure. Guessing it to be that of the singer, she ran and put her arms about the new comer's neck.

"Thou art late. I have counted the moments for thy coming."

But the voice of her lover sounded many steps away, crying, "Faithless one!"

And then, by the light of the moon, which had seemed darkness to her, coming from the illuminated chamber, she perceived how terrible had been her mistake.

"Maurico, thy Leonora thought this man to be thyself; he hath not yet spoken; by his voice I should have learnt my fault."

The count, in a whirl of rage, cried, "He is but a coward or a sinner who wears a mask — remove that mask."

The troubadour took off his mask.

"Thou, Maurico," said the count. "Thou! — proscribed — condemned to death — a rebel."

"Defeat thy rival, count, by calling here thy guards."

"The only guard I call is this — an honorable one."

And the noble drew his sword. "Thou shalt degrade its blade."

The troubadour quickly drew his sword, and the count was rushing upon him, when cried the former, "Softly, count. Brave men quarrel not in the presence of trembling women."

"Follow me!" cried the count; and, spite of all the entreaties of the lady, the rivals strode on to some secluded spot that one might slay the other.

PART II.— THE GIPSEY.

AMONG the gipsies!— the gipsies — then, as now, and as who knows through how many hundreds of years? — daring, brave, handsome, light hearted rovers!

In Spain the zingaras, or gipsies, have ever increased and multiplied. The land seems to foster them kindly; and, at the period of our tale, they were so numerous, that quarrelsome or rebellious nobles would frequently enlist the sympathies and strong arms of the tribe. Often and often the prowess of the zingaras provided the turning points of the Spanish victories.

The band of gipsies to which the troubadour, Maurico,

belonged had taken part in the rebellion against the king. Hence the expressions used by the count when he discovered Maurico in the palace gardens.

The gipsies were encamped within and about a dilapidated old building, amid the mountains of Biscay, not far from the castle of the Count di Luna. In their encampment they sang, and laughed, and danced as though they were masters of the earth, instead of being surrounded by danger, and, possibly, near to death!

The flickering flames of a wood fire, which shone on the faces of the wild band, paled before the coming day. But there was yet sufficient light to see Maurico, muffled in a cloak, lying at the feet of a stern-looking gipsey woman, whom they called Azucena.

Suddenly this woman started from her sleep — stood up — came a step or so forward — and cried, " Look — look ye! See how the flames dart at her, as she is dragged along. Look ye, how they all crowd about, and are merry over her trouble — a poor gipsey led to death! See how their faces are bathed in blood! There! she screams in her agony; and higher, and yet higher the mocking flames rise about her; and now I see her no longer. Gone — gone — gone ! "

Suddenly she came to herself, and half whispered, " Vengeance! I will have vengeance."

" Still that word, mother," said the troubadour, Maurico, rising from his hard bed.

As the sun lit up the shadows in their dark skins, the gipsies moved away in various directions. Presently, the gipsey-mother and gipsey-son were alone together.

Suddenly she began again to speak of her terror. " She was accused of witchcraft — my mother; and they burnt her here — here, on this very spot. I see her, thick chains hanging about her limbs, dragged to this very spot. I stood near, holding thee in my trembling arms. In vain she sought to bless me; they struck down her hands, and drove her forward. Then it was she cried aloud, ' *Avenge me !*' And canst thou not read the words here — here on my face? "

" And thou didst obey, my mother? "

" I stole the old count's son. The child wept and clung

to me. Why should I pity him? They had shown HER no mercy. Here with him I came — a fire blazing as when my mother died. I closed my angry eyes, raised high the child above my head, and dashed it screaming on the burning embers. Then, looking forth again, I saw — I saw — the count's own child still living."

"Then thou hadst destroyed —"

"My son — my own dear son."

And she grovelled on the ground, hiding her face with her hands.

"Then am not *I* thy son?"

Suddenly she looked up fearfully. "Yes — yes, boy, thou art my son — my own dear son."

"And yet thou didst say —"

"Ne'er heed what I say, son, for am I not sometimes daft? Thy mother — have I not been a tender mother to thee all thy life?"

"There's not a day that I recall when thou wast otherwise."

"Did I not save thy life, my son — my own dear son? When they said you lay dead on Pelilla's field, did not I seek thee — find thee — cure thee? Thinkest thou I would do all that for the stranger?"

"A noble wound! If, when Di Luna rushed upon me with his score of men, I fell — I fell as falls a soldier, mother."

"Di Luna! And so he rendered thee reward for the life thou gavest him, when he stood before thee in a duel, and was conquered. Thou shouldst love Di Luna, e'en as thy brother; Di Luna, whom thou, my son, hast spared." And she laughed scornfully.

"I may not know wherefore, but when my sword was pointed at him — when the next moment I should have slain him — some power held back my sword, and I heard whispered in mine ear the word, 'Mercy!'"

"But if again thou meetest him, thou dost promise to slay him — without mercy? Slay him," she said again, as if to herself, and turned away without waiting for his reply.

As she turned, a trumpet sounded near at hand.

A herald appeared, and brought Maurico a scroll from

the rebel chief, in whose ranks he and his people now
fought. The stronghold, Castellor, had been wrested from
the royalists, and Maurico was ordered to take its command. The scroll also incidentally mentioned that the
Lady Leonora, believing in Maurico's death in the late
fight, was about to take the veil in a neighboring convent,

The gipsey-mother saw him turn, and quickly fling his
cloak about him, and place his helmet on his head.

" Whither goest thou ? "

" To duty."

" I command thee, stay."

" But my *general* commands me."

" And thy wound ! thou must not leave me. It may
open again ; and if I am not near thee, son, thou mayst
die ; therefore thou shalt not go."

For answer, he wrapt his cloak more closely about him.

She threatened him, but it was useless. Soon she was
gazing after him as he wended his way down a mountain
pass.

Go we now to the cloisters of the convent, where the
luckless Lady Leonora was about to take the vows that
were to separate her for ever from the world:

Love had humiliated and degraded the count, as it
hath humiliated and degraded many a better man. As
he could not honestly possess himself of the Lady Leonora, he had now come to steal her — tear her away
from the altar. He had not come alone, for love had also
made him a coward. He had brought with him a score
or so of his followers to snatch her from amongst a host
of women.

See them hiding behind pillars, and in shadows, creeping softly and meanly, as robbers and cowards do.

Then came the widowed Lady Leonora, surrounded by
old friends, who would fain accompany her to the door of
her life-long prison.

She sighed as she heard the low religious chant from
within the walls of the convent — henceforth to shut in
all her hopes. But she was determined. He was dead

— her love. Killed on the battle-field, and she would mourn for him in the silence of a convent cell.

"With good, hearty old friends," said she to the attendants about her, "see me to the altar, and then — a long farewell."

But as she turned towards the sacred door the count came quickly from behind a broken pillar, and tremblingly said, "Nought can save thee — thou art mine."

"Mercy!"

"There is no Maurico now to save thee. He is dead — he is dead."

He ran towards her, but suddenly he stopped, and trembled like a coward, as he was. For there, standing between him and his expected prize, was the minstrel, Maurico himself! Standing there was the very man he had seen fall on the field; or — or, was it his shade?

And Leonora? After an instant of doubt and hesitation — for she, too, believed her lover was not of this world — she ran to him, and, with a great cry, threw herself upon his breast.

The consternation of the dastardly count hardly gave him much time for deliberation; but, on a signal, his followers swarmed out from their hiding places, and surrounded the lovers. But they reckoned without their host. The next instant Maurico and the Lady Leonora were protected by trusty arms.

In vain the count drew his sword and rushed upon the troubadour. Twenty swords were pointed at him — twenty swords that in an instant would have touched his heart. But their leader, Maurico, who still suffered from his wound, bade them spare him.

So the count yet stood alive in the midst of his followers. Stood unsubdued by the mercy which had now been shown him; stood, and vowed vengeance against his gentle foe; stood and cursed him as he led the lady away. Away from him, the rival; away from the convent, away to Castellor, which had fallen into the rebels' hands, and whose governor was Maurico, the Warrior Minstrel.

PART III.— THE GIPSEY'S SON.

SURELY, mercy may sometimes be a fault, if extended to a heartless man.

The Count di Luna held his life by the great mercy of the gipsey stranger, but he determined to reduce the castle, whose master was that gipsey, hoping that he might yet destroy a hated rival. No breath of gratitude was in his heart. He thought only of revenge, and turned away his face from the light.

The count's camp was pitched within a mile of the doomed castle. The count's soldiers were lying about — playing, singing, gambling, and polishing up their arms — when the soldier, Ferrando, was seen to run quickly towards the count, who was walking moodily amidst the troopers.

" One hath seized a gipsey woman, general. She is a spy, perhaps."

" Let her be brought hither," said the count, and looking up as the sound of a tramping, mixed with smothering cries, reached his ears, he saw a middle-aged, stern-looking gipsey-woman being dragged towards him by half-a-dozen thick-bearded men. She showed no fear.

" Wherefore do ye thus treat me? What evil have I done ye?"

" Come hither, woman. Answer me truly."

" That shall be as thy questions are."

" Whither goest thou?"

" Whither the gipsies ever go. To the north or to the south, sometimes westward, yet ever gladly to the east."

" What wouldst thou?"

" My son — I only crave my dear, dear son. He hath left me, and I seek him. Thou tremblest — perchance thou hast lost a mother."

" I seem to know thy features. When my younger brother was stolen, the woman who did carry him was like thee."

The noble seemed to be thinking aloud, rather than addressing the gipsey. " Fifteen years — fifteen long years since I lost my younger brother."

"Thou art, then, the Count di Luna?"

She saw she had spoken hastily, as soon as she had uttered the words, so she prepared to fence with them.

"How knowest thou that?"

"They say the gipsies know all things, master. But let me go; I may trace him for thee."

Suddenly the old soldier, Ferrando, cried out, as he peered towards the gipsey, "By our Lady, 'tis she herself!"

"She! who?" cried the count.

"May I never be absolved, general, if 'tis not the gipsey who stole your brother! Did I not see her carrying the child away, hid in her rags? Aye, marry, did I. Did I not tremble when I saw her but just now, as though I knew her? Aye, marry, twice did I."

"She trembles; her lips betray her," said the count. "Bind her — till the cords cut deep into her flesh. Ah! scream — scream; there is no help."

"Help, Maurico!" cried the gipsey, in her agony. "Help, my son! help, my Maurico!"

"His mother — HIS mother!" said the count. And running to her, he raised his hand, as though he would strike her. But he had not yet fallen so low as that.

She looked at him fearlessly. "I defy thee! Thou — the base son of a base father. Frown — hope! — hate, thou monster. Vengeance shall be mine. List to that, I say — "VENGEANCE SHALL BE MINE!"

He turned from her contemptuously. She to talk of vengeance! She a miserable, bound gipsey.

He to his splendid tent — she to imprisonment; and yet she had cried, "VENGEANCE SHALL BE MINE."

Turn we to Castellor, where are Maurico and Leonora.

As they stood near the balcony, all in all to each other, she heard the distant clash of arms. "Prythee, wherefore that sound?"

"Thou art so brave that I fear not to tell thee all. The Count di Luna is encamped but a short mile away. Before the night is gone he will have besieged this castle. Nay, trouble not — your courage and our swords will be victorious. It is, I know, a weary prelude to our marriage, dearest. Of victory I am sure — yet should I fall — my last thought will be of thee — only of thee — Hark! — they await us in the chapel."

As he spoke, the chanting in the neighboring chapel reached their ears, and each knew that the priest was waiting to join their hands.

They were moving towards the holy place when a soldier ran quickly in, saying he had woeful news.

The gipsey Azucena — was taken.

" Azucena ! "

" They say — she will be burnt ! "

" Ah ! the air grows hot and dark about me."

The lady Leonora put her hand to the troubadour's brow, but he put it aside and cried — " My mother — they would slay my mother."

" Thy mother ! "

Then she bade him take arms. No fear had she now. Victory must be with him who fought to save a mother! "Onward !" she cried. She buckled on his sword, and was the first to cry, " farewell." Her last words were " love " and " victory ! "

———

PART IV. — VENGEANCE.

MIGHT is not always for the just. Were it so always, where would be the honor of virtue?

Maurico was conquered, and the castle fell into the hands of his enemy the Count Di Luna. The minstrel languished in prison, with but one consolation in this life — the presence of his mother. They were imprisoned together, that to their miseries might be added the pain of a last separation.

Upon the fall of the castle, the Lady Leonora took flight, hoping against hope. But when she heard he was condemned to death, she came weeping to the foot of the castle, and leant her face against its wall.

With her came the faithful soldier, who had ever been at Maurico's right hand — who had told him of his mother's capture, and who had escaped from the battle at the last moment, when he saw his master taken prisoner, and all hope had fled.

She bade her faithful escort leave her, and then hope whispered that perchance she could save him. And when she trembled she looked at a ring she wore, and found new courage.

Swelling on the night air came the dirge of the monks within the castle —

> " Miserere for him whose death is nigh ;
> Who from life and its joys must be quickly hurled ;
> Miserere for one who, a moment more,
> Must bid farewell to this dreary world."

The solemn words made her tremble and look for a moment with fear upon the ring she wore; but the next instant she started forward with horror, for she heard his voice —

> " Ah — death itself is slow
> When death itself i wooed —
> When death itself is peace.
> Leonora — fare-thee-well ! "

" Great Heaven! — can I believe my senses? "
Again the solemn voices of the monks arose —

> " Miserere for him whose death is nigh ;
> Who from life and its joys must be quickly hurled ;
> Miserere for one who, a moment more,
> Must bid farewell to this dreary world."

Again his voice arose; his last words for her —
" Leonora — Leonora, a last farewell."

And again she looked on the ring as she thought, " her love was as great as his."

Then suddenly she heard footsteps, and she shrank into the shadow of the frowning tower.

The count passed over the very spot from which she had just fled. Then he turned and said to some person unseen by Leonora —

"Thou markest my will; when the day breaks — the scaffold for the son — the pile for the mother."

Cruel, implacable as he was, he even blushed in the dark night as conscience whispered to him that this scaffold and this pile were but a poor return for his life, twice given him. But he had gone too far to recede; and, with a curse, he cried, "'Twas fatality, and Leonora." Then he asked himself where she was — where she had hidden herself, and, in an agony of hot, unrestrained passion, he cried out, "Leonora, Leonora, where art thou?"

"She is here!"

As he started at her voice she came forward, pale and trembling, from the shadow.

Asking himself how she could have reached the terrace, after an effort he said, "What wouldst thou?"

"Canst thou ask me? His life."

"*His* life! Ask me for mine own as well."

"See, I kneel to thee."

"Thou art mad."

"Nay, see how humble I am; look on me — at thy very feet."

"Look in my face; dost thou see pity there?"

"I cannot look upon thy face. Pity — I can say no more; — pity! Hath he not twice saved thy life? Wilt thou not. render back half thy debt? Kill me if thou wilt, for I heard thee say 'twas by me thou art what thou art. Kill me, yet spare him."

"As thou speakest, thou dost but ensure his fate. I would I could make him suffer a hundred deaths. As ardently thou lovest so fiercely do I hate. Let go your hold. Nothing can purchase his life."

"No price?"

"No price."

"Yes, there is one, and I do offer it to thee — myself."

"What hast thou said?"

"What I do mean — myself."

"I dream."

"Nay, open his prison-door, and I am thine."

"Wilt thou swear it?"

"By my dead mother's name!"

"Enough — he is free."

He strode quickly to the door of the tower, and spoke rapidly to the goaler within it; but she had had time to offer herself a sacrifice to her honest love. She took the ring from off her finger, opened a little receptacle in it, removed from it a small grey pellet, and swallowed it. "Thou shalt have a dead bride," she whispered. When he again turned towards her, her hands were pressed to her sides.

"Saved, saved," she cried to herself, as the count — smiling now for the first time for a weary while — took her right hand and courteously led her to the grand hall of the castle.

Enter the hopeless prison, in which the gipsey and the troubadour were trying to console each other as each weary moment rolled away.

She was lying on the bare ground; he sitting at her feet, his hands crossed, and smiling as he looked upon her.

"Dost thou sleep, dear mother?"

"There is no time for sleep, my son."

"Thou tremblest with cold."

"This is a tomb. I would we could escape."

"Escape!"

"Yet, fear not, son; they cannot torture me."

"No; for art thou not a woman?"

"Oh, they would not fear to torture a woman. But look on my face, canst thou not read death there? Nay, cry not, 'mother,' as thou weepest. They shall come to bite their lips with anger; for they will find me dead."

Then, as he buried his face in his hands, she was seized with unconquerable fear. "They come — they come. Save me — save thy mother. I am indeed, indeed thy mother."

"No one cometh; all is quiet."

"Fire! death by fire! I am afraid — I am afraid. I see her now — my mother. They dragged her and bound her to the stake. There! there! See, the flames have caught her hair; how it shrivels up! And her eyes — ah! she can see me no longer. Help! help! save me!"

And she fell back senseless upon the hard earth.

"Mother, if thou dost love me still — if thou wilt hear thy son's prayers, be brave and calm."

As he spoke, she came again to a knowledge of her fate.

" I am worn and weak; or thou shouldst not bid me
be calm and brave.   I am — very — worn — and — weak."

And she fell peacefully to sleep, as in her native mountains; free as the wind, and surrounded by her tribe.

Then he knelt by her side, hardly daring to breathe, for
fear of waking her.

No fear of awaking her; for she is aweary, and *will*
sleep.   They shall come and bear him away from thee,
and still thou shalt sleep on and peacefully; he shall bid
thee his last farewell, and still thou shalt sleep unheedingly.

Suddenly he started, as a light fell upon the prison
walls.   He looked upon his sleeping mother, and thought
it was her funeral pyre.   But as he turned, he saw the
light came from the door, upon the threshold of which
stood the queen of mercy — his dear Leonora.

She ran to him, and nestled on his breast.   Then she
cried, " Thou shalt not die, for I have saved thee."

" Thou hast saved me! how ? "

" Nay," and she hid her face, and pointed to the door.

" And thou — thou comest also."

" My life — my hope — I must stay here."

" Stay here! "

" I pray thee go, go."

" Where thou goest I will also go; and where thou
stayest, I will stay."

" But if thou stayest thou diest."

" Without thee what is life ?   Why do thy eyes turn
from me; what is the price thou hast paid for my liberty ? "

" No price is high for a dear human life.   There is yet
time.   For my sake, go! "

" But he for whom that life is bought may cast the gift
from him as I do, and as I also cast thee away."

" Ah, Maurico — 'tis not the hour to hate.   Peace and
good-will, peace and good-will. "   She turned deadly
pale, and rocked to and fro in agony.

His arms were about her in a moment.   " My transient
hate — my fears, were but excess of love."

" Speak on, speak on, death vainly strives against the
warmth of love.   I feel for thee.   Speak on, oh, my

Maurico. But a little, and envious death shall have his will."

"Leonora — Leonora, thou art dying!"

"Ah — yes, she goes to be thy herald. Unrelenting is the poison. If 'twill let me stay near thee but for a little, little while. Ah, place my cold hand against thy trembling lips, thou knowest now my wealth of love for thee. I did mean to save thee at my life's expense; this was the price. No more, no less."

"And *I* fell back from thee — turned from thee. Mine eyes have fallen from my face. Leonora — look up, look up."

"I am too weak. Keep your hands about me. So let me die! Ah, 'tis well as it it is."

At this moment the count came to the door to claim his bride.

"Good-bye — oh, good-bye!" and she sank exhausted in his arms.

Even this scene did not soften Di Luna. No reverence had he for the poor dead lady — no reverence had he for the maddened lover, straining his eyes upon the dear one's face. The guards, who waited without, came in, and tore them asunder.

"Mother," he cried, "mother."

But she slept on unheedingly. Slept on while they bore her son away to death.

Again, as he was wrenched across the threshold, he cried, "Mother." And now, she trembled in her sleep.

Again, and again, she trembled. Then with a shudder she awoke. She looked round quickly, and clasped her hands about her breast, as she no longer saw her son. Then her eyes rested on the count. With a bound she was by his side. "Thou hast stolen him — thou hast stolen while I slept."

He stood immovable, and uttered not a word.

"Mercy — stay the axe — I will save him — I will save him." And she clung, shrieking, about his feet.

"Save him — nought can save him — see there."

He dragged her to the window, and she looked wildly forth.

"Dead — dead — dead!"

Then she turned from the window a changed woman. No tears. No horror. Smiling even a grim smile.

The noble stepped back in wonder. Then he thought that she was mad. But no.

Proud — erect — she stood before him.

"Have I not said — 'Vengeance shall be mine' — in thy tent, where thou didst cut my flesh with cords. *Vengeance* is *mine*. Thou look'st towards the window. Gazing through it — I say — *Vengeance is mine*. He is dead — thou sayest he is dead. Hear! — thou knowest me to be the gipsey who robbed thy father of thy younger brother. Ah well, I am indeed she — and that brother,— rejoice in the act,— and that brother — look again through the window — mark that body. THOU HAST SLAIN THY BROTHER. Shrink — shrink! — VENGEANCE IS MINE. Hadst thou but have let him wake me that he might say farewell, I should have pitied thee and saved him — but thou didst steal him from me while I slept. Dead! — he will carry thy murderous name with him. Have I not said, 'VENGEANCE SHALL BE MINE?'"

And then her troubles were over, and the last she saw on earth was the bleeding body of him she called, and whom she loved, as a son.

While he, the triumphant count, stood there alone.

Alone. With remembrance. With remorse.

ERNANI. (VERDI.)

PART I. — THE BANDIT.

WHO are these houseless men, lying about amongst jagged rocks, laughing gaily, card-playing and drinking — the setting sun lighting up the place with a red glare, and bathing their brown faces crimson?

The sun writes the truth upon their faces; they are men of blood — lawless, houseless plunderers; singing, laughing, card-playing — waiting for the night, and for their captain, that they may begin their work.

They keep a sharp look-out about them though, and at last, start to their feet with a great noise, as a young handsome man comes suddenly in.

He seems to have nothing in common with these men, for he is elegantly dressed, and looks every inch a cavalier. His face is not ferocious; and yet — yes, they have saluted him as captain, and he waves his hat in courteous reply.

Not a thief by birth! O no! this man really is John of Arragon, the son and heir of the Duke of Segovia and Cordova, killed to please the will of King Carlos of Castille. The son narrowly escaped the same fate, but fortune favored him. He reached the Sierras, which, like all mountains, offered the fugitive safe shelter. Hundreds upon hundreds flocked to his standard, and John of Arragon changed his name to "Ernani." But he dwelt not so far away from his old life, as not to be able to see the Moorish castle of Don Ruy Gomez di Silva. Nor was it for the sake of Don Ruy he kept the castle ever in view. The don had a ward, Elvira, who had held out a hand to save Ernani when the blood-king was tracking him; and for this generous act she had gained his love, giving, however, her own in exchange.

The face of the chief is sad. Would that his men could bear his grief for him, and they would willingly stand between him and death.

"Thank you, brothers—thank you," replied the chief, as he leapt down amongst them; "but my woe is so deep that even your cheering voices cannot drive it away."

"The chief, then, is in love—"

"And likely to lose his love, brothers, if you will not help him."

"Help! Yes—yes—yes."

"See you that castle there, below us, with the red sun full on it. She lives there—she lives there! If you love your chief, you will help him to bring her here—here to the mountains."

"Yes—yes—yes!" replied a hundred voices.

"She would follow me anywhere; she will love the mountains for my sake. You *will* help me!"

"Yes—yes—yes."

"Then let the night be our friend; when darkness has come we will storm the castle, and then she is amongst us."

"Hurrah! hurrah! hurrah!"

And while the noble chief was waiting for nightfall, the lady whom he loved was looking from a window of the old castle towards the mountains, amongst which she knew Ernani dwelt.

A real Spanish lady was Elvira, as could be seen, had anybody been able to spy her at the window. But, alas! no one could, for Don Ruy, her guardian, hid her as a jewel which he feared might be stolen. He was seventy, she was seventeen; his hair was grey, hers was black, and yet he had determined that she should marry him.

As she sat at the window, watching the sun go down, she was at least at peace, for the grandee was away from the castle. And so she sat pensive, and dreaming of Ernani, perhaps, hoping he would come and carry her off. At last it was night time, and still the don had not returned.

Suddenly the door of the quiet room opened, and a procession entered; gay in itself, but of ominous import to the lady at the window — a string of young maidens bearing rich gifts, marriage gifts; for, truth to tell, the old don had resolved that his marriage with Elvira should take place on the following day. Listen what they say to her.

"How many Spanish maidens envy thee, fair lady Thou wilt be the highest lady in all the land. These gifts alone are a mine of wealth. To-morrow thou wilt be a bride."

"I thank you; but the dazzle of diamonds will not lighten hate into love." And she again thought, "I would Ernani were here, and that he would fly with me."

Hardly had they, the present bearers, left the room, than she turned quickly at the sound of a cautious footstep — she thought it was that of Ernani. But no; another had learnt the secret entrance her bandit lover used. Another, who had watched and seen Ernani enter. Not a mean man this. A king — a KING! Don Carlos, King of Castille. She saw her error, shrunk back, and cried out: —

"Sire, you here, at this hour!"

"I love thee, lady, at all hours."

"Ah, no — sire."

"Nay, lady, a king is never told he lies."

"I pray you, leave me."

"I will leave with *thee*, lady."

"With *me!*"

"Ah, if I were Ernani thou wouldst not start thus. Come, thou canst not know the wealth of love I have for thee."

"And my honor, sire?"

"Thou shalt be honored by all the court."

"And by myself, think you!"

"Thou wouldst sooner be honored by Ernani's out-laws — thou lovest the robber."

"Sire, each heart has its own secret."

"And I, have not I mine? Ah, Elvira, from the moment I first saw thee I have loved thee. I love thee for thyself, as I would have thee, lady, e'en love me. But — but if a crown will earn me smiles from thee, I offer you the half of that I wear."

"*With* thy crown thy love is too high for me, *without* it, 'tis too low."

"Thou shalt fall."

"A king — never forget you are a king!"

"I forget I am a king when I am at your feet."

He ran towards her, as her eyes flashed defiance upon him; but the next moment he drew back, for she had snatched a jewelled dagger from his girdle.

"Stand back!"

"You see I do stand back, fair lady. But there are more hands here than mine to pluck the dagger from your grasp."

Suddenly he perceived a great joy flush her fair cheeks. At the same instant he heard a footstep behind him, and turning round, he saw a man, a handsome, daring-looking man, whom he was sure, seeing the lady's joy, was none other than Ernani, looking on him defiantly, with hate and anger! Ernani, who had entered the castle by a secret door — who was there to bear away the lady — who had come to save her from yet further misery.

"Thou art Ernani — I know it by the hate I feel sparkling in my eyes. Hate! Does the eagle hate the worm? No, he despises it. Rejoice — scourge of a peaceful country! Let thy meanness comfort thee. Wert thou greater, I would raise my hand to thy destruction. I have but to call, and thou art lost."

"Thou knowest me and fearest me. I am so mean that thou hast robbed me of my fame; — so mean, that thou hast taken from me my wealth; — so contemptible, that thou hast slain my father! And now thou would'st rob me of my bride. What difference is there between us? Thou, noblest, with a crown on thy head and without risk of life — *I* risk my life to rob where I have been robbed. What difference is there between us? Cowardice! Now — let us be equal. Defend thyself."

"Hark! some one is approaching," cried Elvira, in an agony of fear — "forget your quarrel, at least for a little while, — if you are found here I am lost. So, please you, forget your hates, and leave me."

Still, the two men moved not — still the footsteps nearer drew.

"If you love me, both of you — either of you — leave me — leave this place!   Too late — too late!"

For at this moment the door was thrown open, and on the threshold stood the master of the castle — the Don Ruy — his attendants behind him — witnesses to his dishonor.

"Do I breathe? — here, in the sanctity of my house — to find two men quarreling — as though disputing for some poor booty!"

He was a grand old gentleman, with hair as white as honor.   But his age had not brought him humility.   He was as proud as he was grand, and as merciless as he was proud.   Turning to his court — for this grandee retained a court — he continued: "You, Senors, witness this fall of mine!   This woman whom I loved, but till now I thought as pure as the moonlight streaming on her through the window.   As for these men — my hands are weak, but one can bear a sword — the other a shield.   Yet not here within my house shall blood be spilt.   Go, pass before me."

The last few words were addressed to the king and Ernani, and then for the first time he looked upon them — but the light was too feeble for him to recognize even one of them.

"Gently — gently," said one of these two.   But the don cried out haughtily.   "None but myself had right to speak."

Suddenly, high and loud in the air, sounded a herald's trumpet.

And, within a moment or so, it was whispered among the crowd, still without the door, that it was a king's messenger.

A lane was made for him by Don Ruy — who turned to the herald, imagining that he came to him.   Following the herald came torch-bearers.

On came the herald.   He did not salute the master of the castle — he did not even look at him.   On past him, past one of the men found in the lady's room — past the lady even — up to the second intruder, before whom he knelt.

"The King," cried many, as the herald knelt, and

above him stood, now in the full light of the torches, the brave man who bore a dagger sheath, but not a dagger.

Then said the king, "Don Ruy, I came to consult thy friendship for me."

See! The proud Don Ruy has stooped his head; then he steps forward, and humbly welcomes to his house "the king."

As they crowd about the king — as the latter receives their homage — the robber Ernani and the lady were forgotten, and they stood apart, whispering —

" Until the sun sinketh again in the deep
        Resist the proud tyrant, nor yield to dismay ;
For Ernani unbroken thy precious faith keep,
        And to-morrow from peril I'll bear thee away."

" Thou knowest I'm thine — know also this steel
        Can save me from tyrants — nor do I repine ;
In wretchedness even 'tis solace to feel
        That my heart — that my faith, will for ever be thine."

See, now, the proud noble stoops to kneel before the outraged king, and entreats his pardon. And, graciously, the king accords it.

Hark! the king demands a safe pass for Ernani. He still thinks the eagle should not injure the worm. See, the bandit passes away, out to freedom. The king is gracious, the don trembles, and the Lady Elvira is presented to the king in due form and courtesy.

Part II.—The Guest.

With the next day's sun came Elvira's marriage day. No hope of flight — fate was against her, and so her envious women dress her for the sacrifice.

The great hall of the castle is filling with lords and ladies, retainers and vassals. There is a sudden stir — 'tis the entrance of the duke, dressed grandly, and wearing all his orders. He walks gravely to his grandee's chair, and sits down as the crowd do homage.

In those days — four hundred years ago — it was the custom to give shelter to any pilgrim who should demand it. Hence scarcely a day passed without "the castle" containing many guests of this sort.

The don had hardly sat down when a servant approached and said that a pilgrim was at the gate, craving hospitality.

Gravely and readily was given the order to let the pilgrim enter. The next moment a tall, upright man, dressed in the pilgrim's loose sombre dress, came forward and up to the don as he sat in state.

"I greet thee, noble knight."

"Good pilgrim, be at ease. Nor whence thou comest, nor who thou art, we do not ask. Be welcome for this day and night. My hospitality I promise thee."

"The deepest thanks I have are thine!"

"We do not ask for thanks — the guest is as the lord. But stand aside, good pilgrim." And the don rose and walked quickly to the door to meet a lady dressed in bridal garments.

"My bride," he murmured.

"His bride," said the pilgrim, throwing his cowl from his head a little, so that those who had chosen to look might have seen a handsome, brave face within it. "His bride."

"Senor — as well as others, a poor pilgrim should offer thee a marriage gift — I offer one of price — my head. Let no one fear — I will no resistance offer — I am Ernani!"

"He lives — he lives," said the bride to herself.

The don's face contracted angrily as he saw the pilgrim standing — his gown flung off — fearless among them.

"Deliver me to the king — a price is on my head. Hark! they have tracked me even here. I hear the horsemen near the castle gate. Deliver me, and thou shalt gain a high sum for my head!"

In those old times a brutal ferocity was atoned for by a kind of honor of which, in these degenerate days, we have but slight idea. Above all, the promise of hospitality was sacred, and to keep it inviolate the accorder would run all risk and dangers. When life was so unhesitatingly taken, perhaps this sacredness of hospitality was the only means whereby men lived in society. But for it each man would have kept to his own home as a wild beast does to its lair, and no more have trusted himself in his neighbor's stronghold than that same beast would besiege another's den.

Hence the don, having promised to give hospitality to the pilgrim without conditions — awarding it to him no matter whence he came, or who he was, he was bound to save this guest from his pursuers, even though they were the royal troops themselves.

So far this man whom he abhorred — whom he recognized as the intruder of the night before — for this man the very marriage was stayed, and he, the grandee, left his hall for his ramparts. And soon there was heard the clicking of the lowering portcullis, and the raising of the drawbridge.

As he left the great hall the gentlemen followed him; and the only man left in the room was the false pilgrim, standing in the midst of the frightened women.

Their chief, the Donna Elvira, motioned them away, and soon she stood alone with the robber.

"Ernani — Ernani — they told me thou wert dead!"

"And thou didst believe them."

"Yet I hoped — I would have hoped even to the altar."

"And then — then thou wouldst have sworn to love Don Ruy."

For all answer she showed him the dagger she had wrested from the king. So, she would have hoped till living death were forced upon her, and then she would have welcomed death itself.

"The king — the king!"

Again the cry was heard, "The king was at the gate." The king demanded that it should bow to him, and again the clicking sound was heard as the bridge was lowered before the king.

But ere the king reached the great hall, the lady and the robber had left it. The don returning, discovered them together.

Again, despairingly, the robber offered his life, but the

don was inflexible ; hospitality he had promised, and hospitality he would grant. True, the very necessity of this hospitality would nerve his hand to greater vengeance when the time came. But now his guest's life was as his own ; so the trembling Elvira saw the don open a secret sliding door, and her lover was safe.

"Begone to thy rooms, Elvira — the king — the king."

No second bidding needed she. And when Carlos came proudly into the great hall he found there only the grandee, humbly bowing.

"Fair cousin, why in arms, we are not at war? You bow — enough. Let it be known there is but one king of Castille. When his sword is in its sheath all swords must sleep."

"Your Majesty can never think a Silva dreams rebellion."

"Prove yourself loyal. The chief of the rebels has sought refuge here in your castle. His men destroyed, he seeks to save himself by your protection. Deliver him!"

"If the king will hear his subject. A pilgrim came and entreated hospitality, which I promised. The loyaty I bear the king will not allow me to betray his subject."

"Thou wouldst lose thy head, fair cousin."

"Rather than mine honor."

The king turned and gave some orders to the gentlemen about him. Then again his eyes were upon the door. "Thy head or his, my lord? "

"Mine own."

Yet a little, and the gentlemen of the king's suite returned, saying the royal troops had searched the castle through and could not find the rebel.

"Thy head, I say."

But as he spoke, the king's eyes turned from the grandee, and rested upon the Donna Elvira, coming towards him with hands clasped, and white open lips.

"Mercy — mercy — king! "

"Mercy, fair lady! Thou art mercy's self, and even kings must here obey. But thou shalt be the don's best hostage for his loyalty."

"Nay! my king. Is there no other hostage for a loyalty yet unshaken? She is my only hope, my only joy. I have loved her from her very birth. My king, thou wilt — thou wilt not take her from me?"

"Then Ernani. One or the other."

" Nay, I am steadfast in my loyalty. Therefore — please you, my king — take her — my hope, my life."

"Come, lady," said the king, seizing the hand of the luckless lady. "Come, I'll strew thy path with flowers. Time shall bring thee no heavy hours. Rather let smiles be where now are tears and whitened cheeks. Come, come."

So with his prey the Christian king departed, leaving the old lord bent and wretched with grief.

But not for long — not for long. Now, his eyes sparkled, for hate was there. His head was erect again, and his breath came and went in short angry catches. He ran to the secret door, and as though calling to a dog, he bade the robber chief come forth.

As Ernani stepped into the room, the grandee ran to the wall, and took down a couple of swords.

"Now, robber, doubly robber, vengeance is mine."

"What! will a grandee fight with a poor bandit?"

"At least, thou wast born noble, even if now thou art vile. Follow me!"

"No, no."

"What — has all nobility left thee?"

"I am still too noble to fight with age, Senor."

"See — is my hand firm?"

"Again, thou hast saved my life!"

"That I might take it from thee."

"Ah, well! Kill me, thou hast the right, perhaps."

"Kill thee." And the old lord raised his sword as though a rat were before him.

"Kill, kill. Yet hear a prayer of mine."

"Prayers are for heaven, not man."

"'Tis a prayer to man — to thee."

"Speak on."

"But once again, but once again, let me see Elvira."

"If thou wouldst see her, thou must travel. The king has torn her from me."

"The king, the KING! Old man, the king loves Elvira."

"Loves—loves Elvira! The king loves Elvira! Vassals, vassals," he weakly called as he staggered to a seat.

"Nay, call me vassal, and the strength of this strong heart and arm is thine."

"Stand from me. Aid from thee—from thee! Thou who art doomed to die."

"My life is thine. I know my life is thine. At any time my life is thine. But let me live to hate where now thou hatest so strongly."

"Thy life at *any* time is mine. True. Well, wilt thou promise me thy life at any time I ask it?"

The other hesitated for a moment. Then took from his side his hunting-horn, and placed it in the unwilling hands of the old lord.

> "Take thou this horn, when from it sounds a blast,
> 'Twill tell Ernani that his days are past."

"Upon what dost swear that oath?"

"The memory of my murdered father."

"So be it. Let heaven's darkness fall on thee if thou dost break thy word."

PART III.— THE PARDON.

CHARLES the Fifth was not unforgiving, not even inclined to be harsh; and no one ever disputed his bravery. When he was intriguing for his election as emperor — the election which made him the great emperor, Charles the Fifth — Castille was full of plots to oppose his plans, nay, to take his life; and at the head of these conspiracies was Ernani and Don Ruy.

On the very night when the electors were to assemble to decide on the choice of an emperor, the king heard that this most formidable band of conspirators, formidable because its members were moved by personal hate, were to meet in the subterraneous catacombs of Aquisgrana, the royal open burying-place.

The king fearlessly determined to be present at this traitorous assembly, and to crush it at its work. Soldiers

were posted about the cavern ; the king himself remained
concealed in the tomb of one of his ancestors, and the
hour of the meeting was close at hand.   The king had
given orders that if he were elected emperor, cannon
should roar from the castle-walls, and that thereupon the
lords of the court should present themselves at the cavern, that they might see how a great king treated rebels
and traitors.   Charles also commanded that the Donna
Elvira should be conducted to the gloomy spot.

As the conspirators slowly gathered in the wide central
space of the catacombs, no sounds were heard but those
they themselves made.

Creeping — creeping guiltily, they came, and stood in
a whispering throng.   Then came the casting for a regi-
cide : he on whom the lot fell was to slay the king.

There was a little rustling of papers, and then one slip
was taken from the heap, brought quickly to the light of
a lantern, and the name upon it read.

" ERNANI ! "

" My father — my father !   I will avenge thee ! "

" Ernani, thou knowest my voice ? "

" Surely, thou art Don Ruy."

" I am Don Ruy.   I am the master of thy life ; yield
me the privilege you hold."

" No, no."

" Think ! thou mayst fail, and thou wouldst then surely
die ; yield me the task ? "

" No, no.   And mightest not thou also fail ? "

" See, here is thy horn !   I will give it thee back, if thou
wilt let *me* strike this guilty man."

" No."

" What ! can I not kill thee by a note on this same
horn ? "

" I care not ; chance hath given me the order, I will
not barter it."

" Then fear me, Ernani."

Suddenly boomed over their heads the loud sound of
triumphant artillery.   Victory ! victory !   Charles of Castille was the Emperor Charles the Fifth.

As the sound roared forth, the emperor strode from his
concealment, and the soldiery coming quickly forward,
behold the conspirators were prisoners.

Again the cannon burst forth, and the next moment the courtiers were coming down among the tombs by torchlight, to congratulate the new emperor.

The electors headed the procession, and, kneeling, greeted the emperor by his new title.

"The will of heaven be mine. See these traitors; they have formed against me a plot. Tremble, ye traitors, as ye learn an emperor's vengeance! Let the plebeians be cast into prison; let the nobles bow to the block."

"Accord the block to me, O emperor! for I, Ernani, lord of Arragon, Cordova, and Segovia."

Why does he start and tremble? Is it that he sees his dear mistress again flinging herself at the emperor's feet? Again she pleads for mercy; again she asks for happiness and justice.

"Thou askest, lady, what is already granted; what the king could not forgive, the emperor will not look on as offence. . . . . You are all pardoned! . . . . And as for thee, my lord Ernani, let the memory of the father's death be forgotten in the justice done his son. Thou art again lord of Arragon, Cordova, and Segovia; and thy lady — behold her!"

The new emperor placed the hand of Elvira in that of Ernani. And then again the emperor spoke, "YE ARE ALL PARDONED!"

But how black was the menacing cloud near at hand. The old grandee, sternly frowning, and pressing his hand about a certain hunting horn, whose blast was death.

PART IV. — THE MASQUERADE.

IN Sarragossa, in the palace of the reinstated lord, his marriage was being celebrated. Happy at last — the couple bound together for life.

The palace of Ernani, or rather Don Giovanni of Arragon, was all ablaze with light; and the pale moonbeams, shooting into the palace-grounds, showed numberless mysterious masquers flitting to and fro. It was a grand masquerade the bridegroom was giving.

But among the masquers was one who spoke to no-

body; who took note of nobody; who moved along stealthily from group to group with a firm merciless tread.
They who looked very closely at the mysterious masquer,
noted that his hair was white, and that his eyes glittered
fearfully below his mask.

" Who is he ? "

" See how angrily he looketh about him."

" He seemeth a wizard ! "

Still he took no notice, but went from group to group.

———

" Gentle love — thou hast not seen thy lover's face so
oft to-night that thou shouldst wear thy eyelids down ;
look up, and light my very soul ! "

" In truth, dear husband, I have some mysterious fear,
I know not why, and yet I tremble.   A coming ill seemeth near."

" Those who have felt the storm do tremble when the
lightning flashes. But now our sky is all unclouded, love;
our life as happy as our hearts are light.   See how tranquil all about us seems ; see, too, the guests are going, the
twinkling lights die out each after each, and tell us that
the morn is breaking.   Dost thou still fear ? "

" Who that has had nought but fears for what he hath
— I fear, my love, I fear.   For thee — for thee alone."

A low winding blast upon a horn swept past their ears.

" Why dost thou tremble, love, my Ernani?   Is the air
cold ? or have I frightened thee, perchance ? "

Again the low destroying blast swept past them.

" See, see, Elvira ! dost thou not see his eyes sparkling
in the darkness ? I see his white teeth as he smiles mockingly ! "

" Ernani ! Ernani ! I am terror-stricken ! "

He looked quickly at her, as though he would confide
in her some great terror.   Then a world of pity flooded
his face, and he said quickly —

" 'Twas an old wound, Elvira, which leapt in pain.
Leave me a little, love ; I'll come to thee soon."

" A loving wife doth lovingly obey.   I go."

He followed her with his eyes till he could see her no
longer, in the moon-light, and then he knew he was alone

with death. Yet for a moment hope sprang up; the
sound was surely fancy; the dread of what might be. He
was so little used to joy that now it was come he could
not believe in it. So he let go the dagger he had touched;
and rising, prepared to follow his bride.

Then again came the wailing sound, and following it
were whispered the mocking words —

"Take thou this born — when from it sounds a blast
'Twill tell Ernani that his days are past."

"MERCY!"

Creeping through the moonlight came the mysterious
masquer — his face seen now to be the unforgiving, revengeful face of Don Ruy, come to seek atonement for
the loss of a bride, and to demand the fulfilment of a rash
oath.

"So soon!"

"Aye — so soon!" I come to turn thy myrtles to cy-
presses."

"Think — oh think! I have drunk from the cup of
bitterness all my life — have tasted no happiness till now.
Tarry a little — be merciful — tarry a little."

"'Take thou this horn — when from it sounds a blast
'Twill tell Ernani that his days are past.'"

"Again — mercy!"

"I am a Spaniard."

Then came flitting through the shade the white figure
of the doubting bride. As she came near the spot where
she had left Ernani she saw the grandee, and needed no
words to be assured that her foreboding was no weak
fear.

"See, she comes — thy bride — to see thee fall. Forward, fair lady — forward, fair widow!"

"Don Ruy — art implacable?"

"As death — 'Twill tell Ernani that his days are
past.'"

"Don Ruy — I love him — I love him! Mercy, dear
guardian, mercy!"

"That thou lov'st him is thy fault. Hasten, Ernani, if
thou art of Spanish blood."

"Elvira — do not plead — it weakens my weak arm!"

But she was too loving to obey — too terror-stricken to look upon her husband. She still remained upon the ground pleading hopelessly to the don for mercy. Mercy, she could not tell for what; yet mercy she saw he had the power to give.

"I knew it. Fate hath but spread this feast before mine eyes to make yet blacker the bare truth. Don Ruy — if — if —"

"' Take thou this horn — when from it —' "

"Ah —"

There was a dull thud, a swingeing sound, and the bridegroom was on the ground, pressing his hand upon his side.

Spanish honor was appeased — he had paid the debt of the life he had placed in the grandee's hands, and which he had refused to purchase in the catacombs.

"Farewell — dear love — farewell. Nor seek to follow me. Thou dead, who is there left in all the world to love or think of me? As thou dost love me, live for me — weep for me — guard my grave! Our happiness was but a phantom. I knew 'twould vanish. Farewell — farewell!"

And still with his hand upon his side, his head fell upon her breast, and he spoke no more.

There, on that spot, there were but two living human beings. The young bride mutely clasping her dead husband in her arms; and the remorseless noble standing over her unpityingly — unforgivingly — and glorying in his terrible revenge!

MARTHA. (Flotow.)

CHAPTER I.

THE Lady Henrietta — no, I will not divulge her surname — the Lady Henrietta was ennuyed and bored — though she lived in the sixteenth century. Furthermore, the honest fact is, that being bored, Henrietta was far from agreeable, as two persons knew, to wit, Nancy, her ladyship's sharp waiting maid, and Lord Tristram, who was old and a fool.

A fool decidedly — for courting a young and handsome woman. Hence, by inference, you see that the Lady Henrietta was young and handsome. Yes, young, handsome, rich, noble, healthy, and miserable!

She could not tell anybody why she was miserable, but on one particular day, when her ladyship was rather more miserable than usual, within her castle at Richmond; at Richmond statute fair some hundred yards off, not a single lassie offering herself out for hire, on the dismal conditions of that day, but was happier than my Lady Henrietta.

On that particular morning she was sitting snappishly at her toilette — though, indeed, she was naturally good-tempered; but aristocracy *has* its miseries, or where *would* the balance of things be? — when Lord Tristram arrived. One might have solemnly declared, without seeing my lord's face, that my lord had been tripped up by youth and had never overtaken that early visitor. The way in which the fair Henrietta treated him was a satire upon man's supremacy — indeed, this lord of Cosmos was a supreme fool.

The old youngster coming in, she told him to kneel. He did. She told him to get up. He did. She bade him shut the window. Click went the latch. Immediately he heard the command to open it again. Then and there he did it, and was rewarded by the sight of a pair of scornful shoulders.

And it was just when her ladyship was stamping her foot pettishly, and the lord looking on in a doleful state, that, i' faith, such happy sounds of singing stole through the window! Why, the voices must have belonged to creatures as happy as lords. No, no, no; a mistake, kind reader, a mistake. As happy as — as poor servants not knowing where their morrow's bread lay. Blessed — blessed — blessed hope, which paints that same to-morrow so gaudily that we have not much grief for our rags and crusts of to-day. And the morrow is to-day, and the morrow yet again, and still we hope on, hope ever. Faith, I would sooner be Tom Tumbler at the next show, with the "hope" of getting on Drury Lane boards, than the richest and handsomest peer in England, if he has no aspirations whatever.

These poor servants were going to the statute fair, to get hired, if they could; to hope for hiring if they could not; and, as they went on, they sang merry songs.

Oh! the sudden thought struck her. There was not a poor servant wench but wished to be a lady; why should not a lady wish to be a servant wench? 'Tis but the law of reciprocity.

The very thought made her more joyful, or rather, less dismal than she had been for some time. A moment more, as her natural good-temper came back, and she had decided. Yes, she would dress in that peasant masquerade dress of hers; and she would be — Martha; and Nancy should be — Nancy. And — and would not his lordship join them? Of course his lordship would. His lordship should be — John!

His lordship used plainer language than he had ever before used; his lordship, in a word, declined flatly; but ah! love will lead self-satisfied old-young men the queerest of dances; so, it is but just old parties should go through their little hops and jigs, and puff and blow all the way through the pretty little pas.

So let us just imagine Martha, Nancy, and John, making for the fair; Martha laughing as she has not laughed for years, Nancy playing a polite, impertinent second, and John doing his very best to be gay and happy. Poor fellow!

CHAPTER II.

EVEN in this enlightened hour, at statute fairs English girls stand in rows and exhibit their points — mental, menial, and physical, to as many farmer's wives as have tongues and eyes. 'Tis not a happy mode of hiring servants, choosing them as you would sheep; but let us hope that a better time is coming.

And, of course, in the dark middle age, statute fairs were held in England; hence, we naturally get to that fair for which those blythe singers were bound, and whom Lady Henrietta and her court of two followed.

'Twas the usual scene: stout farmers' wives marching about in the superior manner, the girls looking about in rows of rosy cheeks and giggles, and scandal everywhere; for at statute fairs the way in which the maids run down their old mistresses, and the way in which the mistresses run down their old maids, can easily be imagined.

In one quiet part of the market stood Lionel and Plunket, brothers and farmers.

These two personages had come to hire two servants; but whether the servants were of a very bad kind, or the farmers very difficult to please, certain it is that these latter were servantless, though the fair was half over.

They had not long lost their mother, a good mother, so they were not to be satisfied with any kind of servants.

I love to make all plain, and therefore I may as well say at once that these brothers were not brothers. If affection and sacrifice, and all that kind of thing, made men real brothers, they would have been brothers; but the same woman did not bear them. Plunket was the real son of the mother whose death we have just mentioned, and Lionel was the foundling, though as the

mother had been a good woman, she had always had
enough love for both her own son and the foundling, and
some, indeed, left for the world in general. This old
mother, in a year long gone to sleep, had opened her
door late one night, for being good she had a stout heart,
and there found a man and child upon the threshold.
The man died, the child lived to be her foundling, and
her second son. Who the man was they never learned.
He died, and made no sign. Ah, yes — that little diamond
ring given to the good woman in keeping for his son. If
ever he was in trouble, this son of his, the ring was to be
carried to the queen. But Lionel had never been in any
trouble up to the time of the good woman's death; soon
after which the two farmers wanted two servants, and
came to the fair to seek them.

And thus naturally are we brought back to the fair.

Neither Lionel nor Plunket could find a single servant
to their mind, much less two, and so they went wandering about, and submitted to the hard sarcasm of the
would-be hired.

Meanwhile, in another part of the fair the sheriff was
doing his duty *like* a sheriff. Said duty being to an-
nounce, as usual, that all agreements between servants
and masters were binding for twelve months — said binding to be a legal fact from the very moment the said
servants took earnest money from the said masters. Also
the sheriff was a blessed go-between, announcing to the
servants the wants of the masters, and to the masters the
wants of the servants. 'Twas surprising how clever all
the servants were according to their own showing, and
how doubtful the masters were in believing those same
statements; and indeed, 'tis true these statements might
have led an observer to surmise that all the good servants
in the county had been discharged at one and the same
moment.

And it was just at the precise moment when the
sheriff was going to retreat, overwhelmed by numbers,
that the Lady Henrietta — or Martha, rather — Nancy,
and the troubled John — Lord Tristam — came upon the
noisy scene.

Now, neither Martha nor Nancy were within a hundred

yards of the sheriff, when Lionel and Plunket marked them both, and bore down upon them.

As the lord saw this, he was very urgent indeed that all this disreputable masquerading should come to an end.

Whereupon Martha called out to my lord, "Sir, I'll not have thee for my master." And Nancy added her objection too.

"So please thee, good man, thou canst not force the girls to serve," said Plunket, at whom the old lord stared. However, he could not stare long, for all the servant girls about, hearing Martha refuse the old gentleman's service, pressed about him, each playing her own little trumpet at the top of her voice. And, to be short, the old young lord thought himself perfectly justified in running away. Lady Henrietta was Lady Henrietta, but that was no reason why his lordship should be worried dead, so he thought he had better go; and did.

"Nancy, Nancy, they are looking at us." True, indeed, spoke Martha; Lionel and Plunket *were* looking at "us," and in the act of questioning each other touching "us."

And it was at this precise moment that Nancy told Lady Henrietta she was trembling, and Lady Henrietta told Nancy that she suffered also from the same cause.

The chronicles do not state which of the quartette spoke first, while on the other hand the author was not present at the interview. But let it be admitted that Plunket spoke first, and said — "Hem — do ye seek a service, maidens — will ye bargain with us?"

"A capital bargain," said the other farmer.

"Well," said Lady Henrietta.

"Ha-ha-ha-ha-ha," said Nancy, who, being a lady's-maid, was infinitely scornful at the idea of being a farmer's servant.

"Oh," said stout Plunket to the latter, "I love laughter — work is better done by far when servants all gay-hearted are."

The "maidens" were still doubtful, so the farmer Plunket set to work to show the "place" was not an every-day place — and — and the upshot of it all was that Lady Henrietta, and, oh, more terrible by far, Lady Henrietta's maid, engaged themselves as farm servants to the two stout young farmers—and then took their earnest money (Lady Henrietta didn't know what to do with her Queen Elizabeth's shilling, and so she dropped it)—their earnest money, which bound these two to their masters for twelve whole weary months.

As her ladyship gave up the first money she had ever earned in her life, Lord Tristam came to view again—still harassed by not a few stout handmaidens, who, it seemed, had determined he should choose one of them. However, he flung a good amount of silver about; then, feeling at liberty once more, he came with an air towards the two girls; whereupon he was warned off by their new masters, who seemed rather proud of their proprietorship.

Then it was that the Lady Henrietta proposed to return home. Alas, that despised shilling! Within five minutes more she learned she was actually a servant—bound as surely as any apprentice; and, indeed, the sheriff arrived precisely at that moment, to settle the matter beyond all dispute. Meanwhile, my lord stood in the background, a picture of bewildered despair, and Lady Henrietta stood in the foreground almost in tears. Why, if the court heard of all this she should never be able to show herself in that court's presence! At all events, the truth could not be spoken then and there. Let her be silent before the horrid mob. Hence it was that Lady Henrietta went off quite meekly as a farm servant, while Nancy took the same road, jerking her head and flouncing her garments as only lady's maids of all climes and times could and can manage it.

As for Lord Tristam, he looked as nearly ridiculous as an English lord ever could look!

CHAPTER III.

Imagine that the two farmers and their new servants have arrived at the farm-house — a large, roomy, old building, with deep bay windows of wavy green glass, in the very heart of the forest.

"Home at last," said Plunket, who had pioneered the

flouncing Nancy, as he thrust the key into the lock. As they all entered, Lady Henrietta could not help comparing the place to a prison. However, she did not make the odious comparison in a loud voice.

"There," said Plunket, who was spokesman for the two, and addressing the girls, "there, that's your room."

"Oh — tha-a-a-ank you," said the Lady Henrietta.

"*In*-deed," said the sharp Nancy.

"Good night," said her ladyship, and turned sleepily towards the door; for, truth to tell, her ladyship had never even dreamed of such journeying as she had performed that luckless day. "Good night," and she had her hand upon the latch.

The stout Plunket stared. "Good night — why there's work to do!"

"Wo-o-o-ork," said Henrietta. And Nancy too, shrieked out the little word.

"Of course — take my hat," said Plunket.

Nancy took the hat immediately, but she privately shot it into a corner. Lionel also held out his hat to Henrietta, but he seemed to do so rather because it brought him near her, than as the act of her legal master for twelve months, less one day. Henrietta took it, and knowing no more what to do with it than she had known what to do with the fast binding shilling, dropped it. But Lionel did not mark that fall — his eyes were on the new servant's handsome face. Indeed, he was in love with her, I think.

"Work — work — work," said Plunkett.

"But I'm shivering with cold!"

"And so am I," said Nancy.

"Brother," said Lionel, "brother, she's shivering with cold, you know."

Then Nancy committed herself to this sharp remark, "I'm sure this house is damp!"

If anybody had told the Lady Henrietta on the previous day that she could fall asleep before two strange men of the farmer kind, she would have been justified in denying the proposition, but 'tis a fact that now she sat down, laid her head upon her hands, and was off into a nap. Whereon, it need not be said, Nancy fell asleep

too, for Nancy knew her duty. Indeed, it may be said
that Nancy was very considerably enjoying this comedy
—in her way. However, she did not enjoy the horrid
shake with which rough farmer Plunket woke her.
Plunket, somehow, did not use quite so much violence in
waking up Henrietta. Perhaps this was because Lionel
quietly touched him on the arm. And—and perhaps the
Lady Henrietta was more handsome than ever, with her
eyes closed.

"Hullo—what are your names?" said rough farmer
Plunket.

"Name—name," said Henrietta, as though puzzled at
that plain question. "Name, sir. Oh, I'm—I'm MAR-
THA, so please you." And she made a bob curtsey.

"And *I'm* Betsy," said Nancy, and she made a broken-
backed curtsey.

"And not a bad name for a good girl is Betsy," said
farmer Plunket. "Betsy, put my cloak away."

Which the indignant handmaiden did in the manner of
the hat.

And then it was that Plunket proposed spinning. Why,
neither of the girls knew a distaff from any other staff in
the world. And then, surely, it would have been delightful to hear the great men direct the little women how to
spin, still more delightful to see their great hands pressing
the thin thread. But ah! nor one nor the other could
have given the delight which the young farmer of the
name of Lionel felt, when he found himself bending over
the beautiful, delicate-handed servant, and actually touching those same delicate hands.

Br-r-r-r-r, br-r-r-r-r, br-r-r-r-r, went the wheels, the
industrious wheels, and soon Martha was producing
a highly creditable thread. Meanwhile, Nancy was
making Plunket half wild, for her wheel kept flying first
one way and then the other, and the flax got all manner
of ways, the whole machinery looking as though in a fatal
fit. Meanwhile, Martha was industriously spinning, and
her young master as industriously praising her. At last
Plunket got into a rage as Miss Betsy finally upset the
wheel with a crash, and he was preparing to pounce upon
her in the real old English middle age manner, when the

spinster showed herself deft at running at least, and fled from the room, followed by Plunket, with threats of divers kinds.

As she was scudding round the door post, and looking over her shoulder, Martha looked up from her demure employment (neither she nor Lionel had heard the crash) and no longer seeing Nancy, or Betsy, behold the birr-birring of her wheel ceased, and she started up from the work-a-day, wooden seat.

"Nay, thou art not afraid."

"Afraid — I? Of you — oh no."

And she thought, for a farmer, he seemed very gentle; he also thought she was very superior, for a servant; and, as he was his own master, he had a right to think as he liked. Truth to tell, I think she was beginning to feel kindly towards the gentle farmer.

"So thou art not afraid of me, Martha?"

"Oh no," she said again; still, nevertheless wishing Nancy to return.

"I promise thee, Martha, I will be a kind master — a better master thou shalt not wish for."

"And I promise thee, master, I shall be a bad servant — a worse servant thou wilt never wish to be rid of. The honest truth and the plain truth is, I'm only fit for laughing."

"Well, if thou canst only laugh — i'faith, laugh. Thou doest that bravely. I'll not part with thee, Martha. I'd rather die than part with thee, Martha!"

"Sir," said the new servant, in faint surprise. 'Twas a love-at-first-sight declaration, she knew.

"And can you sing, Martha, as well as laugh? Sing now, sing about this rose," here he took the little blossom from her bosom.

"Give me the rose."

"Nay, thou wilt let me keep it."

"Give me the rose, I say."

"But — but."

"Nay, master, if you *will* keep it, keep it."

And — she sang. The Lady Henrietta was beginning to enjoy the comedy. There was a deal of unlooked-for happiness about it, somehow.

It was at the end of this song, the honest chronicler states, that Lionel went down on his knees before the *new* servant, and in plain straightforward terms told her he loved her. This may appear a highly rapid mode of courtship, but reference to middle age authorities — and the authorities of Elizabeth may surely be called middle aged — will thoroughly set at rest this question in the mind of any sceptical reader, if I have to deplore such a one. I do not know the authorities by name, but that has nothing whatever to do with it.

The lady smiling a little as the impromptu lover tore away all question of inferiority of rank on her part; this latter, as see the authorities again, was for suicide and sudden death, but the perky Nancy coming into the room, followed by Plunket, the young farmer Lionel only got up off his knees.

The new servant, Nancy, it seemed, had drawn a mug of beer, but forgotten to turn the tap off, hence flight on her part and pursuit on the part of farmer Plunket, who, chasing his prey up into a sharp corner, caught a crashing box on her saucy ears.

Then it was that the village clock struck such a late hour as farmers should never hear, except on the nights of fairs.

So the candles were lit, and the new servants respectfully lighted their young masters to the door.

Then left alone, the two girls looked at each other in the blankest manner possible. Beyond a doubt the whole castle was in an uproar; everybody hunting for her, (Nancy said, "hunting for us,") and how should she explain her absence to the scandal-mongers?

"Well," said Nancy, "they seem brave lads and honest."

"And respectful."

"Hum — good rough kind of souls, my lady."

"Yes, I wish heartily we were at home."

"We might as well wish for the queen's diamonds."

And here it was both the girls started, for a very distinct tapping came at the window. They were still trembling when the tapping was renewed, and a weak old voice cried, "Cousin — cousin."

Perhaps Lady Henrietta never heard the old lord's

voice with less dislike than now. She opened the casement herself, and Tristam jumped in as lightly as possible.

Joy! their imprisonment was at an end. But — but
the lady Henrietta seemed a little sorry to go. Indeed,
when she had stepped lightly through the window-case,
she half hesitated, as though she would turn back; but
the impetuous Nancy in a measure drove her forward,
and the next moment she was galloping away from the
farm on her horse's back, kindly brought by his lordship;
but — but her thoughts were at the farm.

My Lord Tristam in making his hurried exit from the
people's place, overturned a table; and barely had he
reached the ground through the window, when Lionel
was up and preparing to enter the room where the spinning machines stood.

He tapped at her door — no answer. Again he tapped
— no answer. Then he called Plunket, who came storm-
ily into the room, but when he heard that the servants
made no answer, he was alarmed, for he felt friendly
towards the troublesome Betsy, and he flung the room
door open. Empty! Then — the window was open! He
went to it; listened! and sure enough in the distance he,
and Lionel too, heard the sound of horses' feet, and at
one and the same moment each felt a blank at his heart.
Lionel fell upon a chair overwhelmed, like a youth deeply
in love as he was, but stout farmer Plunket, boiling with
rage, called out in a voice of thunder to his farm servants;
and when these people came hurrying in, he promised a
golden guinea to the two men who should catch the run-
aways, and he then set to work, to earn his own guinea
by a search after Nancy; but he and the men did not
dream of that fugitive being within the walls of "the
castle," and they passed the mighty building, and went
on hunting, long after Martha, Betsy, and John were
safely housed.

CHAPTER IV.

PLUNKET had a heart, and had perhaps been inclined
to bestow it upon Nancy, for this kind of thing is catch-

ing; but the jade had flown, Plunket was not the man to go about filling the air with big sighs — he set to work, drinking beer, and plenty of it, and singing jolly songs. After all, farmer Plunket was wise. Now, on the other hand, Lionel actually went melancholy mad.

Not three days after the catastrophe, Plunket was out in the woods humming away, when he came up against — Betsy; and in quite a grand hunting costume. She was as full of presence of mind as of sauciness. She stared at the man with lazy curiosity.

In a dozen strong words he told her she was his servant, and the sheriff should decide it.

"'Tis a wild beast!" And giving the view halloo of that day, a number of huntresses were soon about him, and kept him at bay. And indeed, they quite protected Nancy, and Plunket had the worst of it.

Meanwhile, poor Lionel was wandering in this very wood, at this very time, and disconsolate as Ariadne, but not one millionth part as faithless.

It was a grand court hunting day in fact; Elizabeth Tudor had got up that morning at six to chase the deer, and one of many huntresses present was Lady Henrietta. Coming again to Lady Henrietta, I may mention that the company she had most loved since her forced visit to the farm house was her own; indeed, she too had grown melancholy, but hers was very far from such a dismal strait as Lionel's.

Well — in one part of the forest sat on the turf Lord Tristam and Martha (let us call her Martha now and then). The thing which my lord could not comprehend was why her ladyship had left the queen's party — the *queen's* party. He could see no significance in the answer — because she wished to be alone. At last she plainly asked him to leave her, and, hardly believing the testimony of his ears, he ambled away.

And then it was that her tears went tumbling down upon the dewy grass. Oh! if no bitterer tears had ever been shed than Lady Henrietta's what a blissful world it would have been down to that precious May morning!

And thus Lionel, ever wandering in the wood, found her.

The next scene is really so painful that I would rather
shut my eyes to it; but alas, did I do so there would be
such an hiatus in this true history that you might fancy
the printing gentlemen engaged upon it were of the ec-
centric kind. So in a few short and unwilling words let
me tell the cruel truth. He recognized her and she
screamed. Thereupon, Lord Tristam, who, of course,
was not far off, made his appearance, and with him a
perfect posse. Then and there Lionel declared the lady
his servant — the Lady Henrietta! So they declared he
was mad, and were going to fall upon him, when she
interceded for him and prayed that they would let him
go. Then it was that Plunket came on the scene and
recognized Martha; but little said he, smart farmer.

Suddenly, the sound of loud trumpets declared Elizabeth, Queen of England, was near at hand, and, as they
finally drove Lionel back, he, poor fellow and foundling,
thought of the small diamond ring which was to be so
talismanic. He took it from his finger, pressed it within
Plunket's right hand, and bade him give it to the queen.

"Aye — aye, lad," said Plunket; and meant it.

CHAPTER V.

THAT pleasant old farm house, once so happy, was as
dull as the forest at midnight. Lionel grew more and
more melancholy; and, indeed, farmer Plunket was not
very cheerful, though he would not give in.

Plunket was sitting by himself one day, and waiting
for somebody — whom? The Lady Henrietta herself.
Her conscience was at work. So she determined to save
him.

A little and farmer Plunket gave a start of relief —
'twas the arrival of the lady and her maid Nancy, now
no longer the saucy, for she had a kind heart, as she felt
somewhat the gloomy end of the masquerade at the fair.

Well, the farmer and Nancy left the lady by herself.
And then, then she sang the little song she sang when he
asked her to sing on that night when Lionel brought her
home as his servant.

She looked tremblingly about her as she sang on and on to the end of the verse, and then Lionel came slowly into the room.

Ah — I have forgotten to say this farmer Lionel was an earl. The dead owner of the diamond ring had been unjustly banished; years and years before his sentence was declared unjust; years and years had people wondered where the earl tarried, and now, the diamond ring placed in the queen's hands, was the clue to the whole mystery.

I know that the coming of Lady Henrietta to the farmhouse must look interested. 'Tis a pity almost that Lionel does not remain a poor farmer; but there, the queen has the ring — his birth is recognized; and so, Martha must remain under the imputation of telling him she loved him, not for himself, but for his title. For truth to tell, she went up to him, and whispered that she loved him. But alas! he was too sunk in melancholy to feel his heart beat high at hearing those words. He turned away from her with angry pride.

But as the Lady Henrietta did not feel outraged, as she still strove to find a way of leading Lionel back to his old self, perhaps these little circumstances will be set down in favor of disinterested love on her part; and if the gentlemanly reader will remember, I have said *she was very dreamy in the woods*.

Well, this was the lady's next plan: It was as old as romance. It seems if one bereft of sense is brought into a scene similar to one which gave him great happiness, the effect may be so great as to restore him to consciousness. And as the Lady Henaietta knew 'twas a happy hour for Lionel when he engaged her as a servant, she determined to have a mock statute fair, sheriff and all, in her park.

I am always so eager to tell good news that I cannot stand dallying with the trumpet in my hand; and having told it, I frequently find I am at a loss what to say, in continuation, which is a disconcerting drawback. Yet nevertheless, though I could make a fine scene here by borrowing from the chonicle, I prefer at once to say that there never was such a success as this imitation statute fair — for Lionel came to his loving senses and took Martha to his very heart.

And — now, I do not know what to say next! I have told all my news — I am at a standstill!

What *can* come next?

Oh! of course. They were married, and lived happy ever afterwards. 'Tis just like the end of a comic opera.

And stout farmer Plunket was married to Nancy. She made the best of wives, says the old chronicle with a concluding flourish.

THE END.